Missy,

I hope you enjoy the mead.

Best Wishes
Steven Mark Scott
February 2013

CELEBRATE
THE SINNER

A novel by
STEVEN M. SCOTT

ISBN: 0985809507
ISBN: 13: 9780985809508

Library of Congress Control Number: 2012911343
Blue Amber Press, SLC, UT

Cover art by Sheri Doty

Printed in the United States of America

For my father who gave me the place
For Teresa who gives me the love and the space

Oregon's Lumber Industry…has been one of Boom and Bust, an industry whose prosperity has been dependent on wars, earthquakes and other calamities resulting from Acts of God and stupidity of man.

– H J Cox, 1949

It is my opinion that many people thwarted build their desired life behind their eyes and live in it.

– John Steinbeck, 1951

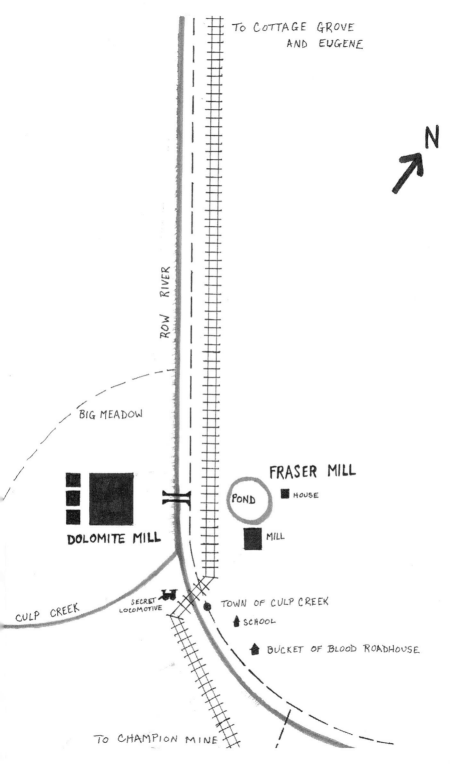

1

I had my problems growing up, my defects as Grandma Lulu called them, but I was no Quasimodo. Some of the ladies said I was cute, and others even called me a doll. My left shoulder drooped lower than the right because I was born arm first and the doctor pulled too hard, but I didn't see it as a problem, not until people started asking. The lisp was still noticeable the year we moved to Culp Creek, but that eventually went away. The two problems that proved to be bigger issues, the defects nobody saw or heard, had yet to be discovered. Miss Cherry, my fourth grade teacher, uncovered one of them. The other remains my secret, and I don't know anyone who can help with it.

I loved my mother, of course, and respected her, I guess. I was in awe of my father, so you might call it love—it was an attachment. I respected what he knew. He introduced me to great ideas, like circumference, pi R squared, 2pi R, and he used to talk about electrical facts: ohms, resistance, and voltage.

Dad's real name wasn't Merle; it was Alfred Merle. He never liked Alfred because it sounded too gentrified, however that was the life he'd have preferred to live. So, Dad went by Merle or A. Merle, and I was "Teddy" because that's what Mother called me.

Dad taught me to love the great trees for the lumber they produced. I learned to calculate board feet in an uncut stand of timber more easily than I'd ever write a sentence. Yet, more than the trees, I loved the machines that took the trees—black, greasy, rusted, every one of them. I'd sit on a log or stump and watch them work. The vibrations that marked their effort traveled through the earth and into me like the rumble of a great heart. Blue smoke, charged with ash and oil, smelled more a part of the forest than did the scent of an evergreen bough, and the undulating scream of the head saw, as it ripped through timber, told stories about the hardness of the wood and the set of the teeth with more clarity than words could ever manage.

Our house was very small, so if I had to say what marked my first winter in Culp Creek, I'd say windows. We had two that I remember. Rain etched them, streamed along their surfaces, rolled over their weathered sills. One bead tracked another, some directed, others aimless, every journey different, but in the end, they all came together at a low spot by the door. Water poured off the porch onto a haul road that encircled our house like a greasy moat. Ruts grew daily in the road and shifted like things alive. When they interfered with the trucks, one of the men would run a blade along the surface to smooth and crown it, but the effect didn't last long, not with heavy machines growling over it day after day. Past the haul road, the rain fell gray against our log pond. Larger droplets dimpled the water; the rest were lost in the trees all around.

Of the two, our front window didn't have much to offer. Just the low picket fence Mr. Mulberger built and Mother painted white, and the weeping willow that drooped inside the fence. Log trucks slowed, nearly stopped, as they turned from the gravel highway onto our property, but in spring, when Mother's tree leafed out, even that view was taken away.

That was about it for the front window.

"Teddy," Mother called through her bedroom door. "I need you."

I left the front window and knocked on her door. She insisted I do that. If she answered, I could come in. If she didn't answer, it meant I should go away.

"Come in," she said.

Mother had just finished bathing. She was at her dressing table, sitting on the chair with the soft embroidered seat, staring into the mirror, studying her image. A white towel bound her hair. I stood in the doorway and watched her pat and squeeze the towel. Her hands traced its length from top to bottom, working the moisture into the towel. As she let the towel fall, with a single hand, she carried her thick braid forward and laid it beside her breast.

"Sit here, Teddy, and brush my hair." She patted the seat cushion and inched forward. "We can make room."

I climbed onto the chair behind her, my legs astraddle her naked hips, my spine pressed against the hard wooden back. The wet length of hair seemed to swell against the loose braid that held it. I released the braid and watched the strands fall apart. As I picked up the hairbrush and started with the damp ends, I knew that when I finished, when her hair had dried, it would ruffle and fan out like the tail feathers of a bright red bird.

I was Mother's spectator, her silent confidant, forever held by the promise of more. Small secret jars, some pink and lavender, some with gold lids, others with glass stoppers, she arranged across her dressing table like figurines. She touched a shade of color with her fingertip and carried it to her cheek with the love of an artist completing a masterpiece. She reached for a second color, sampled it, but chose another. Rarely did she move her eyes from the glass in front. And rarely did I.

Mother's eyebrows were slender because she plucked them, but her lips were full. When she looked down, lids masked her eyes like shades lowered, but the aching green behind them was always present. She wore her makeup bright red across the lips for the world to see, but more subtly along her cheeks and at the angle of her jaw. In her jewelry box, she kept gold hoops and bobs to wear when she and Father went out. During the afternoons at her dressing table, I chose the earrings she wore.

"You are the best little man," she told me as I worked the brush through her hair.

"I know I am."

I carried the brush higher and used it to massage her scalp the way she had taught me. She tilted her head to the left and then to the right to change the angle of view, the cast of light, and I followed her movements, careful not to pull. The thin muscles at the front of her neck tightened and released and slid beneath her pale skin like silk ropes under tension.

Held between the chair back and her spine, I barely moved, the warmth of her bath rising against me, damp like the rope of hair between us.

"I am so lucky to have you," she said.

I searched her mirror for an echoed smile, a flickered glance, the small treasures she'd hide for me to find, me alone.

Mother stood and moved away, but moisture from her thighs remained on the brocade cushion, altering the color of its fabric from blue to purple, which, after years, became an imprint that stayed.

"Go play, now."

I left with only the scent of her bath.

Watching from our kitchen window, now there was a pastime! Men called to each other, engines roared, giant timbers battered unyielding steel. Trucks, trailers stacked with logs, loads wrapped in heavy chain, rumbled around our house all day long. Downshifting, brakes groaning, they dumped the logs into the millpond ten feet from the kitchen window.

With pulleys, cables, and what I thought was magic, the men forced huge logs from the trucks. They spooled out two cables from a tall steel boom attached to the house, passed the cables between the truck and logs, and hooked the ends of the cables to a half-buried log at the edge of the pond. Rewinding the cables over a power drum, they rolled and slid the heavy logs off the trucks into the pond. When the cables began to stretch and pop under the tension, I'd watch for the first log to shift. Fearing the worst, I'd press my hands against my ears and shut my eyes until I felt the release through the kitchen wall. As the timbers bounced over the brow log and thundered into the water, it felt like cannon balls hitting the house.

Dad planned our house with the unloading operation next to it so he could watch the men and make sure they did their jobs. After he built a separate office on the other side of the pond, the trucks continued to unload next to the house because he said it worked best that way. Mother didn't agree. By end of our first winter, she spent less time with me in the kitchen and more of it in her bedroom with the door shut. I had less of her, but I still had my windows.

In the early morning, hours before the first trucks arrived, I'd peer through the low light, searching for movement on the far side of the pond. This told me the men were setting up. When the steam engine that drove the head saw fired up, condensed water from the previous day's work spewed and spurted from its stack. Once the boiler was hot, the steam thickened into a meringue that draped the engine until dusk. A single Ames steam engine powered our mill that first year. Its tall, black stack sailed above the pond, held in place by a web of wires that ran to the ground, to adjacent roofs, and to the walls of buildings. Mr. Cox, who reported the valley's timber business in his newspaper, called our mill a haywire outfit.

I'd watch Dad walk through the mill, checking progress. Every so often, he'd stop to inspect the alignment of a gear or test the tension on a belt. Sometimes he would smile, sometimes look stern. I never saw him yell at a man. He said good men do their best work when left alone, but the boss had to show an interest. I saw Dad at his best from across the pond.

A mountain like a fortress wall rose up behind our mill. Barely large enough to be called a meadow and too small to farm, our mill site was one-tenth the size of the empty meadow directly across the Row River. Dad expected to own that big meadow and the timber that came with it, but he never did. Culp Creek, the small stream that flowed into the Row River from the opposite bank, was nothing special either. Depending on rainfall and the time of year, it flowed with just enough volume to keep a single millpond filled, but never enough for two ponds.

Like the creek after which it was named, little distinguished our community from the other lumber towns that squatted in the wooded shade of the Coastal Mountains. A burg more than a community, Culp Creek had attached itself to our mill like a barnacle fixed to the hull of an unlucky ship. Ours was a hand-me-down spot, an unpromising piece of land that Dad took only because he didn't have a choice. Nobody takes seconds first, I know that now, but that was the foundation upon which my father chose to construct our lives.

2

If you believe the insurance tables, I'll make it to ninety since I'm already eighty-eight and a half, but longevity alone is no cause for celebration. My wife of fifty-three years died of cancer a couple of decades ago. From that day forward, my world has grown steadily, inexorably smaller, and I take credit for it. Once she was gone—no need to name her, since none of this is about her—I sold the house, bought a condominium, sold it, bought a second one, sold it, then a double-wide, and now I'm pretty well settled in my fifth or sixth apartment. I've been evicted twice for salacious behavior, but the circumstances, in my opinion, were totally overblown. The current setup is a ground level unit with three rooms and just enough space for a recliner, a king size bed, and my fifty inch TV. I've given my tools away, and I'm down to one filing cabinet, which I keep in the closet. I made at least four of the moves to hook up with women. It is, after all, easier for Mohammed to travel to the mountains.

I tried a second wife, which turned out to be a mistake when she grew a lump in her breast—there would be no more vomit or hand-holding for me. Since then, I've gone through women like a dose of salts, but with my two hundred dollar a night caretakers (should I say sex therapists), my pump and a ready supply of Viagra, I've fine-tuned the arrangements. It beats the hell out of a nursing home or some other elephant burial ground, and I get to pick the nurses.

I'm not supposed to date women under fifty-one—that's the French rule, and I guess the French should know. According to their academy in Paris, it is permissible to date women half your age plus seven years. My new girlfriend, Rita, is sixty-two and well above that age limit, with wiggle room to move down, and I need my wiggle room. Rita is Mediterranean with flashing black eyes, and she is Hot! Hot! Nothing like the girls I grew up with. She was raised Catholic and taught by nuns at a girl's school. In her health class, she asked, "How long does a man want to do it?" The priest answered, "Until he's been in the grave for three days." With that and a glass of communion wine, what's not to like about Catholics? The French also believe that the perfect breast fits inside a champagne glass, but I'm not so sure about that one. Who's to say the French are right about everything?

My first wife, the dead one—and my kids, too—gave me no credit for self-awareness because I refused to act the way they thought I should. They tried to squeeze me inside their precious snow globe worlds, but I was far too big for that. I'm not stupid, either, even though my 'highly-intelligent' first wife treated me that way. I used to read a lot, and really good books, like The Sand Pebbles with Steve McQueen, until cataracts sponged the letters away. Even with large print, I found myself dragging a magnifying glass the size of a dinner plate across each page, and the selection of age appropriate books turned out to be so limited I was sure the Gideon's were running the presses. Three cardiac stents may separate me from sudden death, but I have no intention of taking up the gospels. My interest in being repatriated with the Holy

Ghost hangs looser than the hairless folds around my knees, and I thank my Grandma Lulu for that.

Each morning at ten, I take a thirty-minute walk to keep my heart ready for any female action that might come along. Then I take a nap. Outside of that, my world has come down to the big screen TV in front of my recliner. It's pabulum for the most part, nearly all of it predictable except for the sports, which do require a big screen. I own a pair of headphones for the TV and I have an amplifier on the phone, but they garble sound more than they improve it. The telephone rarely rings because words and thoughts no longer cross wires without getting jumbled or twisted into meanings never intended. Since my cataracts were removed, the books are better, but my ability to concentrate is worse, fouled by sleepless nights that drift into morning naps.

Spines and bellies soften and round off with the years. Thoughts, too, lose their edge. With enough time, they circle back on themselves, too often circling the drain. The difference between remembering and actually being there is as much a matter of degree as it is a matter of imagination, and I have a world class imagination. Linear thinkers like Dad and my first wife don't have much use for brains like mine, but the world's not any more linear than it is flat.

I read about a sorry bastard who cached his memoirs in a bugproof box, as if someone would ever want to read them. I won't kid myself. Letters, invoices, newspaper clippings—the facts—I've squirreled away in my filing cabinet, but I don't bother to write my memories down. I simply stretch back in the La-Z-Boy and stare at the empty big-screen. Soon enough, images flicker across with a logic that's real, at least for me. These incandescent shadows are no more remote, no less real, than were the bloodless shapes that flickered through eighty-eight years of my life.

Some of the shadows have begun to haunt me. Secrets, it seems, scream for revelation. I've worked through the details of my past, pulled at its marrow, but I don't know how to cast the demons out, and I have no priest to help. I do have space, space enough to step back and see it all whole, so much so, I rattle around in it, but time doesn't grow—about that I'm certain. With what's left, I intend to gather the threads that remain and follow them to the end, more for me than for the rest. There were reasons for what I did, but I'm not sure what it changed. I have no axes to grind since I have accepted the older generation for what it was at the time...far younger then than I am now.

3

I was adopted. Nobody told me so for years, but that was how things were done then. I never guessed that Marie wasn't my real mother, not until 1942, some months after Pearl Harbor was bombed, the day she and Dad put me on a troop train headed for Texas and World War II.

If it were up to me, I'd say I entered the world in 1920 because it makes the math easier. But that's not the way it was. I was born in 1922, most likely in Washington State, but it could have been northern Idaho or western Montana. I tried to unearth the details after I retired, but nothing much came of it because everyone had died by then. The more I dug for answers, the more I desperately cared. After a while, it mattered less and less, and I finally let it go. It was much too late to be forcing rusted locks and peeking through rotted doors.

Gertrude, my real mother, the woman who screamed in pain the day I was born, left me at the Salvation Army Rescue and Maternity Home in Portland when I was two weeks old. In a note to the matron at the home, she promised to come right back. She begged them not to send me away. I've read her letter enough times to wallpaper every whorehouse in the Pacific Northwest.

"Dear Major," she wrote,

"I have accepted a position a few miles from the city, and am writing so you will not worry and think I am abandoning my baby. I could not give him up even if he were a perfect baby, but the very fact that he is not makes him doubly dear to me as I know no one could love him as I do. You are a mother yourself, so you must realize how I feel.

Major, please don't send my baby to the Waverly or some other orphanage. I beg of you to believe me and trust me and keep my little boy for me until I am able to take him. Please be patient with me a little longer. I would go crazy if anything should happen to him."

Grandma Lulu was wrong about her. They all were. My real mother wasn't a prostitute or some loose woman in trouble; she was married to Frank. Gertrude and Frank had a family, and they were saving money to come get me. I can't help but wonder why they never did. I can't help but think that I was the cause of it.

I came to live with Marie and Merle a year and a half after the Salvation Army passed me off to the Waverly Baby Home. When Marie walked through the Waverly, she stopped at my crib and smiled. She said she bent low and spoke softly, but I refused to follow her voice and never once smiled back. She took me anyway, she said, because I had beautiful blond hair and startling blue eyes. She said I looked like the baby she deserved.

I couldn't walk, and I didn't stand until I was two years old. She wrote the baby home asking if I had had polio and was a cripple, or if I'd had rickets, but that wasn't it. In those days, there were so many babies at the Waverly the nurses only had time to warm bottles and change diapers. I never walked because I never got out of my crib. There were far too many of us for that.

I don't remember the Baby Home, but I do recall rows and rows of silent beds. I feel, more than remember, an empty place filled with small, staring bodies, the littlest ones at times crying; the older children, those with the defects, those who had been passed over time and again, lying motionless, increasingly blind to the passing faces and tight smiles. I took philosophy in college, religion, too, and I later subscribed to *Psychology Today*. I've read about the children who were raised like chimpanzees on a wire teat. John Donne wrote that no man is an island entire of itself, but the waves that lapped against Waverly's shores rose from a dead sea. They carried little nourishment and left us wanting for things we could never receive. Had Mother offered a nurturing love, had she made every effort possible, it probably wouldn't have been enough.

As for Dad, I don't think he had it in him to offer anything extra. His roots still wind throughout the green hills that roll in low from the Pacific, but mine never had a chance to take hold and spread like the myrtle that thrives there. Dad's grandfather, Thomas Fraser, brought the family Bible and a willingness to work to the Willamette Valley in 1864. He traveled from Scotland by way of Canada to keep from being a casualty of the Civil War because too many young Scotsmen, not a patriot among them, were being volunteered into Mr. Lincoln's

Army the minute their boots scraped New York docks. Dad, Grandpa Charlie, and Great-Grandpa Thomas—three generations of mill men—sprang from gnarled roots that still cling to Hadrian's Wall. I thought I shared those roots. I believed I made up the fourth generation.

Dad wrote his check to buy the bankrupt Culp Creek mill in February, the time of year when winter rains begin to peter out and days fill with the scent of rot and the promise of new life. But he scribbled the thing in 1929, a perfect example of poor timing, he later admitted. I didn't witness the transaction, but I heard the account enough times to retell it myself. That was just one of his charms. My father told a great story because he was full of bullshit, and that's what good tales come down to. Mother figured this out long before I did.

4

Good or bad, stories have to begin somewhere. Otherwise they'd all fold into one and roll back to Adam. I'll say that mine begins with my dad in 1920—nine years before he bought the Culp Creek mill. I'll also add that perfect people don't hold a monopoly on the right to tell their stories.

1920 marked the collapse of the lumber market in the Pacific Northwest and the arrival of the Ku Klux Klan in Oregon. Unsettled conditions give rise to fear, and fear finds scapegoats and easy solutions. You didn't have to grow up in Pulaski, Tennessee, to see that.

In addition to studying civil engineering at the University of Oregon in Eugene, Dad was commander of the campus ROTC unit and a star member of the baseball team—an honest-to-God big man on campus. However, more than baseball games, engineering problems, and ROTC maneuvers, Dad loved loose women. "The chase is always better than the consummation," he counseled me;

although I'm sure he never had to work at either. Dad developed his taste for whores during rush week of his freshman year, and decades later, he didn't see marriage as a reason to end the banquet. "What's the point of horseradish without a little prime rib on the side?" he smirked, long before I was old enough to understand.

At the time, the girls at the Crystal Palace whorehouse were the hottest around, but that was Dad's personal territory, not mine, although he never tried to keep it private. Half the fun for him was having an audience and bragging. The Crystal Palace straddled the edge of Eugene's downtown district on East Merchant Street and filled the lower two floors of the old Coleman Building. According to Dad, the Palace was a place of higher learning no different than the great university across the river. "Schooling comes in many forms," he said. "Even the best slide rule can't sniff out pi."

As a freshman, Dad had shown great promise in engineering, but his effort stalled along the way. He finished in the middle of his class, well behind "idiots" with far less talent. After four years, he left the university with a degree in civil engineering, but he remained an ardent student at the Crystal Palace long after.

Don't get me wrong. Dad did more than screw beautiful women while at the U of O. He also started as catcher on the varsity baseball team, which, if you know baseball, is the most important position. It was through baseball that Dad met Gust Backer, the first baseman. Years later, when Gust entered our lives at Culp Creek, Dad told me all about him.

"Gust was tall and gangly with wings like an albatross. Everybody on the team called him *big, dumb, and ugly*, but damn, he could hit the ball!"

When I finally got to meet Gust in Culp Creek, after he'd put on a mountain of muscle, I was startled to see how scary-big he actually was.

Dad and dumb old Gust—short for Augustus—attended their first Ku Klux Klan meeting during their freshman year. As a matter of fact, the entire baseball team showed up. At the time, Dad knew next to nothing about the *Invisible Empire* and hadn't planned on going until his professor, Dr. Frederick Dunn, chairman of the Latin Department, and an *Exalted Cyclops* in the Klan, offered to trade the team an *A* in Latin for filling the seats.

"I'm not sure I want any part of this," Dad made a point of telling Gust before they entered the auditorium. He thought Gust felt the same way, but neither varsity player was willing to turn down the chairman's easy A.

"Nobody forced you to come," Gust said in a voice that boomed. Gust was one of those people who had never learned to whisper, and he said exactly what he thought. "Sitting next to Gust always meant calling attention to yourself," Dad said.

Dad leaned away from Gust and surveyed the auditorium. At the front, behind the speaker's podium, a banner caught his eye. In large, blocky print it read: *A Message of Warning to American Manhood and Womanhood.* Dad scanned the rows for examples of American womanhood and was disappointed by what he didn't see. He leaned back toward Gust. "The women here should be wearing the hoods."

Gust grinned, but he didn't respond. Ugly as Gust was, there wasn't much he could say. However, even back then, Dad had suspected that there might be more to Gust than showed on the surface.

On the left side of the stage, the American flag floated like a revelation. On the right, a Holy Bible the size of an encyclopedia teetered on a spindly stand. At the back, below the banner, a cross blazed. Wrapped in gold tinsel, with overhead stage lights shining on it, the cross wasn't actually burning—just made to look that way, glowing orange and red against the purple drapes.

"Who's the speaker?" Dad asked.

"Some preacher from Portland. He's a combination Methodist and Episcopalian."

Posters announcing Reverend Reuben H. Sawyer's lecture papered lampposts and walls around town and on campus. Earlier that evening, a fiery cross had lit up Skinner's Butte, overlooking Eugene. While its blazing arms reached out to the community, four hooded figures on horseback cantered down Main Street in white robes with black symbols emblazoned across their hearts.

Dr. R. H. Sawyer, pastor of the True Christian Church in Portland, strode onstage and seized the podium with powerful hands, hands that looked to have been sculpted by God to carry his Word. He silently surveyed the audience before he unleashed a voice that resonated through every listener.

"The Klan is *not* anti-Catholic!" he intoned. "It is *not* anti-Jewish! We are simply non-Catholic and non-Jewish. But unlike the Catholics and the Jews, we are one hundred percent American."

Gust leaned toward Dad. "Did you know the R in his first name stands for Reuben?" Gust's voice resonated nearly as clearly as the reverend's.

With a shake of his head, Dad telegraphed that he didn't want to hear about it.

"Reuben's a Jewish name, isn't it?" Gust persisted.

"How would I know?"

"Pretty sure it is," Gust repeated. "You never see anybody named that around here."

Two spectators in front of them fidgeted, but dumb Gust didn't pick up on it.

"That must be why he goes by R.H. Sawyer. So nobody knows."

Dad pointed to the podium.

"What do you think?" Gust's full-bodied baritone matched his growing certainty.

"Dammit, Gust! If you have to know, climb onstage and check his dick."

"We are devoted to one hundred percent Americanism and moral uplift," the pastor was saying, "because our forefathers built this country on the same God given beliefs."

The audience had settled in by then, most of them intent on the message. This was what they had come to hear.

Reverend Sawyer turned and studied the glowing cross. "We are in danger of being swept away in a rising flood of color. We control madmen, mad dogs, and other mad beasts, but the Negro, in whose blood flows the mad desire for race amalgamation, is more dangerous than a maddened wild beast. He must and he will be controlled. *We cannot stop there!* Papists and Jews, Japanese, Chinese, Bolsheviks, they all threaten to overwhelm us."

Gust tapped Dad on the shoulder and quietly remarked, "No flooding of color in here."

Dad examined the faces that filled the theater.

"Levees must be holding," Gust added.

"We respect the law," the reverend said somberly. "We do not break the law. Those who say otherwise do not understand us. They choose dark lies in hopes of defeating us, but we are the law's servants. We serve the laws of the land, especially those that make up our constitution. Laws of a higher moral order trump the rest and guide the creation of those that follow. After a few years, America will not regard the Klan as evil or satanic. America will regard the Klan as its savior."

Out of some perverse interest, Dad followed the Klan's activities as it began recruiting in Eugene. The recruiters had reminded him of itinerant preachers, but they were paid professionals, a fact that did not detract from their status as true believers, true Christians, and one hundred percent bonafide Americans. Eugene's first Kleagles, short for Klan Eagles, arrived on the Southern Pacific Railroad by way of Texas and California, and according to Dad, their recruiting techniques were as effective in Oregon, as they had been in the South and the Midwest. That they had to eat while on the road or occasionally take a drink along the way, or got lonely and sought help for the condition, did not in any way diminish their mission or tarnish their standing among Odd Fellows, Legionnaires, Moose, and Elk.

As a rule, Klan recruiters avoided Main Street and daylight when fishing for members. They preferred chumming shallow waters in hazy rooms at the back of Legion halls and among the Masons. Secret recruiting meshed with secret membership lists—fraternal twins invisibly joined against common enemies. "Secrets contain power," Dad said. "They invite curiosity, assume importance, and build intrigue. Secrecy encourages men to act out their fantasies within a web of safe anonymity." Eugene proved to be fertile ground for the Kleagles, as did Cottage Grove, the town closest to our Culp Creek mill.

There was no shame in being a secret member of the Klan because all the best men in town belonged. Within two years of the reverend's speech, Eugene's police chief got canned for being Catholic, and Klansmen won election to every municipal office. The Klan even listed its headquarters in the Eugene phone directory, advertising an office on Main Street.

A few dozen Jewish families and several hundred Roman Catholics lived in Lane County during those years, but you barely knew it. The Catholics were more visible than the Jews because they went to church on Sunday and made a big deal out of it. There were a few black people, too—railroad workers and servants—but you didn't see them together as families. They lived in west Eugene, near the Ferry Street Bridge, and nobody worried about them because there weren't even two thousand in the entire state. Most of them lived in Portland or in railroad towns or the occasional mill town. One of them was living in Culp Creek when we moved there.

5

Wattie Blue was the first black man I ever saw. As far as I knew, he was the only man like him in the world. He may have had a day job, but I only knew him as a musician at the Bucket of Blood Roadhouse. Wattie played the lip harp and had called out square dances for as long as anyone could remember.

Years earlier, long-haul freighters had built the Bucket of Blood as a place to rest the men and change out their teams of oxen before the final climb to the Champion mine on Dolomite Mountain. These men, none of them carpenters, pounded rough-cut planking into a one-story structure with a sloping chicken coop roof. They added split cedar shingles, a covered porch that wrapped three-quarters of the way around, and they went easy on the paint. At one time, a pasture with corrals and a low slung barn had rolled away from the porch toward the river, but the corrals and barn had since fallen down, and the pasture flattened and graveled over to make it easier on the cars.

Music and beer sloshed through the Bucket of Blood most Saturday nights. On a good Saturday night, the beer and music foamed white hot across the dance floor, and the fights cascaded out the low front door into the parking lot, roiling like the spring-fed waters high above them. If the night was hot, the grownups flitted back and forth through the open door with flasks bulging their back pockets or hidden under their jackets. When winter settled in and fog stole the trees, when an endless drizzle ruined their shoes and caked mud to their boots, all sorts of people huddled together under the sagging roof.

Some men entered the roadhouse looking to fight. More came to share a dance and sample a drink. When the music played, they'd dance, or try to, but a few always remained at the margin, leaning against the unpainted walls, hoping that companionship would somehow present itself. I never saw much sense in driving the long canyon road from Eugene or Cottage Grove with no intention of dancing, but the dance floor at the Bucket of Blood on a Saturday night was where the girls were, and for many, that seemed to be enough.

The Bucket of Blood Roadhouse was never meant to be a refuge for small children. However, I was drawn to it just the same. It sat upstream from our mill, and if not for the trees, I might have seen it from my window. I could walk to it in fifteen minutes.

The very first time I saw Boone Shaw—mill mechanic, prospector and roadhouse bouncer—away from the mill, I was standing on a stump behind the Bucket of Blood, peering in through an open window. I had been at loose ends that night and, without really thinking about it, I followed the music and railroad tracks upstream. The band had just stopped playing, and Boone was standing at the bar a few feet from me. With the evening's gloom encasing me, I felt transparent.

Boone was turned toward a scrawny man who looked like an overcooked chicken wing. "How is it tonight, Wattie?" Boone said.

"Just ducky," the scrawny man said, smiling. His shirt was soaked with sweat. He dropped something silver into a pocket and wiped a handkerchief across his dark forehead and behind his neck. He was stringy and brown, and standing next to Boone, he looked smaller than he really was. "Good crowd tonight. Everybody's behaving." He nodded. "Yes sir, everybody's having fun." Pleasure glistened across his face.

"You're in top form, old man. That's why things are going so well." Boone surveyed the crowd as he spoke. "But take it little easy, or you'll have a goddamn heart attack. Then what'll I do?"

Wattie sipped a beer that had been placed on the bar in front of him. "It truly is warm tonight," he said, "but don't you worry. I ain't ready for Freddie, not just yet, I ain't. Mighty hard to kill old Wattie."

Wattie Blue was what everybody called him, and there was nobody else like Wattie. I later asked him how he came to be at Culp Creek.

"Why, that's easy," he said, as if the question were so obvious only a fool would ask it. "I'm here because nobody square dances in Chicago." He laughed at his joke and set me at ease. "Bet you didn't know that about Chicago?"

I shook my head.

"I expect not," he said. "You call a square dance in Chicago, they'll rap you on the head and lock you up for being crazy. So much as try to do-si-do on the South Side, folks be standing and staring, asking what's wrong with you." Wattie grinned and shook his head at the thought. Small sticky tears, the kind that come with sore eyes, stood at the corners, but didn't roll down. "No square dancing in that town, no sir," he said.

"That's why you left, because there wasn't music?"

"Now, that ain't true! There's a whole lot of music in Chicago, the best. But all they care about is the blues, and that's because Chicago is a mean town. Too mean for old Wattie, for sure." Wattie kept his smile going, but the eyes did not match his mouth. "Truth is that ain't exactly why I pulled out. The big town was turning me mean, too. I thought I'd presently be killing somebody, sometime, and for no real reason."

"You'd kill someone?"

"I never killed nobody, but I did start believing it wouldn't be so wrong. Shoot or stab 'em just because I didn't see a reason not to." He smiled again. "If Momma could hear me now! But that's God's truth why I left. A mean town grows a person mean—it just does. I'd find myself wading through all kind of nasty fertilizer. You wade through that stuff long enough, it'll stain you and ruin your shoes." Wattie pointed to his feet. "I am partial to the condition of my shoes and the direction they point. I chose to leave Chicago with my shoes pointing forward, not up. There you have it, young Teddy, as to why I am drowning in these woods. That and a roll of the dice at every crossroad I came to."

Wattie reached for his blues harp. He licked his lips as if he was about to play, but his cracked hands fell back onto his lap, where he watched them settle. "Chicago was a tough, mean city, that's true. But Missouri was a bad, mean place."

6

With everyone scrambling to meet the War Department's orders for biplane frames, life was easy in the lumber business during World War I. Hundreds of mills, some solid operations and too many fly-by-night outfits, came on line in 1916, primed to harvest the rewards of war by meeting the government's demand for strong, light spruce.

"Would you rather be a pig or hog?" Dad liked to ask.

"A pig," I knew to answer.

"Hogs get slaughtered. Pigs keep eating."

Problem was, given enough time and opportunity, every pig grows into a hog. During the First World War, huge inventories built up as pig after pig jumped in feet first, snout down, gorging before the slop ran out. By 1920, with the war over and nobody building houses, with lumberyards sagging under bloated inventories, prices dropped to a third of what they'd been. When margins grew too thin to cover freight costs, the market slid into reverse and raced downhill out of control.

They called it a buyers' strike. If people strike because their wallets are empty, then I guess that's what it was. More than one feedlot of hogs got slaughtered as owners cut back shifts and trimmed employees, simply trying to hang on. It wasn't until 1927, eight long years after the end of the Great War, that the lumber industry finally dragged itself out of the pit the national government had thrown it in. I'm telling you this now so you'll better understand what Dad had just been through when he bought the Culp Creek mill in 1929.

Dad made a point of telling me about a man from that time, named Levi Kellis. Levi and Mr. Vitus co-owned the Vitus Pump Company. Before the downturn in 1920, on the advice of Mr. Vitus, Levi mortgaged his house, his horse, and his car to buy inventory and expand the business. Without seeing it coming, Levi lost it all, including his wife. Since Mr. Vitus had kept the books, Levi didn't know the company was in trouble until the day the bank foreclosed. He came to work one day and found the front door chained and padlocked.

"Levi worked hard, harder than most," Dad said. "He worked as though he'd be paid by the weight of his sweat, but it didn't get him anywhere. If you're not prepared to handle the business end of things, you'll be better off and far happier working for somebody else." Dad took great pride in his own 'business acumen,' as he called it. He taught me to leave the sweat and dirty work to somebody else.

The early 1920's were hard on Dad, too. Fresh out of the university, he partnered with a shyster named Rex Pingree to build a plank mill east of Salem in Elmira. Dad married Mother about the same time and rented a two-story farmhouse with a balcony by a quiet stream. According to her, our time in Elmira was as close to being happy as we ever got. Every morning, she would drink coffee in a big chair, with me on her lap. Together, we'd stare down from the balcony and watch the sheep wander through the pasture, but that time in Elmira didn't last.

Dad's plank mill lost money from the beginning, and he blamed Rex Pingree for the failure. Rex was supposed to supply the logs, but he didn't follow through because he had his hand in too many other enterprises. Without a reliable supply of timber, Dad couldn't meet payroll or fill orders. He lived on the cusp of failure up until the night the plank mill burned. Fortunately, Rex had purchased an insurance policy on the mill, and as things turned out, he and Dad made a nice profit from the fire.

The minute Dad collected his share of the money, he began looking for another mill to buy. Since he had to be away most of the time, Mother and I were forced to live with his mother. Over the course of two years, Grandma Lulu gave me a glimpse of hell I hope to never see again. In that way, you could say she did her Christian duty. For every minute Dad spent in Cottage Grove getting the new mill ready or in Eugene drinking with his whores, Mother and I endured a lifetime shackled hand and foot to the loathsome woman he called Mother.

Grandma Lulu was tall, and she had sharp features, but I remember her more for qualities I never found: she had no soft, warm places. They had been hidden away like acorns lost in a hollow log. Grandma Lulu didn't have cheeks or lips so she bought no rouge and she wore no lipstick. Mother always did. What Grandma did wear was a smell that clung to her like bacon grease gone bad. Grandma Lulu's eyes were set so deep in her head, I never knew their color, but I sensed them shift with tiny movements. When they fixed on me, they always took something away. Safer for me to steal a quick glance when she wasn't looking, although I don't know why I tried. I guess I needed to get away with something.

Grandma Lulu was a devout woman. Above all, she was a careful Christian, and because of that, she never forgave Mother or me for our sins. I was born out of wedlock, or so she always thought. I guess that was my sin. Mother's obvious mark was that she had married my father, although Lulu suspected her of even greater failings. While we lived with her, Lulu also worried about herself. In her mind, intercourse with the devil, proximity to sin, rubbed off on the unsuspecting. If it left a stain, it would detour, forever, her march to glory.

If Lulu ever had sex, and she must have done it twice since she bore two sons, nothing about it could have been consensual—on anybody's part. With the Bible under her head and a hymnal under her butt, she'd have been conjuring up visions of retribution with each successive thrust. At some point during their marriage, Grandpa Charlie, mining engineer that he was, must have run some calculations and realized he'd tapped into a seam of cold, unyielding flint. Long before Mother and I moved in, Grandpa Charlie took off for Mexico, leaving Lulu ripe with a small goodbye present, his exclamation point at the end of a very long sentence.

Lulu was a woman done in by disappointment. When Grandpa Charlie left her with an unborn child to clothe and an empty marriage to dress up, it's a good guess he contributed to her sour world view. Even with that, Lulu's outlook was as much a product of her character as it was her circumstance. Lulu was quick to let the world know that she was Lulu Shaver first and a Fraser second—it was only through marriage to Grandpa

Charlie that she had ended up a Fraser. Lulu put God—and anyone else who mattered—on notice that she cast her lot with the all mighty Shavers, and not with the Frasers, but that didn't stop her from hoarding the Fraser money.

Lulu held on to the three-story Fraser home after Grandpa Charlie left her. The house overlooked the river, the town, and the family's gristmill. A covered porch wrapped the home and sheltered two roaring stone lions that guarded the front door. With her neck thrust forward and her hands clasped behind her back, Grandma Lulu would pace around the porch, smacking her lips and surveying the town from all angles. Lulu's house, with pink shrub roses along the foundation and lions out front, was the type of dwelling people must have envied when they walked by, pointing. Life inside the walls was far different.

"Teddy! Come here this minute!" For whatever reason, Grandma Lulu was hell bent on improving me. If I saw her reach into her housedress pocket, I knew the fiddler would have to be paid. I'd take a few more licks at my nose and then shuffle toward her.

"You are a disgusting little boy!"

I already knew that.

She'd be wearing one of two faded cotton housedresses, buttoned from chin to knees, with large pockets on either side where she carried keys, reading glasses, and used facial tissue. She'd hook me with one hand and wave a wad of moist tissue with the other; she'd be all over me, smearing her crusts across my lips and up my nose. Grandma Lulu never threw a tissue away unless my mucus had soiled it.

This was the Roaring Twenties! Music and fun filled every home in America—except Lulu's. But that didn't stop Mother and me from secretly sharing forbidden melodies. Our favorite was "Lulu's Lament." I still remember every word of it, far better than I do the Lord's Prayer, which Grandma Lulu tried to drill into me. Mom sang best, so she'd start out, and then I'd follow:

Bring Pearl; she's a darn nice girl,
But don't bring Lulu.
Bring Rose with an upturned nose,
But don't bring Lulu.
With her bottom bare, how the boys did stare.
When she hula-hula'd, she stroked her facial hair.

With all she had—the house, saw mill, flour mill, and the town's electricity generating plant—Grandma Lulu never could trust another person, not even her son. She refused to turn any of the business over to Dad, and he wasn't one to work for his mother. So, Dad left Lulu to manage the businesses on her own, and she left him to manage as best he could on his own—without one extra cent to his name.

I'm nearly ninety years old and still thinking way too much about my grandma. Must be some kind of Oedipus complex, a hidden hankering that skipped a generation—what a laugh! Lulu never condoned music, so I love it, and I always turn the volume way up. I explain to people that I'm paying the price for spending too many years around saws and machinery, that the high-pitched sound of whirring blades destroyed the bones behind my eardrum, but there's more to it than that.

My second wife, the one with breast cancer, was always telling me to turn the music down, but between my low volume hearing and the high volume speakers, I could barely hear her. By the end of our mar-

riage, she was as big as a barn, with matching blood pressure. She'd thunder over to me, red-faced, like a hypertensive elephant.

"You're shaking the whole place!" she'd holler. That was the kettle calling the pot black.

She started pushing for a bigger place. "We can afford it," she harped, which wasn't altogether accurate, since I was the only one of us with any money. What she was really saying, without coming right out with it, was that she wanted her own space without me squatting in the middle of it, and she saw no problem in tapping my nest egg to finance it. I can't say I blame her. I wasn't much of a companion.

That, and her cancer, did it for me. I divorced her. No sense in throwing good money after bad, but don't let anyone tell you a prenuptial agreement makes the process easy; it just makes it different. She moved to Seattle to be with her daughter, and I stayed in Eugene, so the bulk of two states now separate us. She got her space, but now that she's gone, I sometimes miss her.

7

Images stay with me, more so than words and facts. I use images to make sense of the world, which might be due to my basic wiring or simply because I spent so much my life watching. I store them and bring them out when I need them. On the empty big screen in front of me—my personal electronic story board—I move images and massage them. I flip and rotate them. The Big Screen has become my last, best window.

I've been watching Dad, thinking about how he came to buy the Culp Creek mill, wondering how he so easily got caught up in Wulf Gehring's clutches. The deal he made to buy the mill turned out to be one Dad's favorite stories; in varying forms, he must have told it a million times. The basic facts are clear enough, but the shadowy spaces lying in between remain open to interpretation. Dad would say different, but I'm convinced that he gave away too much from the beginning.

Dad despised filbert trees. This might seem unrelated to him buying the mill, but it had everything to do with it. Steadfast like the pioneers who had planted them, these filbert trees lined our valley roads like domestic servants. In truth, I don't think he hated the filberts so much as what they stood for: order, patience, and what he called, "an unfounded optimism." When Dad sped past, with row after uniform row of planted trees flickering by, all he saw were men and women, weary generations of them, picking and pruning in the shadows and then disappearing—silent actors moving across another silent screen. Dad never saw the value of planting trees and expending the effort it took to raise them, especially when compared to a stand of wild Douglas fir left by God for him to take. Dad wasn't a silent actor; he saw himself as a hunter.

Dad and Lulu were cut from the same block of hardwood, and to add insult to Dad's injury, Lulu assumed all responsibility for sculpting him. While she gouged and chiseled daily, it's hard to see where Grandpa Charlie had a thing to say about any of it, even before he left. I think Charlie did well just to keep his own pecker out of harm's way.

Lulu and Dad spent their lives chasing goals that drove them nonstop. Lulu sought her exaltation through faith. Step by squeaky step, she pursued it through a narrow spiritual conduit, sized only for her. The way Dad saw things, exaltation didn't come nearly that easily. In his eyes, a Cadillac, rolled leather seats, and a country club membership were goals worthy of his effort. Attaining those rewards in this life trumped valet parking with Saint Peter in the next.

Wulf Gehring set up his first business meeting with Dad in the lobby of the old Bartell Hotel in Cottage Grove. Wulf had developed a lucrative niche with the regional banks by managing mill properties that fell into receivership. Dad knew him only by reputation: although approachable and polite, Wulf never let sentiment interrupt the consummation of a deal.

Cottage Grove was located twenty miles south of Eugene. Because Dad was a stickler for being on time—another of Lulu's traits—he gave himself plenty of time for the drive and arrived early. He circled the hotel twice, but decided to park two blocks down the street because he didn't want to be seen in a Ford, not with an Oakland Roadster and two Cadillacs out front.

He slowed the Ford to an easy stop, but remained behind the wheel, as he listened to the engine cool with the tick-tick sound of contracting metal. He slipped a gold watch from his vest pocket and cradled it against the flat of his hand. He found its weight a comfort, its appearance an anchor. He opened a fresh pack of cigarettes, struck a match, and stripped the tobacco with a long, deep pull. With images and dreams hurtling by, he held the bloom for a few seconds and then slowly exhaled, watching the hazy stream fan out against the glass. He tipped his head back, eyes half closed like a fakir meditating. With dark eyes and gaunt cheeks, Dad nourished the look of an ascetic, although he never would be one.

Ten minutes before ten and another cigarette later, Dad returned the watch to its pocket and angled the mirror down. He examined his tie: a perfect Windsor with a tight dimple. He gave it a tug and reached for the door handle.

The traffic seemed light for a Saturday morning. Older Model T's rattled by, coupes too, and a few pickups. The boys who ran Woodson's Service Station across the street had propped open the big doors and were rolling out their tires. One of the boys nodded a careful greeting.

"Morning," Dad called out, returning the boy's nod with a bonus, his engaging smile. Perhaps without recognizing its power, Dad instinctively knew to mold his face to fit the occasion and frame the necessary sentiment. He rarely passed up an opportunity to cultivate a friendship and calculate its potential return.

The Bartell Hotel was a fixture on Main Street. Gold letters arched across its big front window and spoke of permanence. The gilt edging along the façade had dulled over the years, further adding to its respectability. The lobby, reminiscent of Grandpa Charlie's country club, was where the high muck-a-mucks held court. Dad tried to glance inside as he strode past the large lobby window, but reflected light from the morning sun screened the interior. He might have pierced the glare by squinting or by shielding his eyes with a hand, but he knew better.

A bell jangled overhead when he pushed through the door. The desk clerk and three men in the lobby looked up, and one of the men laughed. Blue smoke circled their leather chairs, and a brass floor lamp washed yellow across an oriental carpet. Wulf Gehring was sprawled in a chair next to the lamp, wearing his comfort like a broad smile. When he saw Dad, he stood up. The other two men remained where they were—backs to the door, chairs tipped up, feet propped on the steam radiator.

Wulf wrapped Dad's offered hand warmly between his two. "Thanks for coming down," he said, telegraphing intentions no less benign than a preacher on the church steps.

Dad relaxed. He thought the man would be tougher.

"Gentlemen," Wulf said, addressing his two associates, "This young man is Merle Fraser."

The men turned their heads enough to see him. Ennis Neet, closest to Dad, had financed every enterprise worth owning in Cottage Grove. He used his bank's money like grease on a gear, sparingly and where it counted. From the looks of him, the blood Neet had sucked over the years hadn't stayed with him. Dressed in a black suit and vest, the pale, wary banker appeared ready to preside over his own funeral. He coldly touched Dad's hand with skin that belonged in another world.

"Well, I'll be damned!" Jackie Sagers, the other man, blurted out. "This can't be Charlie's little boy!" He grinned openly and leaned through Neet as if he were a shadow. He gripped Dad's hand with power and moved with the robust confidence of a healthy man. Flamboyant by most standards, certainly worthy of notice in a lumber town, Sagers dressed in striped suits, silk ties, and he shined his shoes. Sagers was an engineering genius, and everybody knew it.

"How is Charlie?" Sagers persisted. "Did he fall off the edge of the earth?" Grandpa Charlie had been a founding member of the Eugene Country Club, along with Wulf and Sagers. He'd remained a member until he walked out on the family.

"He's in Mexico," Dad said, failing to mention that he hadn't seen Grandpa Charlie in five years, not since Charlie decided to shack up with the Mexican señorita.

Sagers chuckled. "That would explain it."

Ennis Neet smiled for the first time.

"He's developing a mining claim in Sonora."

Dad had come prepared to wade through their shit, he later told me, but he had no intention of making a meal out of it. He fixed his eyes squarely on Wulf Gehring. "Can we get down to business?"

Wulf nodded his approval. "Let's grab a table by the window." Turning back to Sagers and Neet, he said, "Mr. Fraser and I have business to discuss."

"You girls go on," Sagers said, waving a fat cigar. "Ennis and I will be fine."

Wulf guided Dad to a small table. "Those two can get a little full of themselves," he confided. He produced a pack of Lucky Strikes, offered Dad the first cigarette, and wrapped his lips around the second. "For a serious discussion," he said, lighting Dad's cigarette and then his own, "I've always felt that two is the ideal number. When more than two get to talking, there's no telling who wants what." With his wire rimmed glasses and quiet air, Wulf seemed confident and in control. He was respectful and obviously expected the same in return.

Dad pulled in a lungful of smoke, looked out the window, and waited for his heart to slow. His gaze settled on the burgundy Cadillac. The top was down and the white leather seats reflected the morning sun like mother of pearl.

"You can take it for a drive if you like," Wulf offered. "There isn't another car like it in Lane County."

Dad let the offer pass. He arranged his notes on the small walnut table between them. He tapped his ash into the tray and cleared this throat.

"You're married, aren't you?" Wulf said.

The question had to have caught Dad off guard. The whole concept of marriage unsettled him. "That's right."

"And you've got a boy?"

"In a manner of speaking."

I honestly don't know if those were Dad's exact words, but this is how the shadows flow together for me. I wouldn't blame him if they were. I turned out to be the wrong boy, and that was no more his fault than it was mine.

"Does he favor you or his mother?"

"Listen," Dad said, "I drove a long way to discuss the Culp Creek mill."

"By all means," Wulf replied, showing his teeth.

Going into the meeting, Dad had intended to play the rookie. He let a hint of worry cross his face, and then mixed in some embarrassment. If Gehring believed he could take him, the old wolf might get careless. "I suppose you've seen the mill," Dad stuttered.

Wulf studied Dad before answering. "I spent a full week inventorying the assets." Gehring was a financial matchmaker. He scrubbed failure from one bankruptcy and then offered it to the next sucker, as a recipe for success.

Dad had done his homework, too. He knew that Wulf preferred to sell a mill intact rather than piecemeal because it required less effort and resulted in a better return. The bank received a few cents on the dollar, and Wulf did even better. The Culp Creek mill had been sitting idle for months.

"The work and money needed to get the mill running will be staggering." Dad sounded as if he were already struggling through the obstacles.

Wulf lifted a hand and stopped Dad. "I am legally obligated to get as much as I can for the bank," he said. "That is my primary responsibility." He paused. "That being said, I appreciate that there has to be give and take on both sides."

For the second time that morning, Dad relaxed. He wanted Wulf to come up with the first number. Although Wulf's commission depended on the selling price, both men knew that Wulf was haggling over somebody else's money.

"Resurrecting that mill won't be a simple task. It might not even be possible."

Wulf held up his hand a second time, which irritated Dad. "It takes money to buy a mill," Wulf said, "even more to run one. If you don't have it, then we're wasting our time." He stubbed his cigarette against the ashtray's blackened glass. "Are we wasting our time, Merle?"

"I have the money!" The words spilled out much too fast, and Dad knew better. He slowed down. "What do you honestly expect to get for a boarded up, peckerwood mill halfway up the valley? For a mill that's worth less today than it was yesterday?"

Wulf's face took on an air of concern. "If it's so worthless, why buy it?" He was a chameleon, constantly changing his expression, inflexion, and words to gain the upper hand.

Dad wasn't about to give up. "Can't you recognize the fact that nobody else is willing to take a risk on it?"

"What I recognize, and don't think me too crude when I say it, is that a business deal is like a virgin. Pluck it the second it becomes available or forever miss the opportunity."

That was when Dad famously decided to frame the issue in terms that any man, especially an older man sitting on the upside of respectability and on the down slope of opportunity, might understand. "I'll go your virgin one better, Mr. Gehring."

Wulf smiled.

"Ever have a woman with tits like Florida grapefruits walk up, grab you by the balls, and offer her stuff for free?"

Wulf showed no visible reaction. "I don't see the relevance."

"Wait, there's more." It was Dad's turn to hold up his hand. "Hours later, when you're exhausted, thinking you're done with her, when all you want is a smoke and a rare cut of beef, you discover she's only getting started. Before you can grab your pants and run, this insatiable woman locks her thighs around your hips and demands a whole lot more."

Across the table, Wulf swallowed hard.

"Mr. Gehring, as much as you and I and every other son-of-a-bitch might wish for it, a fairy tale like this doesn't happen. If we wait and hope and do nothing more, we'll lie awake at night with an eye on the door and a hand under the covers, and we'll die disappointed."

"We wouldn't want that."

"I know I have to pay a little to get a little. Nothing comes free. But I'll be damned if I'll let the bitch walk off with someone else! For the first time since 1920, the lumber market is showing some life, and I'm sitting on my hands. I can turn that peckerwood mill around and make both of us a few dollars doing it. I guarantee it."

"Six thousand dollars, cash."

Dad finally had a number. He reworked the calculations in his head. He had hoped that Wulf would open at five. To even get into the bidding, he'd have to wrestle a thousand from Lulu—far from a sure thing. Add that to the three thousand he'd received in insurance money, and four thousand was all he had. "Are we talking about the same mill?"

"I expect we are," Wulf said mildly.

Dad pointed to the street. "I don't see any buyers lining up."

"It only takes one."

"I'll give you four thousand," Dad said. "The extra business the railroad picks up by shipping my lumber will be added gravy for the bank." Dad had taken time to understand the railroad's finances. Its revenue had fallen nearly to zero since the closure of the upstream gold mine two years earlier. Neet's bank now owned the OS&E railroad. The bank and its shareholders had much more at stake in keeping the railroad solvent than in the sales price of a small sawmill.

Wulf glanced toward Neet and Sagers who were still seated across the lobby. He seemed to be working some calculations of his own. "You have a deal," he said finally, "but with one small condition."

"What's that?"

"You agree in writing to use me exclusively as your lumber broker."

This stipulation surprised Dad. It gave Gehring complete power to dictate the price he'd be paid for his lumber. Wulf would be able to rip Dad's heart out in a single blow or slowly bleed him to death. "I can't do that."

Wulf pushed his chair back from the table.

"Unless," Dad said before thinking things through, "we agree on a limit, say a dollar per thousand." Wulf looked interested. "You remain my exclusive broker unless I'm able get a dollar per thousand more somewhere else. I need a little protection here."

Wulf's smile returned. "Bring a check on Monday."

"I can't make it Monday," Dad said. He had to nail down that extra thousand dollars—the money he hoped to get from Grandma Lulu.

"Tuesday, then."

"I'll see what I can do."

Red erupted across Wulf's forehead. "Come up with the money by Wednesday. Otherwise, the price to you becomes eight thousand." Wulf slapped two dollars on the table. "Here's a start. The rest is up to you."

Dad's heart was pounding in his ears. Sweat tracked cold along his ribs. He didn't move from the table until he'd seen the burgundy Cadillac disappear at the far end of the street. Only then did he reach for Gehring's dollar bills. He stopped at the front desk and laid Wulf's money on the counter.

"Will this cover the gentlemen's tab?" he said, pointing toward Sagers and Neet.

"That's more than enough," the young clerk answered.

"Keep the change," Dad said, loud enough for his audience to hear. "I won't need it."

8

Dad's head hurt when he stepped from the Bartell Hotel, and his mouth was dry. Sunlight shimmied off the parked chrome and danced along the wet street, disorienting him. He steadied himself against the building's brick. The mill felt real one moment, and then it evaporated. Somehow, he had to find a thousand dollars. On top of that, he needed a logger with timber and a couple of trucks, a steam shovel, a crew, and God knows what else. He dreaded the fact that he'd have to beg his mother for money. Subtlety was a variety of rose Lulu's garden never grew.

When Dad reached Woodson's Chevron, a dilapidated flatbed truck was sitting next to the pump with the hood up. One of the attendants was checking the oil and chatting up the driver. The other attendant was topping off the gasoline. The driver inside the cab looked vaguely familiar, but Dad couldn't place him and didn't stop to consider it further. He stuck his head inside the garage and asked to borrow the phone. The owner was easy about it when Dad offered to call collect. It took the operator ten minutes to put the call through and another three before Lulu agreed to accept the charges.

The green Packard truck was gone by the time Dad emerged from the garage. He stared at the empty spot and again tried to make the connection. When he reached the roadster and slid behind the wheel, he was still thinking about the truck and driver. He tapped the dashboard with his fingers and glanced down the street. The Packard was parked across from the National Guard Armory with several dozen uniformed soldiers out front. The weekend warriors were drilling; that was the reason the traffic had been so light. Dad knew all about spit and polish and close order drill from his ROTC days. One quick look told him this group of warriors wouldn't be winning any competitions. Amused and a little curious, Dad idled down Main Street for a closer look. He pulled up behind the green truck.

The Cottage Grove guard unit, like so many others throughout the country, had devolved into a social club for members and served no real purpose. After President Wilson and Congress had tallied up the country's losses from WWI, they swore the United States would never again fight a European War. Some officials argued for no military at all. As a result, the U.S. ranked nineteenth among world armies in 1929—just behind Portugal and Bulgaria. Judging from the level of expertise Dad was witnessing, he would have pushed the country's fighting ability farther down the list—on par with Luxembourg. The Cottage Grove unit's official mission was to man an artillery battery at the mouth of the Columbia River, but the only real security the unit provided was a monthly paycheck for its members.

Age, a little luck, and some close order maneuvering on Dad's part had prevented him from participating in The Great War. But once the war was over, well after the smoke had cleared, Dad began to look upon his lack of military service with mixed feelings—relief and regret—but he voiced only regret about missing the action. However, he never uttered one word of regret about pushing me into the next war. In 1942, it was easy for him to be a patriot.

The truck's cab door swung open ahead of him, and a tall, athletic man climbed out. Dad finally made the connection—August Backer, a.k.a. big, dumb, and ugly Gust.

Dad rolled down his window. "Gust, is that you?"

The man turned and grinned. It was no surprise to Dad that Gust recognized him right off. "Indeed," he said. "It is I." That sounded just like Gust, either butchering the King's English or overdoing it.

The muscle covering Gust's chest had grown thicker, the shoulders more powerful, but poor old Gust hadn't gotten any prettier. Dad shook his head at what he saw.

"What's it been," Dad asked, "eight years?"

"That may be so."

Dad waved toward the bustling uniforms. "You part of this?"

"No," Gust said, scratching his scalp and checking the fingernail. "Not yet, anyway." Gust seemed unsure. "But they're looking to hire."

"I thought you were on track to play pro ball."

"I never made it to the Big Leagues," Gust apologized. "And in the minors, you can't hardly make your way." He dug at his scalp again. "I'd be gone all the time…it wasn't working."

"I see," Dad said.

"I have a family now," Gust added.

"Ahh, so here you are."

Gust pointed to a little man with captain's bars on his shoulders and hands on his hips. He was barking orders. "Sid Mackenzie told me to come by. That's him."

In addition to his small stature, Mackenzie had a tiny chin and an even smaller mouth, but that wasn't what Dad saw. Mackenzie had stage presence. He looked like a small, wiry dog—a Jack Russell terrier—who had long since concluded that size was not a measure that applied to him.

"This unit is in the midst of a big shakeup," Gust said. "The government is set to build a new two-story armory with a drill hall big enough to play ball in, and Mackenzie was just made commander. The armory job, by itself, is worth half a million board feet of lumber.

"Didn't hear word one about it," Dad said.

Gust winked. "Mackenzie got the job on a who-you-know basis. He commanded a logging platoon in Europe during the big war."

"That was all it took?" Dad was already grieving an opportunity lost. "Any more openings?"

"Not for officers. One of Mackenzie's high school buddies is second in command. His lawyer is next in line. The three of them are tied to Dolomite Lumber, which Mackenzie owns. Mackenzie calls the shots as to who gets into the unit, and he approves all bids for new construction."

"That should buy him some friends," Dad said.

"He's got plenty already."

"Was he some kind of war hero?"

"I wouldn't go that far." Gust thought for a moment. "If you want a piece of the armory contract, you'll have to join the unit. The Klan, too," he said.

Mackenzie glanced their way. He spotted Gust.

"Gotta go," Gust said. With several long, muscular strides, he was at the commander's side.

9

Dad had planned to take Highway 99 from Cottage Grove to Eugene, but instead turned onto a back road. He needed time to think. The roadster's spoked wheels splashed through puddles where the road ran straight. At the turns, he sent power to the rear wheels, forcing them into a controlled slide, consumed with the thrill of crossing a line and pulling back. As he pushed the roadster faster and faster, Dad chased Gehring and Neet down the winding descent into the Willamette Valley.

Dad accelerated with a change of gears and felt the familiar press of the seat against his back. The roadster hummed at the upper end of its range. Ahead of him, an ancient covered bridge squatted over the road like an old troll. Tucked in a shady hollow, spanning a modest stream, the forgotten bridge had grayed with the years. Neglect had blistered its paint, and it sagged toward the water. Dad didn't notice. His thoughts were lagging miles far behind, still stuck at the Bartell Hotel. When he finally sensed the danger, it was much too late.

The roadster exploded across the uneven threshold; it was sent airborne inside the covered bridge. A shadow followed, draping the coupe's windshield and blinding him. The tires struck the rotten planking with enough force to launch Dad into the windshield and drive his teeth through his tongue, and when the injured roadster exited the covered bridge, Dad was unconscious. Slowing, it veered onto the soft shoulder and then disappeared off the road.

When Dad came to, he was flopped forward against the steering column. The car's front end was tipped down the bank toward the river, somehow suspended. Red spattered the dashboard and windshield in front of him. At first, he didn't feel pain, but he tasted salt and he smelled raw gasoline. His tongue felt too large for his mouth, and then his skull began to hurt, and so did his ribs.

He pushed against the door handle, stepped out, and cautiously tried to stand, but nearly blacked out. Black bile resembling last week's coffee splattered the dirt around his shoes. He sucked a clot from behind his nose, coughed it out, and then wiped his mouth on his shirt. He stepped over the mess and began to slowly circle the car, leaning on it for balance.

The bridge had taken paint from three fenders and had crumpled a wheel well. The right front fender had carved a groove into the rubber, but the tire hadn't blown. Beneath the chassis, the rear axle was high-centered on a boulder, and the gas line was broken. Gasoline coated the undercarriage and was pooling in the weeds. Dad gripped the bent fender and pulled, but the sharp metal gouged his hand, and his breastbone crackled painfully.

"God dammit!" he yelped. "It's a goddamn day from hell." Giving up on the car, he slowly retreated up the bank on his hands and knees. The road was not well traveled, and since he wasn't up to walking, he settled into a nest of pine needles and wished—didn't pray—for salvation in any form.

"If wishes were horses, beggars would ride." The familiar words rose red from Lulu's lips, and that pissed him off even more.

The rumble of a truck engine roused Dad. The driver downshifted as the truck approached the stream from the other side. For several minutes, the covered bridge blocked Dad's view. In due time, an old Packard truck slid out from under the shadow and slowly stepped across the rough transition between the bridge and the road. When Dad tried to stand, his rib popped again, and he let out another yelp.

Gust jumped from the cab and ran toward him.

"Your timing is impeccable, Gust." Those were the words Dad wanted to get out, but he only mumbled. His lips were stuck to his teeth, and his tongue didn't work.

Gust took Dad by the elbow and sat him back down. "Let's make sure you're not killed." He pulled a handkerchief from his pocket. "Wipe the blood off so we can see what we've got."

Dad tentatively touched the handkerchief to his face.

"That didn't do shit," Gust said, actually laughing at him.

"It's stuck down," Dad said, trying not to sound offended. "Haven't you got any water with you?"

Gust grinned and laughed even louder. "You're as ugly as me, now!"

Dad grinned, too, but didn't believe a word of it.

Gust returned from the stream carrying two bottles filled with icy water. Dad was well into the second bottle before he thought to ask Gust if he was thirsty. "Want some?" he said, extending the nearly empty container.

"I filled up at the stream."

"You don't have anything stronger, do you?" Dad said.

"I stay away from the sauce these days."

It hadn't always been that way, Dad recalled. Not even close.

Gust walked to his truck and began rummaging through the back. He dragged out a logging chain and hooked one end to the Packard's front bumper. He wrapped the other end around Dad's rear axle and had the truck engine roaring before Dad could get out of the way.

"Let me know when the slack's out," Gust yelled over the engine noise. Without waiting for an answer, he revved the engine and slipped the clutch. The chain stiffened, the truck's rear duals dug down, and the roadster lurched off the boulder and up the bank. Gust jumped from the cab.

"How'd you get into this mess?" he said, gathering up the chain.

"I blew a tire."

"The tires seem fine now."

The revelation caught Dad by surprise. "It's a strange deal," he said.

"That it is," Gust said. "Add one more to life's endless mysteries."

Dad limped to the roadster and pulled a pint bottle from the glove box. The alcohol cut through the dried blood and cleared his mouth. When it found his tongue, he thought he'd been stabbed.

"Sure you don't want a hit?" Dad gasped. "One can't hurt."

Gust waved away the offer. "I don't want it, and don't ask again."

The two men stared at each other: one with a bottle in his hand, the other holding a heavy chain.

"You won't be driving this wreck any time soon," Gust said, more gently. "What say I pull you in?"

Dad shook off the suggestion without considering it. "It's a great idea, Gust, but it won't work." Dad had been through enough catastrophes for one day without Gust adding to them. "You'll snap the chain or pull off a bumper."

"Have some faith."

Dad wanted to remind Gust that a college dropout without an engineering degree didn't have the background needed to understand centrifugal forces and inertia. Instead, he said, "You don't need to do this."

"Consider it a sip from the milk bottle of human kindness." Gust gave Dad's steel bumper a solid kick. "This shouldn't take long."

By the time Gust finished, Dad acknowledged that the contraption might work. Gust had bolted the center of his logging chain to truck's rear hitch with the two ends angling out. Those he bolted to the Ford's front end, forming a triangle. He pulled a railroad tie from the back of his truck, cut it to length, and notched the ends. He wedged the railroad tie between the truck and car so it acted like the tongue of a wagon with the triangular chains serving as side braces.

"If we tried to pull you with the chain alone," Gust said, looking satisfied, "your little roadster would chase after us like a loose cannon." He signaled for Dad to get in. "Let's give her a go, Orville."

Gust smoothly shifted through the gears as he accelerated. He and Dad stared into their side mirrors without speaking.

When the truck's speed leveled off at thirty-five, with the damaged roadster tamely following, Dad began to relax. He glanced at Gust with more than a little interest. Gust's eyes were moving systematically from the winding road to his mirrors and back as he concentrated on his driving. Dad was beginning to see Gust in a different light.

Dad surveyed the cab. An old horse blanket covered the bench seat. Under it, a coiled spring prodded him with every bump. The steel knob that capped the gearshift lever had been polished to a dull patina through years of use. Grease rags and newspaper fragments littered the cab, and near the brake pedal, where a two-inch hole had rusted through the floorboard, the gravel road slid by. The engine's heat rose through the floorboards, carrying strong vapors of gasoline and transmission fluid.

"Turn the heat down," Dad said.

"No can do!" Gust yelled over the engine noise. "There isn't any heater. It's just hot as hell in here." He spread his ugly grin. "In winter, it works out fine."

Dad leaned as far from the engine as he could get. He opened his window. "How did you come up with the towing idea? I've never seen anything like it."

"Me neither," Gust said.

"You've never towed a car like this before?"

"Nope," Gust said. "But it seemed like a good idea...even if it wasn't going to work."

Dad ignored the comment.

"I like solving problems," Gust continued. "I loved geometry at the university. I could have made a good teacher if I'd stuck with it."

"And I figured you were there just to play ball."

"That was the problem."

Gust double-clutched at the crest of a steep hill and slipped the truck into low. "Might get a little tricky here," he said. "These brakes are well shy of new."

Dad held his breath.

When the hill leveled out, Gust continued, "Nobody in the family has any college, and it was baseball that got me there in the first place. Before I even knew what college was about, I let baseball pull me away. I didn't think school compared to a minor league try-out."

"You were a sure bet."

Gust slipped a hand from the steering wheel and waved the thought away. "That's old water under the bridge now. I've got a good home, and once I drop you off, home is exactly where I intend to go."

"Wish I could say the same."

"Don't you have a home?"

"Gust that is a great question. An honest-to-God Hamlet question."

Gust didn't seem to follow.

"Hamlet: 'To be or not to be?'" Dad said, smiling at him. "You know, one of those really big questions."

"It's Shakespeare. I know that much."

"I do have a roof over my head," Dad said, "but it's not my home. It's my goddamn mother's." He looked over to Gust and softly shook his head. "To tell you the truth, I don't know what I have, but I am looking at a place along the Row River."

"My uncle and me," Gust said, "we log a tract on the Row. I can't see anybody calling that area home unless he's some kind of woodpecker."

"Why the national guard?" Dad said, changing the subject.

Gust shrugged. "It's only a weekend a month, and the pay isn't bad. Mackenzie says he'll hire me on full time if I join the guard. Working for my uncle doesn't pay regular. He for-gets I have a family, and family has to come first." Dad didn't respond. "I haven't decided that I'm doing it."

"What exactly are you talking about?" Dad said.

"I don't know that I want to join the unit. It's thick with the Ku Klux Klan." Gust looked over. "All the boys have more than one uniform hanging in their closet, if you know what I mean."

"I thought that shit was over."

"It's not, and it's bigger in Cottage Grove than it ever was in Eugene."

10

Mother and I escaped in the dark, beneath a sky with no stars or moon. With our fingertips stretched out in front, we groped through the night, playing blind man's bluff. Grandma Lulu was the real reason we started out so early—she hadn't been able to sleep, worried sick we'd miss our train. I stumbled against one of her lions and ran my hand across a mane that was rough and cold.

"Can you see?" I whispered to Mother.

"Can you?"

"No."

We pushed through the heavy gate and crunched along the gravel drive toward Grandma's ancient Ford. She was already inside, waiting for us. I quickly slid past her and moled my way to the back seat through bags and boxes, where I stretched out among handles, rivets, and corners. Reassured by the growing distance from Lulu's house, I was asleep in seconds, not waking until we reached Cottage Grove.

I felt the car rattle over washboard. The tires were dropping in and out of potholes, and the suitcases were shifting underneath me. I lifted my head and peeked out. The night's rain had softened, and only an occasional drop troubled the brown pools sliding past. Grandma and Mother were bouncing on the seat in front of me. They looked like puppets caught on the same string. Grandma made no effort to miss the holes, and Mother didn't comment on the driving or the bumps.

"It's better that way," she'd always say.

At the end of the street, a platform began to grow out of the gloom. In the early morning light, people and things were taking shape. A kerosene lamp glowed yellow behind a small window, but did little to brighten the platform. Beside the lamp, a bald man was leaning over a desk.

Grandma braked hard in front of the depot, causing the car to slide through the mud. "This is where you get out," she said, acting as if she meant for us to sit crossways in the street.

"Where do we get our tickets?" Mother said.

Grandma pointed to the lighted window. "Ask the agent. That's what most people do."

Mother fumbled beneath the seat for her purse. She put a hand on the door handle and struggled with it, as well. Smiling a soft encouragement, she helped me out of the backseat into the morning gray. When I stepped from the car, an inch of fresh mud closed around my shoes with a pleasant slurp. I shifted my weight to test its grip, not really wanting to break free.

Thinking I should say goodbye, I looked toward Grandma. From her perch behind the steering wheel, she was staring straight ahead, watching the vibrating headlights dance against a featureless wall. I changed my mind.

Mother leaned through the open car door. "Thank you Grandma Fraser for all you've done for us." I don't think she expected an answer—her lowered eyes said that much—but still she waited for something. When it didn't come, she tried to close the door, but she couldn't manage with a bag in each hand.

Grandma reached a bony arm across the seat and yanked the door shut. Revving the engine and hunting through the gears for first, sounding as if she meant to murder them all, she killed the engine with a lurch that rocked the car. Without looking at us, she tortured the starter until the engine caught and then whipped the car forward with mud flying behind.

Mother smiled brightly at no one I could see. But who could have missed her waves of red hair and the spring flowers that floated across her summer dress or the fact that she stood in the town's only patch of morning sun? Mother was the most beautiful woman I have ever known. She could never understand people who hid their hearts behind their ribs, people with tiny muscles that beat only because they had to. And because her own heart pulsed so fully, I think she felt more alone than most people could have believed possible.

As soon as I was out of the car, I forgot about Grandma Lulu, even before she rattled off. I was far more interested in the mud oozing around my shoes. With a nice slurp, I pulled free of the muddy grip and began following a string of puddles, intending to wade through them all. Off to my left, a tired looking steam locomotive was wheezing in the damp air and coughing up black soot. White letters circled its stack, and blasts of steam erupted between heavy iron wheels at its belly. A coal car trailed the locomotive, followed by a single passenger car, two half-filled flatbeds and a red caboose with a lantern hanging from rear platform.

"Teddy!" It was Mother's frightened voice.

I looked back. She was on the platform, trying to find me, twisting her neck in circles. She spotted me and called out even louder, "Don't get your clothes muddy!"

"I won't," I promised, promises being what they were in our family—short-term commitments. I eased a shoe into the nearest murky pool, controlling its entry so as not to splash—she didn't need to remind me to be careful. At the end of the puddle, I checked for telltale spots on the white sailor suit. Nothing! Not a single splotch.

"I so want you to be dressed nicely for the trip," she had said before we started out, doing her best to convince me that the sailor suit made me look handsome. The cap and matching tie served no purpose that I could see, other than guarantee I'd be noticed. I was certain that real sailors wore them only because they had no choice in the matter, and that day, neither did I.

A crowd was forming on the platform around her, and more people were pressed together beneath the station eaves. The men standing in the most sheltered spots wore black coats, felt hats, and flashy ties like they were going to church with Grandma. The men in the open had on overalls and boots. I stuck out a hand and looked up. Gray filled the sky, but no rain. The promise of untracked mud and fresh puddles kept me moving forward.

"God dammit! Straighten this prick up!"

I jumped at the sound and turned toward its source.

Four workmen were struggling to roll a wooden crate onto a flatbed car. The crate was tilting dangerously, about to fall off the plank. Underneath it, a purple-faced man was pushing up with all his strength. A second man jumped down to help. When they finally got the crate righted and onto the car, the men threw a chain around it and snugged it down alongside the rest of the load.

I edged into the mix of people.

"Teddy! Be careful. Don't fall!"

I looked back again. Mother had moved to the edge of the platform. She was flailing her arms. "Teddy! Can you hear me?"

I have always preferred corners, quiet places away from people, like the warm kitchen floor near the stove with my Erector Set or a seat at the back of a classroom. These were hopeful places, free from the scrutiny of others. Mom never operated that way; she could be so big and dramatic, and that morning, with all those people watching, she was at her best. She wanted me at her side, out of harm's way, but I wasn't ready for that.

Two men standing next to her were following our exchange and grinning. The man closest to Mother was dressed in faded overalls, a denim shirt, and looked ready for hard work. Big muscles, the kind you see in draft animals, rippled under his shirt and down his arms. He stood soldier straight with a smile I liked, not like the man next to him whose smile edged out sideways like he thought Mother and I were some kind of dirty joke.

I worked my way farther into the growing thicket of strangers. A fat man, carrying a box of apples and puffing from the effort, stumbled into me. "Watch it, Sonny!"

It wasn't my fault.

Just the same, I moved off the street, onto the less crowded boardwalk. Supplies and crates were stacked along it, with barely enough room to squeeze by. I studied an especially large wooden crate. The stenciled letters on its sides had bled black in the rain. I made no effort to decipher the words, but even without the streaks, the letters would have roamed wild and senseless in front of me. I ran my fingers across the lettering, feeling for changes in texture at the margins of the paint. I sniffed the crate. The wood smelled like fresh pine, not hemlock or cedar. I dabbed at a blob of sticky yellow pitch and toyed with it. The pitch spread along my fingers, binding them together, creating a lobster claw that I repeatedly opened and closed. From the opposite side of the crate, I heard an angry man's voice.

"Wulf," the voice said, "why can't this sorry excuse for a train pull out on time, just once?"

I cautiously peered around the crate.

Three men were huddling together. One was skinny and pale, dressed all in black. He looked like Count Dracula. He was staring at a pocket watch. The man next to him seemed friendly enough—at least he was smiling. He had a bright red handkerchief in his jacket pocket. Off to the side, a third man was dressed in gray and didn't smile. He looked like a wolf.

I slid behind the crate and rubbed my hands against the clean wood. The pitch hung on, worse than any booger. I needed a rag and considered using my shorts, but I didn't dare. Instead, I pulled a pocket inside out, and in what seemed like a fair and magical trade, the pitch migrated onto the pocket liner in exchange for white cotton lint between my fingers. I used a second pocket for the other hand, confident that the crime would never be discovered.

"If Merle Fraser actually makes a go of it," I heard the wolf say, "we'll deal with him when we have to. The revenue his mill is generating for the railroad is useful right now. But change is on the way."

At the sound of Dad's name, I listened harder.

"Where will that leave Fraser?" Dracula said.

"I promise you, he won't be a problem," the wolf said.

The men moved into a doorway, and I suddenly remembered Mother. I looked for her on the platform, but she wasn't there. I jumped as high as I could, but everything around me was too tall. I tried running back, but people, wagons, and supplies blocked the way. She was about to leave without me.

When I reached the platform, people were spilling off the steps. Above me, the two men who had been laughing at me were there, but not Mother. I shouldered a doughy thigh, elbowed a kneecap, and began fighting my way up the stairs.

"Ouch!" It was a woman's voice, but I didn't care, and I didn't slow down.

If I had slowed, I might have noticed that countless winter rains had tortured the decking and had caused it to buckle. If I had hesitated, I might have seen the rust stained holes where nail after defeated nail had strained against the lumber before pulling through. I might have realized that thanks to the morning rain and a parade of muddy boots, the deck's surface was as slick as axle grease.

I was still struggling through the forest of legs and skirts when the train's whistle shrieked right on top of me. The harsh sound shocked my heart and surprised my legs. One shoe snagged a nail and the other shot out in front of me. I went down hard and fast, sliding in the direction of the train, not stopping until I smacked into a pair of ladies shoes and matching umbrella.

The fancy shoes shook me loose. Face down, I opened an eye and searched the depths of an empty knothole. Through the waves of laughter, I prayed for Jesus to pull me through the hole into the dark below the platform.

A voice reached out to me. It wasn't Jesus and it wasn't Mother.

"Are you hurt, son?" Big hands pulled me to my feet. "That was one hell of ride you took."

I started to sniffle.

The voice carried a smile at its edge. "Give you a nickel to see it again." A callused finger found my chin and gently pried my gaze from my shoes. Attached to the finger was the strong man I'd seen earlier, the man with the nice face.

The lady with the pointy shoes wasn't far way. She was clutching a Bible and pointing with her umbrella. "The little idiot," I heard her say.

"Don't listen to that," the big man said, laying a broad hand across my shoulder. "Her brand of Christian business can be a little light on charity."

"How could you, Teddy?" Mother said, running up, sounding and looking even more dramatic than usual. "Why do you do these things?" Always the same questions.

Since I didn't have an answer for either, I kept quiet and waited for the eruption.

"He slipped, ma'am." It was my new hero. "The footing here is treacherous."

I sneaked a peek. Mother was staring hard at the man. I could tell she wanted to say something cross, but for some unknown reason, the fire cooled, and she smiled. The immediate source of her pain—me—was forgotten.

"I don't think we've met," the big man said, holding out a hand. "I'm Boone Shaw. I live upstream."

"My name is Mrs. Marie Fraser," she said, formally taking his hand. "I live upstream, too, but just not yet." She sounded flustered. "Actually, I'm not sure where I live." She turned back to me. "Where we live." The pain again registered on her face. "We were, we are, traveling to be with my husband."

Cold water was seeping into my shorts and trickling down my legs like icy pee. I moved closer to Mother and tried to tuck in behind her skirt.

She pushed me away. "Don't move." She reached inside her purse. By the time she found her lace hankie, the trickle had become a torrent that forced me to stand bowlegged.

"Well, well, well! Didn't we catch us one sorry looking little mud puppy?" The scrawny man who earlier had been standing with Boone decided to join in. He laughed big at his joke. All his teeth were black near the gums and pointy. "This one ain't no keeper." He lunged toward me with dirty fingernails that looked like claws. "We better throw him back."

Boone stepped forward and blocked him. "Not today, Mohl."

The nasty man stopped, stepped back and shrugged. "Sure thing, Big Boone." He stared at me. "We was only having some fun. You got to wonder, with him dressed prissy like that and falling down for no reason, the kid must be some kind of glass ass."

Then, as quickly as he had started, Mohl forgot about me and turned his gaze on my mother. More than likely, she had been his primary interest all along. He smiled widely at her. In addition to being pointy and black, his teeth were sized way too small for his mouth. They looked like they had been filed.

"The name's Rodney Mohl," he said, not waiting to be introduced. "Me and Boone are partners. My buddies call me Mohl, but you can call me Big Rod." He rocked back on his heels and stared into Mother's eyes, laughing when she blushed. Dirt and grease stained his bib overalls. He hadn't shaved in several days. His beard grew in clumps with the bulk of the stubble clustering around his chin and directly under his nose. Hair sprouted from his nose holes, and with each whistling breath, the hairs slipped in and out like hungry caterpillars. Above the teeth and the sly smile, Mohl wore a narrow felt hat pulled down low so that the brim obscured his eyes.

"Uh...hello," was all Mother could manage.

"Hello to you, too, sweetheart," Mohl said, under his breath.

Mother immediately turned toward Boone. Since her back was all Mohl had to address, he returned to me.

"And hello to you, Glass Ass." He played with the brim of his hat, patting and creasing it, all the time staring at Mother.

"Mr. Shaw," Mother said in a voice louder than usual, "my husband, Merle Fraser, bought a saw mill near Culp Creek. Have you heard of it?"

"I've already done some work for your husband," he said. "Mohl, too."

The train whistle shrieked again, but I was ready for it. Boone and Mohl started toward the passenger car. Mother started on my clothes with her hankie, trying her best to make me presentable, but she quickly gave up. Shaking her head, she also started toward the passenger car.

Boone and Mohl hadn't yet climbed aboard. They were standing near the door, watching a piece of cargo being loaded.

"I need to be sure that my shipment gets strapped down," I heard Boone say. The crate in question was the one I'd been interested in earlier, the wooden box with the black, stenciled letters. I wanted to know what was inside and dropped behind Mother to ask about it.

"Yes, sir," Mohl was saying, "I'd like a mouthful of that titty. The bitch knows what she's got." He licked his lips when he saw me and grinned. "I'd give 'em a little twist, and she'd like it fine."

All I could see were his teeth. I turned and ran as fast as I could toward Mother, not caring if I fell.

"For Christ's sake, Mohl," I heard Boone's harsh whisper, "for once, just shut the fuck up!"

11

With Mother behind me, pushing, I stumbled up the portable step into a dingy passenger car. A crow in a blue uniform scowled at us. "Don't let that dirty boy touch a thing."

"He'll be careful."

We edged past the sour conductor and moved down the aisle, past rows of scarred wooden benches. We squeezed between the other passengers and their luggage. "Excuse me. Excuse us, please," Mother kept saying.

When we found an empty bench. Mother pulled a newspaper from her purse and spread it across the wooden surface, thought better of it, and then added a second layer before allowing me to sit.

"Madam, please!" The conductor's voice was higher than you'd expect from a man.

Mother was still rustling newspaper, so she didn't hear. As far as I could tell, the pain she was taking to cover the bench served little purpose since my backside had escaped the mud, but that didn't matter since her actions were for show. She was letting everyone know that she was a good mother.

"You are blocking the aisle!" The conductor's command was another octave higher.

Mother heard him. She blushed, and her hands moved faster as she worked the newspaper into position, patting and smoothing.

The conductor began pushing through passengers to get to us. "We have a schedule to keep!"

"And just when did that start, Chivas?" Boone's words resonated like thunder after a brief squall. He had taken the bench in front of us. Mohl chose the seat across from him.

Mother turned her worried smile toward the conductor. "We're ready now," she said brightly, giving me a shove. "You, get in and slide all the way to the window."

The sailor cap, tucked inside my back pocket, had gotten through the disaster unscathed. I considered putting it on to please her. Had she asked, I'd have done so without complaining, but she didn't ask. The layered paper stuck to the back of my legs as I scooted across and began to shred. As it pulled apart, it revealed a stained, gouged, and well-worn bench.

"Look at this!" I shouted, pointing to the scarred wood. "It's already wrecked." The seatback in front of us was no better, its varnish worn down to raw oak along the top. I tugged on her sleeve to show her, but she jerked her arm away.

"Don't do that!"

I slouched against the window, making sure my head was below the top of the seatback.

"All aboard!" the conductor called out. He was hanging halfway out the door, scanning the platform. He pulled in the wooden step with a single hand and set it to the side. The locomotive started forward with a jerk, a hesitation, and another jerk. The string of cars gained momentum and moved forward like ripples across a pond.

I peered over the seatback. Most of the passengers were staring straight ahead or looking out their windows. A few heads were tipped into newspapers. Nobody seemed to care about me. Feeling better, I turned back to the streaked window as structures began to advance and retreat with increasing speed.

The flour mill, a white building with a low peaked roof, rolled into view. Two flatbed trucks, each stacked with flour bags big as me, were being readied in front. Next to the trucks, an empty buckboard wagon, hitched to a solitary horse, stood unattended. The animal followed our progress and switched its tail across a broad, brown rump.

A second set of tracks kept us company through town, but veered off when we turned toward the mountains and began to follow a stream.

"That other track heads south to Roseburg and California," Boone said, turning around to face me. His shoulders filled the bench in front of us. "We go east."

Black fields, square farmhouses, and rows of nut trees filled the window. Rainwater puddled the soil. The naked trees seemed to shiver in the morning air. We crossed the river though a white, covered bridge and skirted a large lumber mill. Rafts of half-submerged logs filled the millpond. Rows of stacked lumber waited beside a rail spur.

"Goddamn!" Mohl said. "Still no boxcars for Sager's lumber. That's sure to give Jackie a bright red rash. He's got three months of inventory sitting here with no way to move it."

I looked to see if Mother had noticed the word he'd used.

She cleared her throat and leaned forward in her seat.

"Mr. Shaw," she said uncertainly, "how do you pronounce *Row* River?"

"Row is frog talk for red," Mohl interrupted. "Some Frenchie came up with it."

"Oh," Mother said.

"That's God's truth," Mohl said, encouraged. "Frenchmen traipsed all over the place before us Americans showed them the door."

"I see," Mother said, but I was pretty sure, she didn't.

"I don't know where the name came from," Boone said. "But most of us rhyme the word with owl." While Boone talked, Mohl kept sneaking looks at Mother.

Boone reached up to open a window. His pointer finger was cut off at the first knuckle. He gripped the latch between his thumb and thick middle finger and strained. A layer of fine white sawdust rode across his shoulders, but he didn't seem dirty and he didn't smell bad. When he stood to get a better grip on the latch, fluffy armpit hairs, blond like the sawdust feathering his shirt, poked through a small tear in the fabric.

When the latch released, morning air, thick with a mix of smells—burning wood, evergreen trees, cut lumber—rushed in. I breathed deeply, appreciating the freshness.

A woman's voice swelled behind us. "Well done, Boone Shaw!"

Boone flinched, but didn't look back. Everyone else turned toward the voice.

"If you could open your heart like you did that window, you would feel the sweet breath of Jesus blow down. Can you feel it?"

I thought I felt it.

The voice belonged to the lady with the pointy shoes, the one who had called me an idiot. She was standing up and leaning against the seatback in front of her, rocking with the movement of the train, swaying with the conviction of her words.

There wasn't much of her to see, just thin wrists and a narrow, sickly face. The rest of her was hidden beneath shiny leather gloves and a long-sleeved, baggy dress with a flat ruffled front.

"Give your heart to Jesus and leap from Hell's fire!"

The lady's tired eyes sat behind wire-rimmed glasses that were awkwardly attached to a narrow face and an ungainly nose that ended in a bulb. Billie Mackenzie, I later understood, would never be beautiful. By then, she had long since stopped trying for something that could never be. In the place of beauty, she took pride in a brain that spun circles around most men.

She bowed her head. "We pray for Jesus to cleanse this man's—"

"Billie, *please*," Boone said.

She paused in mid-sentence and unshuttered one eye. She stared at Boone as if he were wearing Satan's own blood-stained overalls.

"Can't you find a better time and a more worthy place to witness for Jesus?" Boone said.

"Amen to that," said Dracula.

The train rounded a curve. Billie gripped the seatback with both hands, but as soon as she was stable, she aimed a bony finger right at Boone's heart. "This *is* the Lord's place," she intoned. "We *are* His church. Today *is* His time."

Each syllable hammered into me. Her every word pounded into my chest and made me afraid. She could have been Grandma Lulu.

"It is *always* His time."

I closed my eyes and covered my ears.

"If you wait, Grace will pass you by. Drink from the fountain while you still can."

Then, as quickly as Billie Mackenzie had begun her sermon, she ended it. She turned from Boone and abruptly strode down the aisle toward the thin man who had made the mistake of saying, "Amen to that."

"Ennis Neet," she called toward the pale man, "you and your secret confreres have so much. And yet, you give so little."

At the rear of the car, Dracula shrank from God's light.

"Use your gold for Jesus. He will return it with interest. Do not starve your soul! Empty souls feast in Hell." Billie flicked a set of leather fingers at Neet and signaled for him to slide over.

"Ennis is in for a long ride," Boone said quietly. "Teddy, have you ever heard anything quite like that?"

"My Grandma Lulu talks a lot about personal sin."

"Billie has plenty to say about that, too." She attends the Assembly of God Church and dabbles with the Pentecostals."

"Is she a Holy Roller?" Mother asked.

Boone nodded. "Not all Pentecostals are like Billie. Most save it up for Sunday and then cut loose, but not Billie, not now." He lowered his voice. "She hasn't always been so forceful, but lately, her sense of urgency has grown."

"Why?"

"She 's sick," Boone said, "which explains her impatience. To make things worse, she's married to a man who doesn't pay any attention to her, either. Her husband, Sid Mackenzie, is part owner of Dolomite Lumber Company. We'll pass it on the way."

The door at the front of the car opened, and the conductor stepped in. He began taking tickets with one hand and punching holes in them with the other. Clip, clip—a double click for every ticket. I strained to see how the clipper device worked, wondering what kind of ratchet mechanism was involved.

"Tickets," he said when he reached us. His voice was cheerful, and his face showed interest. Given enough time, most men responded to Mother like that. "How are you two getting along?" He smiled at Mother without seeing me and then punched two small holes in our tickets—clip, clip. I really wanted to do that!

"Very well, thank you," she said, also smiling. Mother always smiled and laughed when she met strangers or felt nervous. "I am so sorry about the mess, but at least he's starting to dry out."

The conductor looked at me for the first time. Releasing a little bark of a laugh, he said, "I observed his entrance at the station. Has he thought about a career in the circus?"

I turned toward the window. I really wanted a few minutes with the ticket puncher, but I wasn't about to ask him for anything.

"I can bring the child a towel," he offered.

I shook my head.

"That would be wonderful. Otherwise, I'll have to strip his clothes off and hold them out the window to dry."

I knew she was joking, but I looked over to be sure.

The conductor laughed out another little bark. Mother's green eyes flashed, and her red hair reflected happiness. She could do that so well.

Outside the window, the stream we were following slipped over smooth black river rock without a ripple or a splash. That was where I wanted to be.

"I like your railroad," Mother said. "What does O S & E stand for?"

"Old Slow and Easy," Boone answered for the conductor. "Because the railroad's so damn old and slow, it can't take itself seriously. Chivas here is the exception."

"The letters abbreviate *Oregon and Southeastern Railway*," the conductor snapped.

"Come on, Chivas. The name has changed four times since then," Boone said. "Each new name has signaled a failure and a resurrection, a bankruptcy followed by somebody else's new money."

The conductor frowned. "Say what you want, but the railroad has carried on nicely for twenty-seven years."

"I like your train very much, Mr. Chivas," Mother said.

The conductor took obvious pleasure in his small victory. "What's the boy's name?" he asked with a fake smile. I heard a lisp rattle behind his cheeks as he spoke. Up until then, he had hidden the lisp, but now, it sounded worse than mine. With each 'S' I could hear spit shoot out from the sides of his teeth. It had to be pooling inside his cheeks.

"Teddy," Mother said.

"Like the fuzzy bear cub?" The conductor smiled through clamped lips. More saliva was gathering between his teeth and cheeks. It sounded juicy. I began to wonder if he'd stop talking long enough to swallow before the spit leaked out.

"No, like the President," Mother said.

The conductor studied me for a moment, as if testing the comparison—me with the President. I didn't blink. And then it happened.

It was a large gulping swallow, followed by a satisfied, encompassing lick around the lips and deep into the corners. "What's waiting for you in Culp Creek?" he said, swallowing a second time. "There's not much there, an abandoned logging camp west of the river and a broken down sawmill on the east side."

Boone's head had fallen to his chest and was rolling side to side with the motion of the train. I felt drowsy, too. I looked to see if the other passengers were getting impatient, waiting for the conductor to come by, but nobody seemed to care whether or not he punched their ticket—a procedure that, until then, I believed was vital for the success of the railroad company.

I propped my head against the glass window and watched the country change.

The wide valley had narrowed and deepened. A patchwork forest that was thick in places and stripped bare in others had replaced the farms. Smoke and steam blossomed from many of the clearings, usually signaling a mill or a logging operation. At each clearing, I looked hard for Dad. With every structure that moved into view, I hoped we had reached our destination.

12

The conductor's voice yanked me up through a dream of thorns, roses, and a high castle wall. "Culp Creek, just ahead!" he shouted from the front of the car.

I resisted opening my eyes at first, reluctant to throw off the warm web that held me, but then struggled upright. "Where?"

"A little farther on," Boone said, shuffling through his things. "Don't blink or you'll miss it."

The riverbed had shifted to the opposite side of the train and now lay to our right. The actual stream and riverbank were hidden behind blackberry vines. A gravel highway ran between the train tracks and the river. I stood for a better look and heard the dried newspaper to crackle beneath me. I reached around and collected bits off my shorts.

"Throw that on the floor and you'll pick up every piece." The conductor had appeared out of nowhere. A grim look now replaced his earlier grin.

"I won't," I promised.

"Of course not." Mother's response was automatic like her smile, but she wasn't paying attention. She was perched on the edge of our bench and staring out.

After the conductor pushed past, I wadded the paper and crammed it between our bench and the wall. I mashed it down with my shoe so that it remained hidden.

Mother watched and said nothing.

I reached inside my shorts and adjusted the mud-encrusted goods. It was getting raw down there. "Can I change before we see Dad?"

"We don't have clean clothes."

"Well," I said, not willing to just give up, "where are they?"

"In the luggage compartment. In the big suitcase."

"Let's go get it."

"You will just have to wait." Her voice had that final—this is the end of the conversation—sound to it, but I was desperate. I started to argue, but she wasn't listening. A puzzled look crossed her face. And then she covered her mouth with a hand. I followed her gaze.

Gray buildings dotted an irregular clearing. Some looked like tiny houses, but most were sheds or lean-tos. I saw no regular blocks, no straight streets, not even a stop sign. A wide dirt path, maybe it was a road, wound through the clearing. Weeds grew in tufts among scattered machines, tires, piles of lumber, heaps of dirt and splintered tree stumps. At the far end of the clearing, stacked lumber circled a hodgepodge of weathered walls and rusted roofs. In the middle of the rust, a tall, black, smoke stack sailed above it all like the mast of a ship.

"That's your mill," Boone said, reaching for his bags. "And here's your new home." He pointed to a squat, unpainted square sitting on four tree stumps, two feet off the ground. Gray vertical boards separated by wide cracks with tarpaper showing through made up the walls. "It's a little rough right now, but once your husband tacks up the batten strips, it should hold out the worst of the weather."

A mountain rose up just behind the mill and the house. It hovered above the clearing and threatened to push everything below it into the river. At its highest reaches, trees filled the hillside; down lower, they'd all been cut out. With the river in its face and a mountain pushing from behind, there seemed to be little room and no future for our mill. Yet, across the river, a second clearing ten times the size of ours lay empty.

"I don't see the station," Mother said in a voice I could barely hear. "My husband will be waiting for us."

"It's on the left," Boone said.

I didn't see a train station. Stacks of lumber lined a loading dock, but nothing much else.

"At least, that's where we get off," he said. "You'll have to pick your way through the boards."

Mother looked confused.

"Follow me." Boone turned sideways in the aisle, and with a bag in each hand, he pushed forward.

"Teddy, grab your things and don't forget anything," Mother said, trying to keep up, fighting with her bags and bumping into seated passengers. "I'm so sorry. Excuse me," she offered after the worst offenses. She sounded ready to cry.

At the head of the car, the conductor was squeezing his watch. He pointed to two suitcases and a box resting on a small gravel pad beside the train tracks. "Your things are already off." He signaled to the engineer with the same crisp wave he'd used before. When we were off, he leaned out the door and smiled down at Mother. "Enjoy your stay."

The locomotive began rolling forward. Once again, I counted the cars from engine to red caboose, and as the caboose and lantern moved past, Dad appeared. He had been standing on the other side of the tracks. I ran toward him.

He saw me coming and stepped back. He raised both hands to stop me. "God dammit, Marie! He looks like a pig in a sailor suit."

"It was an accident," she said. "He slipped in the rain."

Without waiting for the explanation, he grabbed the two bags and started walking away faster than either Mother or I could easily manage.

Mother hurried after him, doing her best to carry the big box, with her purse swinging awkwardly at the elbow. She ran to keep up, talking non-stop about the trip and the train and Grandma Lulu. It was a one sided conversation, and not meant for me, so I stopped trying to hurry. I slowed down and let the distance between us grow.

13

Mother didn't make me finish out the last two weeks of second grade at the new school, and Dad stayed out of it—my schooling had become a sore subject with him.

"Teddy doesn't belong in the third grade. In good conscience, I can't pass him along." That was what Mrs. Watson, my second grade teacher, had said to Mother before we left Fraser Mills. "But we are going to miss him." Then she and Mother stepped away and began whispering.

I couldn't read: that was the main problem. Letters refused to stay put long enough for me to make sense out of them. I could easily recite the alphabet from memory. That skill had been enough to move me from the first to the second grade, but according to Mrs. Watson, it wouldn't get me any farther.

When Mother reported her conversation to Dad and Grandma Lulu at supper that night, there was no whispering. "Mrs. Watson wonders if there might be some kind of brain problem," Mother said, unable to look at me.

Dad was sitting at the head of Grandma Lulu's table, as he had done once it became clear that Grandpa Charlie wasn't coming back. At the opposite end of the table, Grandma glowered, listening and nodding, shaking her head and looking at me in a cycle that kept repeating itself.

"Other than that, Mrs. Watson says he's a fine boy."

"Let me see it," Dad said.

Mother passed my report card across the table, and Dad silently began to read.

"Why don't we all hear what the teacher has to say?" Grandma Lulu said.

Dad handed the card back to Mother without comment.

"Teddy is a very fine boy and a joy to have in class," Mother read, "but he does not seem to have the capacity to read." Her smile was supposed to tell me this wasn't a sin. "Although Teddy shows good ability with numbers, he is not yet ready for the third grade."

"This is what happens when you put your hand in a bag and blindly grab," Grandma Lulu pronounced.

Dad looked at Grandma and considered her remark, but again said nothing.

"That's not fair, Merle," Mother said. "You were with me when we decided."

Dad weighed his words. "I didn't say 'no' at the time because with you, there was absolutely *no saying no*."

Mother glanced away.

I didn't want to look at them either, so I watched my fork reduce my peas to puree. I didn't understand what all this meant. I felt that my not being able to read was only one of my failings.

"Don't play with your food," Grandma scolded. "Plenty of children would be grateful to have it."

A single tear slipped from my eye. With more welling inside my nose, I wiped away the one and tried to snuff up the rest.

"Use your napkin and don't snivel," Grandma said, once again concentrating on me rather than on her own food.

Dad's fork clattered against his plate. "Let me have the damn thing!" He reached across and ripped the card from Mother's hand. "We'll see about this!"

Two days later, I found my report card sitting on the kitchen table. Mrs. Watson's earlier writing had been lined out with black ink. Right below, in her handwriting, squeezed in above her signature was a single letter, 'P', for Pass.

We didn't talk about it afterward, but we all hoped the problem would fix itself over the summer—I know I did. I was hungry for so many things then, but that lonely place in the woods soon served up little more than soggy, unsalted vegetables. Mother tried to spice the fare up with stories and songs, games for two and little walks, but she had her needs, too. She promised she'd teach me to read, and we tried for a few days, but it was just too hard. Honestly, she and I didn't know what I needed, and I didn't have anywhere else to look.

Rita, my hot sixty-two-year-old girlfriend, is a little like my mother in that she tries to spice things up, but Rita has never demanded anything from me. She has her life, I have mine, and we meet in the middle. That's usually on a Sunday afternoon. We alternate weeks. One Sunday, I'll take her out for lunch; the next Sunday, she'll bring groceries and grill for us on George Foreman's grilling machine.

Rita and I met on the net. Then we met in person in a mall parking lot, and I must have passed inspection. She told me she'd be over at six that evening. When she arrived, she charged up the stairs, shed her clothes along the way, and put her jewel out on a silver platter.

If it isn't raining, we'll sit on the concrete pad outside my kitchen door. When it's cold or wet outside, we pull the grill into the kitchen and open the French doors. Rita always fixes a salad to go with the meat, which is nice, since the only other salads I eat are from McDonalds. I can make one salad last two or three meals. After lunch, we go up to my bedroom. I have green satin sheets on a king size bed. We call it our soccer field, and since there is no reason to hurry things along, we scrimmage for two or three hours, and then I score!

14

Nineteen twenty-nine was a funny year. Spring came and went. Summer followed with little to mark it except our move. But once August's heat had passed, after the wild flowers had spilled their petals like corn flakes across a kitchen floor, at a time when the world was supposed to turn gold and slide into winter, that's not at all what happened. The world slowly seized up.

Little towns in backwater states far away from New York City didn't topple over the day the stock market fell, but their roots had been cut. In the months that followed, different parts broke down, wore out, couldn't be fixed, and, like an engine choking under a tank of bad gas, the markets sputtered, slowed, and then stopped for good. That's what later caused lonely, even desperate, men to show up asking their families for help. Uncle Normal, my mother's brother, was one of those men.

Most nights, when Dad read the newspaper, he would worry about business, and in his own way, he worried about the men who worked at the mill, about how they'd support their families if there wasn't work. From the kitchen, I'd hear his newspaper rustle as he moved through the pages. Occasionally, he'd listen to the radio while he read or worked, but he usually preferred quiet. Two knobs, which I was not allowed to touch and a huge dial in the middle, commanded the radio's polished front. The kerosene lamp that sat beside his chair hissed and sent an even halo of light across his paper. A small brass knob at the base of the lamp fed its winking flame. I was not to touch that either. Twist the knob one way, the fire blossomed into gold, twist it the other way, it disappeared.

If the news was especially bad, I'd hear Dad mutter over the hiss of the lamp, "God dammit." This was usually followed by the click of his glass tumbler against the ceramic coaster Mother kept beside the lamp. Dad drank his whiskey over two ice cubes. He'd slowly pour and watch it coat the ice like yellow oil. I suspect the whiskey lubricated his soul in the same way. He'd close his eyes before the first sip and breathe in the perfume, as if willing it to carry him to another place.

When Dad learned that the big meadow and its timber across the river had been sold to somebody else, and that a new sawmill was to be built there, the muttering and lubricating increased. In August, he started running short shifts. By September 1930, there were days when the mill didn't start up at all after lunch.

During those bad months, the men had to know there'd be no afternoon shift. Yet, at the break, they still shuffled to their regular eating spots—some by the head saw, others on a crate by the green chain, where they opened their tin boxes and ate. When it was time to go back to work, they folded the wax papers that had wrapped their sandwiches and stowed them back in the tin boxes to wash and use another day. When the whistle didn't blow, they gathered up their things and word-lessly walked home, to what, I don't know.

Uncle Normal came to live with us in the summer of 1930 because he had no work, no family, and no other place to go. When Mother first suggested the idea, Dad was totally against it. "I know a hundred good men who need a job," he said. "I can't find work for the men I've got."

Mother kept at him every night, and this time she won out, maybe more for her than for Uncle Normal. She made up a bed for him in the bunkhouse, where he lived with the other single men, but he didn't stay long. Dad had him build a shed to store the dry slab lumber, and while he was at it, Uncle Normal added a little space for himself along the shed's back wall, just big enough for a cot and a two-drawer dresser. Mother sewed a quilt for his bed.

Uncle Normal was a skinny, nervous man with ears that stuck out. He looked like Ichabod Crane on Halloween night, always checking over his shoulder. Dad called him high strung, and Mother worried that he didn't get enough to eat. Dad made fun of him and got on him like a hungry wolf chases an injured deer, but Uncle Normal seemed to take it well enough. Anyone could tell he wasn't strong. For me, he was someone who would sit next to me on the porch steps with time enough to listen, and not just talk.

I think Uncle Normal would have come for supper every evening if Dad had allowed it, or maybe if Mother had insisted more strongly. It is hard to know for sure. Had Mother pressed Dad harder about Uncle Normal, she might have pushed events along faster than they were meant to move, and she may have sensed that to be so. That's because Mother had horse sense, as Dad called it, but no real education. Mother attended elocution school after the sixth grade where she learned to form her vowels, where she became expert as to the correct way to pour black tea from a white china pot. They taught her that and whatever else it is that a good wife needs to know, but they taught her nothing of any substance.

"Norm, you are a regular up-to-date Christopher Columbus," Dad said one night, as he passed along the bowl of mashed potatoes. "Don't you think so, Teddy?" Dad winked at me to let me know I was in on the joke.

I nodded back, more out of reflex than understanding, but I knew what was coming.

"Isn't that so, Norrrrmal?" Dad said. "Aren't you a modern day Christopher Columbus?"

Uncle Normal stared at his plate. "Well, I don't know." He always was careful with his words before he released them, which made him sound slow. "I don't have no boat, so I guess not." He looked at Dad, knowing that he'd come up with an answer, certain it was wrong.

When you grow up alone, surrounded by adults only, it's like living in a dirt packed yard with high walls and no grass. You can throw rocks and chip at the gray walls, but you'll never pull them down, not by yourself. Without other children to distract, you become expert about adult conversation—when to tap into it and when to shut down, when to pull inside, and when to quietly will the weariness of their words to pass on by.

Dad breathed his drink in, sipped it, and let the oil slide along his tongue. "You do know who Christopher Columbus was, don't you, Norm?"

Uncle Normal froze.

"I know who he was," I nearly shouted.

Dad didn't look my way. He had hooked Uncle Normal by the lip and wasn't about to let him go until something tore.

Mother forked salad onto my plate. "Merle, would you and Normal like some salad? I made Thousand Island dressing with my dill pickle relish."

Uncle Normal reached for the bowl. "Thank you, Marie. I sure would." He scooped the lettuce and tomato onto his plate and passed the bowl to Dad. "Good food tonight, good enough to be our own Mother's, but even better, Marie, lots better."

Uncle Normal smiled at the salad while he spoke. He rarely looked at people, not directly in the face, except for me; he'd look at me. He'd look at a dog, any dog, didn't matter what size or disposition. He'd look at it square in the face and talk to it just like he was having a regular conversation, like he expected the dog understood. Most of them did. They would nod back and smile, especially when he cupped his hands around the base of their ears, his careful fingers gently pulling and sliding from base to silky tip.

"Christopher Columbus," Dad said, staying the course, "was a man without a compass, a soul who set sail with no idea as to where he was going." Dad dipped a questioning finger into the dressing and tasted, nodded his approval, and spooned particles of green suspended in pink over his salad. "After months of sailing, when Columbus finally arrived in the new world, he landed on a white beach, stuck a flag in it, and christened it for Spain, but you know what, Norm?"

Startled, Uncle Normal looked up from his salad. "No, I don't know what."

"Columbus had no idea where he was going when he started out, and once he arrived, he hadn't the faintest clue where he was. After he returned to Spain and bowed before the goddamn king and queen, Columbus still had no concept at all of where he had been...not the faintest goddamn idea. The man thought he'd been to China and back!"

Uncle Normal stared back blankly, and so did I.

"Norm, I have to believe that you are on some kind of Christopher Columbus expedition. You sure as shit don't know where you're going, and you don't have any idea where you've been. Tell me, Norm, do you have any idea where you are right now, right this very minute?"

Uncle Normal stirred gravy into his potatoes like a man without an appetite.

"When it's all over, Norm, will you know any more than you do right now?"

Careful like always, Uncle Normal sucked on his words like corn caught between his teeth. "I suspect not," was all he said.

"I suspect not," Dad mimicked.

Uncle Normal died twice. The first time, I watched from my window in the kitchen. The second, I didn't actually see.

15

Since Uncle Normal was a pond monkey, he knew a great deal about muskrats. The similarities a pond monkey shares with muskrats are considerable if you take time to think about it. Both live in the water, and when not in the water, they stay out of sight in musty little holes. Since neither are readily seen, their importance to the overall scheme of things registers below the water mark, except for the fact that a sawmill owner needs the one and wants to be rid of the other.

It took balance and desperation to succeed as a pond monkey, and the task nearly always fell to the youngest workers since they were agile and desperate for a job. Uncle Normal wasn't the youngest monkey by any stretch, but he may have been the most desperate. With poles in their hands and cork soles on their boots, pond monkeys took charge of the logs after they had been dumped into the water. Riding logs of their own, they herded each load across the pond to the wooden ramp that rose from the water to the mill deck. When the wind blew the wrong way, they'd struggle, poling and fighting to keep the logs from turning. In the rain, they'd often slip and fall in, but they always got right up. If Uncle Normal saw me watching, he'd wave and grin and do a little dance or run along the length of his log, making it spin and bob. Uncle Normal had never learned to swim, but that didn't stop him from putting on a show for me.

A cable had to be attached to each log at the base of the mill ramp to drag it onto the main deck. That job also fell to my uncle. Up to his armpits in nasty brown water, with a cheek pressed against the slimy bark, he'd belly onto the log and reach around with the cable and choker. He was supposed to separate the logs by size and type and have them lined up in the water and ready before Mr. Sharpe, the sawyer, needed them. Or else get yelled at, which happened way too often.

Uncle Normal and I visited nearly every day after he got out of the pond. When it was sunny and dry, the porch was the best place for us, but when it rained or was cold, we didn't have a good place. Rain or shine, we could talk about anything. I'd take a turn with him listening, and then it would be his turn to talk, and I'd listen.

"If you can get rid of those stinky water rats, your dad will like you for it," he said.

"He will? Why would he want that?"

While he considered my question, I picked a scab on my elbow that was about done. People thought Uncle Normal was slow, but, although he never was one to have a quick response, he wasn't stupid. He had good ideas, lots of them. He just couldn't get them out before people lost interest. He took his time before answering out of respect for the question. If a person cared enough to ask his opinion, he considered it his duty to give the best answer possible. Problem was, people didn't show him the same respect in waiting for him to work things through. That was their loss and his, too.

About the time I got my scab to bleed, he pointed toward the river and said, "Lookie there!"

Two small creatures were running along the river bank, one tearing after the other. Within seconds, both animals dropped out of sight behind the bank.

"I'm afraid them two little critters won't be choosy enough about where they park their burrows," he said. "It's always the same story. One pair starts out at the river, living along its banks, and that's fine, but once the little ones come along, trouble starts."

"Why?" I asked, thinking a big family would be good.

"The youngsters have to find their own roosts."

"Can't they all live together?"

"If the kids stay around too long, some time when the momma's out, daddy bites off their heads and makes a meal of them."

"I don't believe it."

"Given the chance, the daddy will eat his youngsters. Every bit, but for the tail and teeth."

I glanced toward the living room.

He smiled. "Good thing for us people aren't muskrats." He got to his feet and slowly straightened up. He pressed his knuckles into the muscles of his low back and then worked his knees around to get them going. "By the end of the day, I get a little creaky." He started down the steps and motioned for me to follow.

"Knowing that," he said, "if you were a little muskrat, you'd naturally be inclined to pull up stakes and leave before your daddy could get crossways with you."

I tried to imagine it. "How do they know when it's time to leave?"

"It's one of those things they have to get right." He slid a finger across his throat. "If they get it wrong, daddy won't need to fish for his dinner, will he?"

We climbed onto the dirt berm that wrapped our pond and paused at the top while Uncle Normal added more thought to my question.

"The muskrats that get their timing right seem to know when to leave. The ones that don't get it right, well, their kin aren't around to puzzle about it." He pointed to the pond wall across from us. "Do you see them little holes above the water line?"

"I see three," I said.

"Them burrows are the current home for some smart little muskrats, ones that left the river in time. A week ago, they took a swim in your log pond and decided they like it."

"Is that so bad?"

"By itself, there's no harm," he admitted. "But with their digging, these new rats have burrowed through your pond wall and out the other side." He pointed to a puddle collecting in the weeds along the outer bank. "Get enough of those holes, your daddy ends up with an empty pond and a pile of muddy logs. You can't float logs through mud."

"Dad told the night watchman to drive boards through their holes and cover them with dirt. He said that would slow them down."

"No hunk of wood or heap of dirt will stop a determined muskrat. He'll gnaw 'til he's through the board and dig until he reaches daylight. In a day or two, probably in the middle of the night, a new leak will sprout, then another, and so on." Uncle Normal smiled. "Animals, especially the small ones, are never as dumb as people want to believe. Wouldn't you say so?"

Small and dumb would be a bad combination, I thought.

"This whole section will wash out if nothing's done to stop them. That's why your daddy doesn't like them. Nobody does." Uncle Normal stared me in the eye. "Would you like to get rid of them nasty rats and make big money? Make your daddy proud of you at the same time."

"I'd like all of that," I said.

"You've seen mouse traps?"

Not only had I seen them, I'd hear them in the middle of the night, in the quiet after everyone was in bed. Whap! Followed by the frantic scratching of feet. The first time, I wondered about helping them. I thought the scratching was the little animal trying to escape, but Dad said it was just their nerves acting up. Later, when I saw the havoc the spring had done, I knew my opening the trap wouldn't have changed a thing.

Mother refused to touch dead mice, afraid she'd get the bubonic plague. I don't know that she really believed the part about the plague, but still, she made me carry the bodies away. With the mouse hanging by its wiggly neck, I'd carry the trap to the outhouse, dump the body, and then sprinkle it over with lye. If I had to use the growler later that day, I'd worry that resentment was about to rise up and bite me where I sat. Before I shut the door and dropped my pants, I'd check the hole for movement. In less time than it takes most people to settle in, I'd be up and out, still looking over my shoulder.

We always had three traps going at a time, and we used them over and over because you didn't waste a good piece of equipment. Dad set them, I cleared them, and Mother did her best to ignore the issue altogether.

Uncle Normal's comments weren't always so practical. One evening, while we were on the porch, waiting for supper, trying to stay out of Dad's way, he told me that my mother's name wasn't Marie.

"She, herself, took on that one," he said. "Mary is her God given name."

Uncle Normal had been drinking, I could smell it, but that wasn't unusual. He was drinking every night by then if he could get hold of a bottle. I didn't think the drink talking for him, but it was likely helping out.

"Are you sure?"

"Ten of us kids grew up calling her Mary, so I should know. But don't let on I told you." He lowered his voice. "Your mother won't have any part of that name now, so it's best we never talk about it." He hugged my shoulder in a loose-limbed way. "Promise not to tell a soul."

I promised, not understanding why.

"Uncle Normal," I said, thinking it was my turn to talk, "why would she change her name? I thought we kept our names forever."

For once, he acted like he expected the question. "For her own reasons, your mother had to become another person. That was how she went about it."

I stared ahead, trying to make sense out of it. I had never heard Uncle Normal put words together like this before, but, he thought a great deal of my mother. He was, I believe, her sole connection to the past.

"Mary was the mother of God," Uncle Normal solemnly stated. "You know that, don't you?" More to himself, he added. "It's a fine name."

"You mean, Jesus." Uncle Normal looked at me with his blank stare. "Mary was the mother of Jesus," I repeated.

"I suppose that's right, too," he said absently.

16

During the summer of 1930, with hot, dry days filling July and spilling into August, I searched for reasons to leave the house, not so much to get away from Mother as to find a door into Dad's world.

And every morning, Mother reminded me of my chores. "Go on out," she'd say. "It's time to carry water for the men." She had reasons for getting me out of the house, too.

Mother loved music and parties. She had thrived on them before I came along, had used them like salve on an open wound. Later, she began to apply straight gin to the same end. Gin dampened the main saw's shriek when it tore through her afternoons. Gin warmed her rainy evenings when the stove's fire lost its heat. Although Prohibition and its chorus of fine Christian women slowed the flow of liquor in many places during those years, that was not so in our home. Dad saw to that part of Mother's happiness. When Mother was alone, or thought she was alone, she'd rub her fingers over the cool, smoky glass and mumble a soft incantation. She'd conjure a magic carpet from the corners of her bottle and fly away.

"Your mother never showed any interest in being 'some oaf's drudge' as she called it. The day she turned eighteen, she walked away from our farm in Molalla. That same day, she found a job at the movie house because they were looking for a cute girl to take the tickets."

Just as easily, Mother learned to dance and she began to drink. While her brothers and sisters went to church and worked every day as if having fun was a sin, she took pride in being the black sheep of the family. Mother made mistakes after she left the farm, some of them so bad they could never be fixed, but I don't think she had a choice in leaving. Years later, when she returned home and tried to see her dour parents and their dismal church with fresh eyes, all of it was just as she had left it.

"Neither my parents nor *The True Christian Church of Molalla* will ever change," she told me. "Not the moss that has taken root on its cedar roof, not the dark boughs that fold over it like great hands in prayer, not the coarse shake siding—painted white and probably an afterthought—that scrolls along its outer walls. *The True Christian Church of Molalla* was built to look like gingerbread with creamy vanilla frosting along its sides and mint green on top," she said. "But none of it was *True*, and all of it so *Christian*."

"Your mother used to sing in the choir," Uncle Normal said. "At sixteen, her notes were so round, so perfect, they floated above her like halos over baby Jesus. She could send them flowing across the congregation like wild honey over a buttermilk biscuit. I saw parishioners touch their tongues to their lips, as if hoping to sample her sweetness. At times like that, you were supposed to be filled with the Spirit, eyes on God, but all we ever saw was Mary."

A church is supposed to be a sensible building. Mother and I learned that much from Grandma Lulu. Flourish in design reflects a lack of humility; imagination among the pews demonstrates an absence of discipline. Oak doors at the entrance are sensible because they hold the Spirit in and keep the demons out. "Those heavy doors knew to open and reach out for the chosen," she said. "They also knew when to swing shut and lock the chosen in." Behind the oak doors, far above the pews, a narrow band of windows, each no bigger than a King James Bible, sat so high on the church walls, so far out of reach, that only heaven and the very tops of the trees could be seen from below.

"I couldn't breathe," she said. "The room was too small, the light too dim, and the doors much too unreliable."

By the time we arrived in Culp Creek, Mother had traveled farther from her childhood congregation than miles alone might suggest. She still sang, and her voice remained as clear as ever, but she never again sang in church. At times, she'd sing for me. More often, she sang for herself, private melodies that embraced the dark and searched its spaces.

I had three official jobs by then. The first was to keep muskrats out of the pond; the second was to carry water to the men; and the third was to watch for fire. Dad constantly worried about fire. He talked about it nearly every night at dinner and didn't pick just anybody to be a fire lookout.

Everything the mill produced burned. The main saw that squared the logs left behind thick slabs of bark. Rough lumber from the main saw traveled over steel rollers to the edger where it was squared into boards exactly the right width. From the edger, the boards moved to the trim saw to be cut to the right length. Slabs, sawdust, shavings, oil, and grease piled up daily and had to be cleared away from saws, rollers, and carriages. Under the main saw, the sawdust was the size of pea gravel with corners. Beneath the edger and trim saws, it was much finer. The planer left behind sweet-smelling shavings that felt like talcum and curled like wisps of smoke.

To run the boilers, to fill the pond, to prevent fires or put them out, we had to have a constant supply of water. We siphoned what we needed from the only source available: Culp Creek. Unfortunately, the creek flowed into the Row River from the far side, across land we didn't own. We used gravity and sleight of hand to route the water onto our property by way of a four-inch pipe that ran beneath the railroad bridge, under the highway, and into our pond. We had no choice but to appropriate the Culp Creek water since there was no reliable way to pump water out of the Row River, which flowed twenty feet below us.

Our drinking water came from a spring that broke through a patch of moss high on the hillside behind us. The men preferred to drink spring water, but that's not why Dad piped it to the mill: river sediment formed a mineral scale on the inside of the boilers and shortened their lives.

After the cool of morning had fallen away, as flies began rising to the scent of men's sweat, I'd bang through the back screen door and follow a narrow path through tall blackberry bushes that grew between the pond and the slope behind our mill. I'd fill the water jug with spring water and carry it to the men before their morning break. A few of them nodded a greeting, but most didn't seem to notice. Each man would take a swig from the jug and pass it around; they'd share it, snoose and all. By the last man, flecks of tobacco and swirls of brown spit coated the bottom of the jug, forming something far worse than river sediment. I rarely stuck around long enough to witness the whole gory process—that was too much communal living for me. Instead, I preferred to spy on the men from my hideout below their boots, and they never knew I was there.

The space beneath the mill's decking was too low for a man to comfortably move through, but it was perfect for me. I used knotholes and gaps between planks to follow their conversations. I learned to recognize the men by their voices and by the manner of their movements. With time, the faceless silhouettes all took on flesh. Separated from these living shadows by four-inch planking, I floated unseen below. Caught between their world and the cool packed earth, I was a ghost.

Sawdust and planer shavings layered the ground. Bug-eaten posts spaced every four feet supported the planking overhead. Since Dad had just bought the mill, I expected everything to be new, but the wormy lumber underneath the mill was years past new, all of it pocked by earlier nails, driven and later pulled. The hidden surfaces were weathered: curled and gray, lifeless like the feathers of a sparrow dead too long to be of interest. From the bottom looking up, nothing was new, none of it as it appeared from above.

Bill Sharpe, the sawyer and lead man, called out above the murmur one morning. "Be a good kid, Duff. Bring me that jug."

Above me, Duff's image jumped from crack to crack, as he sprinted across the decking. Duff was Sharpe's opposite in every way; in no particular way, was he special. Sharpe ran the main saw and decided how to cut the logs. Duff pulled boards off the green chain at the end of the mill. He sorted and stacked the green unseasoned lumber by hand. Sharpe used brainpower and savvy to do his job. Duff needed nothing more than a strong back, willing arms, and a brain he could turn off for hours on end. I always assumed I'd be in Sharpe's position one day.

"It's been a good day, so far," Sharpe said, setting the jug down. "Clear timber with no rot to work around."

Dad liked Sharpe because he was ambitious and had once played catcher, same as Dad. And, like Boone, he had fought in the Great War. "We mostly fought the mud," Sharpe said, "with an occasional German mixed into the mess." Dad liked to get Sharpe talking about his battles in France, something I never understood since Dad had done everything possible to get out of the war.

The success or failure of any mill depended on the sawyer's output, and Sharpe had high expectations, which was good and bad. Good when he came up with new ways to cut more lumber in less time without waste. Bad when he wanted more for himself. "Managing a top man's expectations can be a tall order," Dad said, "but it's a hell of a lot easier than coping with his disappointment."

"Duff," Sharpe called out, "be a good lad. Run to the tool shed and fetch our millwright."

Duff's slim shadow bounced up and disappeared.

Minutes later, Mohl's shadow filtered through the cracks. The unwelcome form was listing to the right from the weight of a toolbox. When he stepped above me, sawdust, fine as bakers' flour, sifted across broken beams of light. All I could make out were his boots, but that was enough. I retreated deeper into the shadows. I detested Mohl because of the way he stared at my mother.

"The top saw's running to the right," Sharpe said. "I must have hit a goddamn rock."

All saws run after hitting a rock because the teeth pull toward the dull side. This causes the blade to wobble back and forth, resulting in thick and thin lumber. It takes two people to cut perfect boards: the sawyer who runs the carriage and plans the cuts, and the millwright who keeps the teeth sharp and hammers out the saw to keep it stiff in the cut. Bill Sharpe and Rod Mohl were best at those jobs.

"I hear they're about to open up the Champion gold mine," Groot, our Norwegian edgerman, said.

"You hear that every ten years," Sharpe said.

"Might be worth a look-see."

"Look all you want," Sharpe said, "but don't crawl back begging for a job when it doesn't pan out."

"Boone says they've got a new way to pull out the gold. He thinks it'll pay."

"Boone ought to know," Duff said quietly.

"What was that?" Sharpe said loudly.

Sawyers, who stand three feet from whirring blades day after day, lose their hearing because they constantly lean into the saw, checking their cuts and watching for hang-ups. What Sharpe hadn't known at the time—and couldn't have done anything about anyway—was that the steel teeth he used to rip the logs were no less kind to the small bones inside his ears.

Groot turned directly toward Sharpe. "Boone says they've got new machines at the mine that should make it pay."

"Boone ought to know," Sharpe said. "He's been chasing two claims since the war."

Groot laughed. "You're deaf as a post, same as me." When Groot first started, he said the sound of the main saw "had hurt like hell." For a month, he had to grit his teeth just to make it through the day. "After that, it wasn't nearly so bad."

"The only reason Boone works in this rat hole," Mohl said, butting in, "is to stake another year of prospecting."

"Work at the mine is gonna pay three bucks a day," Groot said. "That's sure to bring in the Italians and Greeks."

"All Italians are fucking papists," Mohl said, "but at least they're Christians. The goddamn Greeks don't even believe in Jesus Christ."

"Holy shit!" Groot said. "That can't be true."

"Look at their cross. It's broken, deefiled by the anti-Christ."

"Italians and Greeks working the mines and stealing our jobs is plenty bad," Groot said, "but not believing in the Lord God…Christ on a crutch!"

The whistle blew, sounding the end of the break.

"Back to work, ladies," Sharpe said.

The main saw powered up with a moan that rose to a shriek. Sharpe started working the dogs, rotating the log for the next cut. The carriage began rolling forward, pushing the log into the spinning teeth. The pitch dropped as the saw hesitated in the cut, and then, beneath a curtain of raw splinters, the one substance passed through the other.

I slid back from the noise and dust, preferring to search for hidden treasure among the junk. Pallets, some splintered, a few still intact, littered the weeds alongside beer bottles, scrap lumber, crumpled cigarette packs, and snoose cans. I kicked at a dandelion, and a new cigarette pack bounced up. The fresh cellophane wrapping crinkled when I squeezed it.

"Lucky Strike," I announced in my best radio voice. "Good for what ails you!" A red bull's-eye with a background of dark green and gold dominated the pack. "It's toasted," I pretended to read. Lucky Strike was a man's cigarette. It was my father's brand.

I sniffed the open top. It smelled sweet inside like Dad's jacket pocket. I ripped away the top, stuck my nose inside, and inhaled. I licked the inner walls, trapping the remaining flecks of tobacco with my tongue. My mouth watered, and my nose started to run. I rubbed the tobacco over my gums and against the roof of mouth. I swallowed a juicy mouthful of spit and threw the crumpled pack back in the weeds.

The discarded pack settled beside a book of matches. I retrieved the book and opened it. Three dry matches remained. I struck the first one and watched it flare along the thin paper shaft. When the flame threatened my fingers, I dropped the match, and with the toe of my shoe, I ground the smoldering remnant into the planer shavings like the men did with their cigarette stubs. I studied the tiny grave for a moment and then pushed the small book deep inside my pocket. I left my hideout to see what else there was to do.

17

When Dad announced that Mr. Rex Pingree and his wife, Daisy, were planning to drive up from Salem to visit, Mother was happier than I'd seen her since before Christmas. Mr. Pingree owned a car dealership in Salem and had been Dad's partner in the plank mill that burned. Mother and Daisy were good friends, too, but the real reason for Mr. Pingree's visit was business.

"I can't possibly get ready in time," Mother said, worrying about the rough state of the house. As she said it, she had the mop out and had started scrubbing.

The Pingrees didn't have any kids to bring along, so I didn't share the same anticipation.

"Make the best of it," Mother said.

They were to be our first official visitors at Culp Creek, and this would be our first fancy meal in the house. Mother worked hard to make it a great occasion—cleaning, cooking, and arranging flowers.

The afternoon they were to arrive, she put on a new summer dress that showed off her legs. She said it made her feel pretty. Each time she heard an engine in the distance, she ran to the window to stare out. Then she'd tell me to wash my face and hands and not get dirty. I'd wave my pink fingers to remind her I'd already done it.

"You're a good boy," she said without looking.

I spotted them first. A tree was sticking out of their car. The branches waved when the car bounced over the ruts.

Mr. Pingree stuck his head out of the car window. "It's spring planting time!"

I ran to the trunk of his car, where he joined me.

"It's a weeping willow," he said, lifting the tree from the car, "because we miss you. You most of all, Marie."

Mother beamed. "What's it for?" she said. "It's certainly not spring, and there are no holidays in August."

"We brought it as a house warming gift," Daisy said, "so you'll have company and a little shade."

Mr. Pingree carried the tree by its root ball, which was wrapped in burlap cloth. "Now, where do you suppose we should put it?" he said, taking care not to break the branches.

Dad had been watching from the sidelines. He strode to an area well away from the house. "This spot will do fine."

"Not there." Mother said.

Mr. Pingree hesitated.

"That's not the right place." She began marching off the corners of her planned fence. "We'd hate to have to replant it." She sounded a little out of breath.

Mr. Pingree set the tree down and watched Mother whirl around a perimeter only she could see. When she was satisfied, he carried the tree to her designated spot. He changed into a pair of boots and began digging with a shovel he also pulled from the trunk of his car. With some easy conversation directed toward Mother and Daisy, Mr. Pingree planted the young tree near our front window.

"Now, it's a home," he said, giving the soft earth a final pat with the flat of his shovel.

We stepped back to admire it. Mother's new weeping willow was the only living tree on our property.

Mr. Pingree gave Mother a big hug, and she kissed him on the lips. She built a low dike around the tree with her bare hands and patted the soil. She emptied a jug of water over the roots while Mr. Pingree tapped the shovel against the underside of his bumper and stowed it back in the trunk.

Mother was standing beside her new willow, petting its leaves and looking very happy, when she started flapping her hands. She turned toward the house and started running. "My God, no!" she screamed, "I've ruined our dinner!"

Mr. Pingree's eyes followed her as she ran up the steps. "Will you be having a little chicken for dessert tonight, Merle?" he said.

I quickly looked at Mother to see what I had missed. The thin fabric of her new summer dress had ridden up. It was clinging to her bottom and *really* showing off her legs and the backs of her thighs, too.

"No chicken tonight," Dad said. "It's grown a little stale."

Mr. Pingree noticed me staring. "I like dark meat when it's really juicy," he said. "Especially the drumstick and thigh. What about you, Teddy?"

"I like dark meat, too."

Thinking back, I suspect Mr. Pingree could talk like this about Mother because he had made lots of money in business. He drove an air-cooled Franklin that Dad said was better than a Cadillac.

Mr. Pingree ruffled my hair. "Little Teddy," he said, "I swear, you look more like your Daddy every day."

Dad told me to wash my hands before following Mr. Pingree into the house.

The adults ate their supper in the living room while I sat at the window seat. The kitchen smelled of fresh paint because Mother had only finished painting it the day before. The walls were covered with sheets of thick brown paper tacked to boards with wood screws and washers. Before the paint, the walls had looked like grocery bag paper, but with the new white paint, the screws and washers reminded me of rivets on a new steam boiler. We didn't have insulation in the walls, just tarpaper on the outside, and this thick wallpaper inside. In the fall, when it got cold, Dad had the men move a new stove into the kitchen. It had an inner cast iron box surrounded by an air space and an outer porcelain cover. That helped, but we were rarely warm as toast like he promised.

"From the looks of the things," I heard Mr. Pingree say from the other room, "You're still up and running. Are shipments going out regularly?"

"We're cutting lumber, if that's what you mean," Dad said. "But I'm down to running short shifts."

"The times are tough on everybody," Mr. Pingree said. "I was over the border in Canada two weeks ago. The Vancouver dock looked like a wasteland."

"Lumber sales are half of what they were last year," Dad said. "I'm getting sixteen dollars per thousand compared to twenty-five." The words caught in his throat.

"Look at the bright side," Pingree said. "With our little arrangement, you've got an extra source of income, which brings me to the point of my visit. We have to get another shipment out soon. Our clients back east are beginning to feel slighted, and that's bad business for everybody."

"As soon as I put together an order big enough to fill a boxcar, I'll ship," Dad said.

"You'll ship now," Pingree said. "I'll fill the boxcar myself, if I have to, but it's going out Monday."

"It's your nickel," Dad said.

"No," Pingree argued. "It's my ass."

Mother was flustered during supper because her roast was dry, and the end pieces had burned black. When she stepped into the kitchen to get a sharper knife, both of us heard Dad from the other room. "Marie must have used the beef to fire up the boiler." She opened the cupboard above the sink and reached for the bottle she kept there. She filled her glass for the third time and gave me a wink before drinking it down. Then she hurried back to Dad and our company.

"Merle's right," she said, joining them. "I *was* trying to get double duty out of the roast. These are hard times, so we make do as best we can."

Mr. and Mrs. Pingree laughed and told her the meal was fine. Still, she apologized and made sure her guests got the best pieces from the middle. Her heels clicked on the hard linoleum as she circled the table, filling plates and glasses. More than once, she stumbled in her high heels because she wasn't used to wearing them—that was what she told them.

"As you can see, Temperance spreads her legs in our home," Dad said, much to Mr. Pingree's amusement. When Dad had made the same comment once before, Mother had objected. She said nothing this time because she was so happy to finally have company. The married mill hands who lived nearby kept to themselves. Out of principle, nobody hobnobbed with the boss's family.

I finished my supper and traded my chair for the kitchen floor where I started working with my Pelton waterwheel. The axle wasn't turning freely, so I crimped the hub and paddles with pliers and then climbed on the chair to test the waterwheel in the sink. While I was splashing in the water and waiting for blackberry pie, Dad and Mr. Pingree walked outside for fresh air.

They stepped off the porch and started toward the earthen berm that contained the log pond. I followed at a distance, carrying my waterwheel. As long as I was seen and not heard, I could go pretty much where I wanted.

"When does the booze roll in?" Dad said.

Mom stuck her head out the door. "I'll wait to serve the pie. Don't be too long."

Dad and Mr. Pingree acted as if they hadn't heard. "Late Sunday night, after dark," Mr. Pingree said without so much as looking up. "The crates will be labeled as surveying equipment, same as always, but with one change. We're moving four crates, instead of two, so save room."

"No worries there," Dad said.

The clatter of dishes and women's voices receded as we moved away. At the pond's edge, Dad and Mr. Pingree stopped to survey the evening. The night's first star hung overhead, and a single cricket was tuning up; it was early August, the time of year when night was slow to come. Since there was no urgency for men or insects, Dad reached for a cigarette, and Mr. Pingree did the same.

"Do you have the custom timbers I asked you to cut?" Mr. Pingree said.

"Forty cedar cants, as ordered," Dad said. "Twenty by twenty inches, sixteen feet long, but I have to warn you, this isn't clear timber. It's pecky in sections, and there's some rot."

"I promise not build bridges with it," Mr. Pingree said, "at least none I'll be driving on. The rot's not a problem, but they do have to be absolutely straight. I need to see them."

They rounded the pond, following a footpath that took them to the mill. At the loading dock, Dad took hold of the ladder and climbed the four feet onto the deck. Mr. Pingree followed, and I slipped underneath.

"Any other changes in how you'll move the liquor from Canada into the States?" Dad asked.

"We still plan to use sailing schooners out of Vancouver. Small ships can change docks at the last minute and off-load just about anywhere. You can't do that with a heavy steamship. We'll truck it here at night from the docks."

"Who'll be riding with the load after it leaves the mill?" Dad asked.

"Nobody. That's why I asked for the special timbers. When you load the boxcar, stack the timbers around the crates so nobody can get to them. We want to discourage unwelcome interest by a bum or a Fed."

"It's no simple matter distinguishing between the two, these days," Dad said. "Everybody has a hand out."

I scooted between posts until I was directly beneath them. I couldn't make out their shoes in the low light, but Dad's voice was easy to follow. "Here they are," he said.

Pingree counted the timbers and paced off their length. He checked for twists and warping. "Most people I deal with," he said, "especially those paid to be curious, lack imagination. The Feds will continue to search for crates and barrels while I ship legitimate lumber." He propped a foot on one of the timbers and leaned down to tie his shoe. "And it all stacks so nicely."

"Why the change, now?"

"The California docks are a mess. We can't trust labor unions or cops anymore—too many unfriendly eyes and, as you said, too many hands out. We intend to bypass the docks altogether and stick to the rails. Big and heavy as these timbers are, nobody will try to move them."

Dad grinned. I could see his teeth in the moonlight. "Once they're stacked inside the car, it will be impossible to turn them or get to the ends."

"Starting with this shipment, my crates and your lumber travel non-stop to a stud mill in California in the central valley. From there, it's on to Chicago and the East Coast in a quarter of the time it takes to sail around South America."

"Sounds like you're a small part of the process," Dad said.

"Just a cog in the wheel," Pingree said.

"What about problems unloading in Portland like you've had in California?"

"We have a solid partner in Portland: McCormick Steamship. McCormick controls Portland's docks top to bottom, including labor. We'll sail through Portland."

Dad took a seat on his special timbers. "Rex," he said, almost too quietly for me to hear, "do you think we'll get through this with our skins intact?"

"You're not getting cold feet, are you?"

"That's not it. I'd twist off a nut if it would buy me a place on top."

Mr. Pingree chuckled. He reached for another cigarette, but Dad placed a hand on his arm.

"Too easy to burn the place down, Rex."

Mr. Pingree slipped the pack back into his pocket. "You know the Latham mill burned to the ground this past Fourth of July. It was quite the fireworks from what I gather."

Dad pointed toward the clearing across the river. "Can you see the vacant meadow across the way?"

Mr. Pingree stood to look. Scattered throughout the overgrown meadow were remnants of an abandoned logging operation. I had picked through all of it. The machines and trucks were rusted out and missing parts. A boarded up cookhouse and several ramshackle buildings still stood. I'd been inside those, too. A railroad spur still crossed over to the meadow from our side of the river by way of an old timber bridge. At one time, the spur had been used to carry logs. Now, it ran into the empty camp and wasn't used for anything.

"Not much to see," he said, sitting back down.

"That property is going to be up for sale soon," Dad said.

"This isn't a good time to be moving," Mr. Pingree said. "Why not wait until the market improves."

"I don't plan to move. I just want the logs. Polk and Chisholm Lumber fell into bankruptcy last week. They own the timber rights to the property."

"I don't know anything about it."

"Fifteen years ago, Polk and Chisholm Lumber—out of Wisconsin—went on a buying spree throughout the Northwest and over-leveraged its assets even for the best of times, which this ain't. Along with the Latham Sawmill, Polk and Chisholm bought land, timber, and a majority interest in the OP&E railroad. The assets are now tied up in receivership. The court named Wulf Gehring receiver and ordered him to liquidate it. I want the timber sitting in the Culp and Sharp Creek drainages; that's ten years of production parked on my doorstep."

Dad stood and stretched. He glanced toward the house. Mother had lit the kerosene lamps. I watched her shadow slide across the window.

"We had better start back," Dad said. "We don't want the girls mad at us."

"More to the point, I need a cigarette."

"Thinking I'd have an in with him, I paid Gehring a visit and offered a fair price for the timber, but damned if Wulf didn't give me the time of day. He told me he had no interest in peddling the property in pieces, preferring to sell the timber as a package, *with* the Latham sawmill.

"You can't argue with that."

"I suppose not," Dad said. "But once the Latham Mill burned, wouldn't that approach have to change? Without the mill, Gehring no longer has a package to sell. All he has is the railroad and these timber rights."

"He didn't change his mind after the fire?"

"I figured I'd get the timber at a discount," Dad said. "I expected him to eat crow, but the son-of-a-bitch still refused to give me the time of day."

Dad and Mr. Pingree stopped to talk some more, but I'd had enough. I slipped inside and found my pie on the kitchen table. When they finally stepped inside, Mother and Daisy were shuffling cards and playing music on the gramophone. I was in my room, wide awake, with instructions to go to sleep. Instead, I was listening to the music and the happy voices. With strangers in the house, I could no more go to sleep than stop breathing.

"I'll tell you what," Dad was saying, "if Hoover had a decent Congress, we'd have this stock market mess solved. There is nothing wrong with Herbert. The real problem is the crackpots and communists who have the ear of the Democratic Congress. They all want Hoover to fail. If the Democrats get their way, they'll destroy every business in the country."

"Pie is on the kitchen table, coffee, too," Mom said, getting up from her game and walking to the kitchen. "There's cream in the white pitcher to pour over the pie."

"Marie and I want to play pinochle," Daisy called from the other room. I could hear her shuffling the cards.

"I always have time for your cooking, Marie." Mr. Pingree said, "but we can't stay for cards." Mother murmured her disappointment. "I have an early start in the morning."

"Don't say that, Rex!" Mother complained. "Tomorrow is Sunday."

"And God has a full day of work cut out for me. I have to get a shipment together for your husband."

Chairs scraped and voices shifted toward the door. "If you're serious about getting hold of those timber rights," Mr. Pingree said, "you had better work on your business connections."

"I attend the Lumbermen's meeting every month."

"That's not enough," Mr. Pingree said. "You need to join the Cottage Grove Klavern. Every wheel in town is a member."

"That's the Ku Klux Klan, isn't it?" Mother said. "Should we be talking to them?"

"It's a different organization, now," Pingree said. "More of a business group, and they're all Christian. I've been a member for five years, and we've never made an issue of dark people. This is about Catholics and Jews taking over our schools. It's not about coloreds. The Klan is for an independent government and safe schools, nothing more."

"That doesn't sound so bad," Mother said.

"I know more than you think about The In-vis-i-ble Order," Dad said. "The Klan recruited hard while I was at the university. It didn't fit me then, and I don't see it fitting now. I'm not one to parade down Main Street dressed like a cheap ghost."

"The Klan is big in Oregon, and it's getting stronger every day," Mr. Pingree said, his voice tight. "If you want to do business in the big leagues, you'd better think again about what fits and what doesn't."

"No harm in thinking," Dad said.

18

"Two ways a mill burns," Dad said, the first time he sent me out to watch for spot fires. "You need to know what they are."

I stared at him and waited because I didn't know it was a question.

"What are they?" He already sounded irritated.

I thought about it, stalled, and reluctantly said, "They burn with fire and smoke." I had also considered wood and gasoline as possibilities.

"That would be *how* they burn," he said. "That's not what I asked. I want to know why they burn."

I didn't give it a second try because that wasn't the purpose of the question. I had played my part.

"Mills burn," Dad said, settling into a tone that Moses likely used when he spoke to the apostles from the mount, "either through bad luck or bad judgment."

I tried to see it. Lightning dropping from the sky would have to fall into the bad luck category. Laziness and stupidity would run in the company of bad judgment, which might not be obvious to somebody who hadn't already heard Dad's thoughts about the matter. "Hiring a lazy or stupid person," he'd say, "comes down to bad judgment for employing such a person in the first place." Ending up with a lazy or stupid son, well, that could only be attributed to bad luck. Dad never said that outright. It was me just thinking it.

Dad lost his first mill, the plank mill in Elmira, to fire before I was born. He never told me whether that fire was due to bad luck or bad judgment.

To go out and watch for fires, now that was no joke since a mill fire could start anywhere, at any time. Hot summer days were the worst, but lumber burns in January, too. To fight the fires, all we had were wooden buckets hanging on water barrels and canvas hoses to drag around—and a gasoline-driven water pump that we'd have to crank to start.

A spot fire usually starts deep inside a pile of sawdust, near the bottom. The spark is spawned from the heat, but starved for oxygen. Without air, it burns cold with little more hope than Dante's damned praying for the resurrection. Still, it creeps through the airless underbelly, and if lucky, it finds an edge, where it peeks out. In the air, the spark celebrates; it dances and leaps.

"Spontaneous combustion." That was what Dad called it. "But it feels like God exhorting sinners, and we are all sinners. Isn't that right, Teddy?"

"Grandma would say so." Dad often used Grandma Lulu's words, but they didn't carry the same meaning when they passed from his lips.

So, I would walk from one end of our mill site to the other, looking for spot fires. On especially hot days, I'd move sprinklers three or four times to splash the cold deck—the pile of logs waiting to be sawed. Other days, I'd carry a small shovel through the tangles behind the mill to clean up the three-foot wide firebreak that looped up the slope behind the boiler and then rolled down to the highway. The firebreak needed constant tending to keep brush and thistle from growing back. If a fire started at our mill, it was supposed to keep the flames from wiping out the forest behind us. From the highway, it looked like a bad scar slashed through the stubble on somebody's head.

I believed that fires were mostly bad luck. All mills burned sooner or later, it seemed. The new Darby Mill in Cottage Grove had four boilers up and was only half built when it caught fire. Old man Darby had sunk thousands of dollars into the construction and hadn't yet cut a stick when a summer lightning storm rolled in and grounded through the structure.

Babe Ashman, who worked on the green chain with the Norwegian, Alex Groot, described the Darby fire one night at the bunkhouse. Babe was sitting next to the wood stove, watching me and Ray Luke play checkers. Uncle Normal wasn't with us. As usual, he was by himself in his room by the woodshed. A steady rain rattled the tarpaper overhead, but we were snug inside. It was getting dark outside, but I wasn't ready to go home. Before dinner, Dad had left for Eugene with his tie and good jacket on. "I'm off to the lumberman meetings," he'd said. He skipped dinner because he was in a hurry, and then so did Mother.

"We were just standing around," Babe said, starting into his story, "watching a storm roll in." He stretched back in his chair and stared into his recollection. He tipped onto the back legs and made the chair creak. Babe Ashman was big like the blue ox, which was why he got the name and the heavy jobs. "When lightning hit the mill that night, I felt like Lon Chaney in the movies. If Frankenstein's monster had been there, it would a lit him up to the last bolt."

While Babe talked, Ray and I kept at our checkers. Ray had lost an arm several inches below the elbow, but even with one arm, he played checkers better than everyone else. His remaining arm looked strong enough to do the work of two.

"I've seen a storm or two like that," Ray said, studying the board even though it was my move.

"Not so," Babe said. "This storm was a thousand percent different than any typhoon you ever saw. Black like diesel smoke, it boiled down on us with no rain inside." Babe leaned even farther back and propped two crusty socks on the old horsehair leather chair by the barrel stove. Ray and I both caught a whiff. We looked at each other, but didn't say anything. Above Babe, the stove's shaky metal chimney climbed to the ceiling and disappeared through a rough-cut hole. Water had stained the wood dark brown at the opening where it seeped through. More water had left orange stripes down the length of the stovepipe.

Since Babe prided himself in telling a good story, he eyeballed everybody to be sure we were with him. I tore my eyes from the checkerboard long enough to let him know I was listening.

"Before the lightning struck," he said, finally satisfied, "there was an unnatural glow on the horizon that turned the trees into black cutouts. Struck dumb, we watched it come and never moved, not even when the air started buzzing. If we'd had corn in our pockets, it would have been popping."

Pulled in by Babe's words, I forgot about the game.

"It's your move," Ray said. "We're still playing checkers here."

I slid a piece across the board and lifted my hand, but immediately regretted it when Ray smiled.

"When the buzzing thickened into a swarm, I dropped my wrench and jumped away from it. The lightning bolt hit and sparked the wrench like a magneto so bright I had to close my eyes. The thunder that followed tore a hole in the sky wide enough to drop a locomotive."

With the hand he still had, Ray moved one of his pieces onto my back row. Ray never wore a hook or strap on the stump, he simply folded his shirtsleeve over and pinned the cuff up by the shoulder.

"It changed color where it touched down," Babe said.

"What did?" I asked.

"God's righteous spit," Ray said.

I turned from Babe to Ray. That was something Grandma Lulu might say.

"God's righteous Spirit, I meant to say," Ray corrected. "When God gets really pissed off, he starts screaming and yelling, and lightning flies like spit, just like with Babe here."

Babe seemed more upset with the interruption than with the insult. "I'm talking about the electrical charge where it hit the ground." Pulling his bulk forward until he was almost on top of me, Babe looked me in the eye.

"What started out as a white bolt of lightning," Babe said, "turned blue and came alive where it touched down. Pure energy flowed through the place and sparked anything metal. The fires that followed melted Darby's four boilers into a pile of sludge that had to be dozed away and buried."

"Like bodies in a lime pit," Boone Shaw said.

Babe glanced over. Boone was lying on one of the bunks. "Not something I've ever seen," Babe said.

"I saw plenty," Boone said. "When we lost count of the bodies, we made up a number. The only thing the officers cared about was having that number to pass along to the brass."

"Can't say I've seen it either," Ray said, "but I have heard that lye bubbles meat off the bone." Ray was still concentrating on the checkerboard, even while he spoke.

I thought about the dead mice I'd dumped in the outhouse. How many bodies had I sprinkled with lye?

Ray's hand edged toward the middle of the board. I waited quietly for him to finish his move because he didn't like me talking while he was thinking. Drops of water fell onto the hot stove and disappeared in tiny puffs of steam. Ray jumped two of my pieces and landed on kings' row. "Crown me," he said, looking pleased.

I stared at the board, trying to assess the damage. I checked Ray's eyes to see if he'd cheated.

"You got to be ready for anything," he said.

While Ray dished up two bowls of hot beans and biscuits, I started setting up another game. The Darby fire had to be an example of bad luck, I thought.

"His ma know where he's at?" Babe asked nobody in particular.

"She knows," Boone said.

"Mother likes me to get out and see people," I answered with my mouth full. Since my first fearful visit to the bunkhouse, something that had started out as an adventure had grown into a necessity. I was spending more and more time at the bunkhouse even though it wasn't always fun: grownup men can be hard even when it's not their intention. Still, it was better than being locked inside a silent bubble.

Silence can be a relief for some. At times, it's a haven for everyone, but too much silence presses down the way black at the bottom of a well must feel. I've never been down a well, but I've stared into plenty. The black at the bottom of an endless hole is worlds apart from the dark that fills a moonless night. It's the difference between despair and hope. Mother said a quiet house and a dark room calmed her. For me, it felt like the bottom of a well.

"Speaking of fires," Ray said, "you have to wonder whether the recent Latham mill fire happened on its own or if somebody helped out." Ray would talk plenty between games, just not during. "It started in broad daylight on the Fourth of July without a cloud in sight." Ray was arranging the red and black pieces faster with one hand than I could with two.

"No lightning anywhere near with that one," Babe said, "but more money owed on it than we'll see in a lifetime. The insurance investigators poked through the ashes for weeks. From what I hear, they still haven't paid the claim."

"You're right about that," Ray said. "The mill was shut down with nobody around, not even a watchman. It could have been spontaneous combustion that started it. More likely it was simple debt management, and nobody could prove a thing."

"I hear the owners disconnected the mill from the town's water system a month before the fire," Babe said, "to save money." Babe smiled like he knew something. "Pretty fuckin' hard to fight a fire without water."

"Who actually owned the mill when it burned?" Ray asked.

"I never saw a title, if that's what you're asking," Babe said. "But it doesn't take a genius to figure how it likely played out. With the original owner, Polk and Chisholm Lumber bankrupt, Neet's bank was left holding the bag."

"That was my guess, too," Ray said.

"It serves the little prick right to get a taste of his own medicine."

"The way I see it," Ray said, "Wulf Gehring tried to sell the mill as a package, but couldn't find a taker. It was becoming an expensive problem for Neet and the bank."

"Did the fire get Neet in the clear?" Boone asked.

"You bet it did. The insurance carrier paid out last week," Ray said. "Neet deposited a check for the entire amount, and I know that for a fact." Ray was interrupted by footsteps on the porch.

A man in a rain slicker banged through the door, stomping loudly and shedding the rain. He halfheartedly scraped his boots against the threshold and shook his coat over the floor. I slid my chair away from the table. It was time for me to go.

"Let's play some poker," Mohl said, sitting down.

Boone watched him settle in. "Aren't you on night watch?"

"I think it's time for a break," Mohl said. "Nothing's going to burn in this rain."

"Does Fraser know he's paying you to play poker?"

"With what Fraser's paying," Mohl said, pulling his chair up to the table, "he's lucky I don't torch the place." He spotted me and curled his lip. "Isn't it past your bed time, sonny?"

Ray began clearing away the checkers. "I think you better go," he said to me. "Your mom might start to worry."

"Careful near the pond," Mohl said, showing his teeth. "I just saw the biggest, meanest muskrat ever slinking through the bushes. Looked like a real carnivore." He laughed so hard I could smell his breath. "You know what a carnivore is, don't you?"

I buttoned up my coat.

"Ease up," Babe said. "What do you say?"

Mohl slipped a flask from his pocket and pulled hard on it. "What do I say?" he muttered, swallowing. "What. Do.

I. Say?" He set his flask down and then leaped at me with his claws open. Growling and hissing, he screamed, *"Meat eater!"*

I ran for the door.

"That's what I say," Mohl added, slurring his words. "Pound for pound, a muskrat eats more than a bear and is meaner than a cougar. Especially in the dark."

If he had anything more to say, I missed it. I was on the porch, staring blindly into a steady drizzle. The thermometer on the wall, advertising *Symmonds Saws*, showed fifty-three degrees. I didn't believe Mohl's lie about the muskrat, but it made me uneasy. In the near dark, the pond was gone and the smokestack had faded into the hill. A silhouette, larger than real, loomed above me; it was all that marked the mill and the loading dock. The gurgling that normally rose from the river was also absent, muffled by the fog and the falling rain.

I stared across the pond and tried to find our house, but night had taken it, too. No lighted window, no moving shadow suggested a presence. No voices and certainly no laughter would be tapping against its empty windows. I hoped Mother wasn't in her room, even if it meant she was sitting in the dark, silently watching the black stare in, winding and rewinding the Victrola, listening over and over to songs that played through our house like orphans.

19

Music and Mother's voice woke me. She was bustling around the kitchen, singing the one tune that always seemed to make her happy. With my eyes open, I lay in bed and listened: to her footsteps, to doors opening and closing, to pans clanking against the sink and stove—warm, wonderful sounds that crackled like kindling. Not wanting it to stop, afraid I might do something to ruin it, I stayed in bed and breathed it in.

"Oh, dem golden slippers
Oh, dem golden slippers
Golden slippers I'se goin' to wear
because they look so neat"

The music stopped. I waited. The gramophone started up again with her clear voice joining it. Covers pulled to my chin, toes wiggling beneath, I began to hum along.

"Oh, dem golden slippers
Oh, dem golden slippers

Golden slippers I'se goin' to wear

To walk the golden street."

"Teddy," she sang from the kitchen. "Time to get up, darling. Breakfast is ready."

I jumped from bed and raced toward the kitchen in my pajamas. I opened the bedroom door, and breakfast smells carried me the rest of the way. Mother was at the kitchen sink with her hands busy in the suds. A fire popped in the stove behind her, and her feet were tapping the linoleum. She had on a dress and an apron, and she was still singing along.

I stopped at the threshold, unsure, afraid I might be intruding. "Hi, Mom," I said carefully.

She turned toward me and beamed. I so loved my mother when she was like this. She danced over and picked me up with warm soapy hands. We hugged. She twirled me around as if I were her dance partner.

"Good morning, Teddy Sunshine," she said.

I started to speak, but she put a finger to her lips and pointed to the music—she was already back to her singing. Not once stopping to rest, we danced around the kitchen until the song finally wound down.

She patted my bottom. "That was so much fun!" She was radiant. "Now, slide *your* golden slippers to the table and get started. I made your favorite breakfast." She glided into the living room with an invisible partner and restarted the music.

After the gramophone wound down for the third time, I said, "This is really good!" And it was good, even though eggs and bacon weren't my favorite breakfast. Waffles were. But it was really good anyway.

"Mom," I said. "Is this a special day?"

"All our days are special, Honey."

"Oh." I took another bite.

"Don't you think so?"

"Yes," I said carefully.

"We are going to have many more special days. Wait and see."

I wanted to believe her. I looked outside through the kitchen window. The boilers were up with steam filling the sky. The men were all working. Uncle Normal was at the far end of the pond. I didn't see Dad.

"Where's Dad?"

"He's with Mr. Sharpe, looking for new timber."

Mother moved to the living room while I finished eating. She was curled up in a chair, reading a book, when I walked in. I quietly looked on, over her shoulder. She almost never read.

"This story is so wonderful," she sighed. "It's how my life is going to be when my ship comes in." She turned back several pages and pointed. "This is where young, beautiful Tess of the Storm Country learns of his love for her."

"Whose love?" I asked.

"The handsome biology student, Mr. Graves, who is nothing like his father."

I stared at the page.

"They meet when he is out chasing butterflies. He sees her beautiful red hair and falls in love with her. Then they get married. After suffering for so long, her ship comes in at last. She has all the money and love she could ever want."

Mother's page marker sat in the middle of book, not at the end. "How do you know that already?" I asked.

"Because he happens to be the love of her life and because I've already read it twice."

My mother was a happy on the outside person who tried to make the best of things. She painted my room and put up wallpaper and planted flowers. She was a good mother who fixed my meals and made sure I wore a coat and hat when it was cold outside. Once, we made play dough out of flour and tried to build zoo animals with it. When she was in the right mood, she could float and never touch the ground. Those were the times when she loved everyone, and they loved her.

Later that morning, I was at the kitchen table, working on my water wheel and watching Uncle Normal and Lewis Woolsey herd logs across the pond. Lewis had just moved up from Venita, and since he was new, he got put in the pond with Uncle Normal. They were wearing thick coats and rain gear because the day was so cold and drizzly. Uncle Normal saw me and started dancing on his log, causing it to bounce and roll. I waved. He laughed and ran from one end of the log to the other, which Lewis didn't like it, probably because he was new. He poled his log to the other side of the pond.

Uncle Normal was still goofing around when he fell in. I'd seen men do that before, but they always popped right up, sputtering and mad. Uncle Normal didn't pop up. All I saw was a hand reach up. He tried more than once to pull himself out, but the log kept spinning away from him. His waterlogged cold weather clothes were dragging him down. Then he started thrashing, struggling just to keep his head above water. He couldn't get his feet underneath him for some reason.

"Mom, come quick," I said in a regular voice, too scared to yell.

"Just a minute," she said.

His face came up and then disappeared. The raft of logs closed over him.

I looked over to Lewis to see if he would help, but his back was turned.

"He's drowning!" I yelled.

Mother ran from the bedroom.

I pointed to the rocking logs and the circle of ripples. She didn't ask who. Her feet pound across the floor behind me. I didn't leave my window; I was afraid to get any closer.

Mother ran straight into the water, quickly up to her shoulders. Her skirt billowed up and held her back. She had to struggle against its weight. She was taking too long. When she reached the nearest log, she reached down and groped blindly, but came up with nothing. I knew he was already dead, but she didn't give up. She plunged her hand under a second time and found something. Uncle Normal's hand came to the surface inside her grip.

Refusing to let go of him, Mother leaned her shoulders against the logs and forced them apart, just enough for him to squeeze through. I wondered how she could do that when he couldn't, but Uncle Normal had trouble managing a lot of things when he was drinking. Still holding onto his hand like he was two, she walked him to the shallow water at the edge of the pond. Lewis Woolsey saw them and came over, but she waved him off.

Mother was wet to her shoulders, and Uncle Normal was shivering and blue when they reached the kitchen. She seemed only to be thinking about him.

"Let's get you out of these clothes," she said, stripping off his jacket and shirt. "Teddy, fill the teapot and set it on the stove. Bring all the towels you can find."

Uncle Normal had shed his long underwear top and was sitting on a kitchen chair when I returned with an armload of towels. Mother was on her knees in front of him, unlacing his

129

boots. She pulled them off and peeled away his trousers, socks, and flannel underwear. Starting with his head and shoulders, she began toweling him off, rubbing the mottled skin as hard as she could, to the point where it had to hurt.

"Teddy, start drying his legs and feet," she ordered. When we met in the middle, she made Uncle Normal walk over to the stove.

Shivering and chattering and uncertain of his balance, he swayed next to the stove. He reached a hand out to steady himself, but Mother grabbed him first.

"Don't touch the stove!" she scolded him.

Uncle Normal was so skinny, it hung from his frame. The muscles men carry on their arms and chest, he didn't have, and where a round butt should have filled out his pants, he had bones and hollows. Uncle Normal looked like a man half gone. Even his skin was gone. All that remained was cellophane with blue worms crawling through it.

Mother took a damp towel from his shoulders and replaced it with one she'd warmed by the stove. With the towel draped across his narrow shoulders and his head sagging, Uncle stood in the center of the kitchen, naked. I had never seen a man so laid open. Mother put her arms around him and pulled him close.

"You can't do this, Normal," she said, drying her tears on his towel. He didn't answer.

She took a step back. "Teddy, hold onto your uncle while I slide a chair over. Don't let him fall."

I wrapped my arms around his thighs and hugged them. I felt the pressure of his open hand on the top of my head. Mother slid a wooden chair behind him and sat him down. His wrinkled member curled against the cold wood and appeared less significant than my own.

She dressed him in Dad's clothes and fed him scrambled eggs with sausage. They sat together at the kitchen table, sipping coffee, saying nothing. The cuffs on Dad's pants were rolled up to mid-calf so Uncle Normal could soak his feet in a basin of warm water. Black coffee steamed in their mugs. Neither of them used milk or sugar because that was how they'd been taught to drink it. Since Dad liked two teaspoons of sugar in his coffee, the sugar bowl always was at the kitchen table even if he wasn't.

The three of us silently stared at the pond. Lewis was still out in the rain, rafting the logs by himself, doing the work of two. "Why do you do these things?" she asked, watching Lewis work.

"I wasn't thinking," Uncle Normal said.

"At worst, you might have drowned. At best, you could lose your job."

Uncle Normal said nothing.

"Merle isn't happy with the way things are going."

"He already told me."

Mother retrieved the coffee pot and filled their cups. She dipped her fingers into his foot bath. "More hot water?" she asked.

Uncle Normal shook his head. "Tomorrow is Nels' birthday," he said in a soft voice. "Did you remember?"

"I remembered," she said.

"I suppose it don't much matter to him, now," Uncle Normal said.

"It matters to me."

"Who are you talking about?" I asked.

"Your Uncle Nels," she said. "Nels was our brother. He died when he was nineteen years old."

"You know what he told me before he left?" Uncle Normal said.

Mother looked at him without expression.

"He said we'll soon settle this." Uncle Normal turned away from Mother. "I should have been with him."

"You had a wife and a small baby. You had no business going to war."

"And since Nels was young and not married, that made it his business?" Uncle Normal pulled his feet from the bath. He reached for the wool socks Mother had placed on the table.

"The draft board made it his business," she said. "He was happy to go, proud even."

"I can tell you this," Uncle Normal said. "There is no pride in staying behind." He turned to me. "Your Uncle Nels was a brave man." He slipped wet boots over the dry socks and gathered the rest of his soggy clothes into a bundle. Without bothering to lace up the boots, he walked across the kitchen, leaving a trail of boot prints. He stopped at the door, but didn't look back. "Nobody saw fit to send me with him, and God didn't see fit to send Nels back." He placed his hand on the knob. "Thank you, Mary," he said before he closed the door.

Mother stood at the window and watched her brother disappear in the direction of the slab shed. The fire crackled in the stove, and the rain tapped against the window. She brushed her palm across the glass to clear the condensation.

"Teddy, you ate such a late breakfast," she said, "you won't need lunch, will you?"

"No," I said, even though I hadn't eaten any more eggs or sausage with Uncle Normal. I had learned how to manage when I was hungry. "Mom," I said, "where was Uncle Nels when he died?"

She moved to the table and sat down. "Nels died in France, so far away from here. We know that he fought with the Marines at Belleau Wood. We think he fought at Verdun. We just don't know for sure."

"What don't you know for sure?"

"Your Uncle Nels was killed, that much is certain. But he never came home, so we never got to bury him." She hesitated. "We have no place to go, and we never got to say goodbye."

"Doesn't he have a grave?"

"We hope he does," she said. "He has to be buried somewhere, but we're afraid he might be tangled with others like him, and that idea has always troubled us."

Like bodies in a lime pit, Boone had said. "Doesn't everybody get his own grave?"

"Not always."

"What do they do with soldiers who don't come home?"

Mother bit her lip. "I don't really know," she said. "I try not to think about it."

I didn't know either, but I thought about Boone's 'trench sweeper,' the big shotgun he kept behind the bar at the Bucket of Blood. The trench sweeper could fire six shots in less than ten seconds. "They built that gun during the Great War," Boone said, "to wipe Germans out of trenches."

If Uncle Nels had had Boone's trench sweeper, he would have come home, and Mother would have known where to visit him.

20

"Marie, something wrong's here."

Dad said it more than once while he looked at my homework.

I asked Mother what he meant by it. She said, "Don't worry, honey." But I did, and so did Dad, and to his credit, he was slow to give up on me.

I was *not* a stupid bump on a log at school. I pondered any number of subjects. Problem was they seldom had anything to do with the lessons at hand. Mrs. Ames, my teacher in Culp Creek, followed the Palmer method for writing, a series of endless tasks designed to cripple the imagination. Under her watchful gaze, we copied our letters into a little book every morning and re-copied them in the afternoon. In between writing assignments, we worked on sums and multiplication tables, scratching at them over and over inside the same tired book.

I was eight by then. I had barely made it into the third grade, and I worried I wouldn't go any farther. Everything about school was grim, and being in the spotlight as the mill owner's son didn't make it any easier.

With all the practice I was subjected to, you'd think my handwriting would be good, even legible, but I never applied myself. I did just enough to get by, at least what I considered to be enough. Some of the older girls liked helping the little ones with their letters, but I wasn't interested. I preferred to stare out the window and wait for the morning train to rumble by. After lunch, I watched for the afternoon train. But even when I tried, I had trouble joining in. The upturned branches outside my window would wave at me; at times they'd almost reach inside and touch me. With any breeze at all, their blue-green arms would sweep me away.

Parents didn't send their children to school for inspiration. They sent them to get an education, which was a simple thing: reading, writing, and figuring numbers. Those who brought an exercised imagination to school were best equipped to survive the day, but least suited for that kind of education. If you were one of those who managed to pass the eighth grade, you went away to high school in Cottage Grove, where you boarded with a well-meaning and poor town family during the week. If you didn't go to Cottage Grove High, you went to work in the mines or started pulling boards off the green chain, the lowest, hardest job at the mill. Or you moved away.

The one good part of school was walking there. I took my time, and I was never early. From the house, I'd round the pond and stop to check for muskrats. From there, I'd meander through the mill, past the bunkhouse and through the yard where we stacked the finished boards. On cold mornings, I'd stomp across the frozen millpond and pitch rocks at logs that lay like stiffs in brown corrugated ice. At Boone's garage, I'd try to guess what he might be working on, wishing I could stay with him. After that, I had a choice. I could follow the train tracks, the quickest and shortest way to school, or go another way and loiter along a quiet path made soft and crunchy with pine needles. Moss-covered and slightly scalloped from use, this narrow path wandered from the mill to school, sliding like a banana slug, through the rot of ten thousand great dead trees. Along the way, I'd kick at puffballs or squat in the shade to watch the yellow slugs slide on their slime.

By the end of third grade, I still couldn't read. Mrs. Ames held me back, saying I'd probably never figure it out. That was enough for Dad and the school board to tell her to leave. When the mill owner and school board president were the same person, they could do that.

There are places better suited to learning than school, and the best teachers can be found far from a desk and chalkboard. Boone Shaw was one of those teachers; and in his own way, so was my dad. What I know about gold and prospecting I learned from Boone Shaw. Most of what I know about fixing engines, I learned from Boone, too.

Dad was an idea man. He viewed himself as a salesman first and mill operator second. Nothing pleased him more than getting the better end of a transaction, which he almost always did. "With any deal," he liked to say, "it is far more important to know the rock bottom price at which you can make a profit than it is to ask for the moon. Don't expect to get the moon because the minute you start to count on it, it disappears." Then he'd smile his cat-eating-the-canary smile. "But it never hurts to *ask* for the moon because people might surprise you." So, there's a difference between asking for something and counting on it.

During the week, Dad worked hard at his business. In the evening, while Mom did the dishes and I played at her feet with my Erector set, he'd be in the living room, worrying a pencil between his teeth. He'd stare at his green pad, open a leather case, and pull out his ivory slide rule. Milled from an African elephant's tusk, he called the slide rule his sole trophy from engineering school.

Dad respected men who did their homework, but said they were few and far between. "Too often, the idiot across the table from you isn't prepared, doesn't know his shit from Shinola." During one business discussion that was going badly, I watched him glance around the room; he looked puzzled. He stood and walked to a window and then scanned the horizon like a buffalo scout. "I believe this has the look of a Christopher Columbus operation," he said to the room. "The Santa Maria has to be here somewhere." At times like that, Dad typically excused himself and walked out. That is to say, he walked out if there wasn't money to be made at the idiot's expense.

Because he was an idea man and a college man, he held himself apart from the other men who lived in Culp Creek: the sawmill hands, loggers, bookkeepers, and anybody else he didn't have time for, but he was a gentleman about it. Most would leave thinking he had paid them a compliment. Dad could make a man feel good one minute, and later gossip about the guy like he was the biggest fool in the Northwest.

Dad had wanted me to be an engineer like him. He had hoped that I would study at the Colorado School of Mines, but that was his pipe dream, not mine. "Nothing is more important than an education," he repeated more times than I needed to hear. "Nobody can take it away from you."

I knew my limitations long before he was able to acknowledge them, at least to me. Early on, he had wanted me to be him. I had wanted it, too. That turned out to be our one shared pipe dream.

Boone Shaw never tried to set himself apart, although by his size, his temperament, and a number of qualities hard to put into words, he was a man well apart. Most obvious was his raw strength. Less obvious was his faith in friendship and his loyalty; traits that were difficult to see, much less understand. During the day, Boone was either packing a hundred pound piece of mining equipment miles to his claim on Dolomite Mountain or tearing into a boiler or diesel engine. The power that rode beneath his shirt was testimony to the kind work he did. When he strained to lift an engine or pull against a balky wrench, the thick bands of scar that covered his chest and arms blazed red like the fire that had raised them.

During World War I, Boone had enlisted in the navy and had served as a master mechanic aboard a destroyer in the South China Sea. He had been popular with the enlisted men because he never lost a wrestling match against another ship. "I also ended up in the brig more times than was good for my career. There are times and places suited for fighting, or for walking away," he said. "I had trouble sorting them out."

After the war, Boone left the navy, but he continued working as a mechanic. In exchange for his services, Dad supplied him with a house and garage on our mill property. He had piles of *Popular Mechanics* magazines lying around his shop, but he never took them inside the house. "Tools and mechanic magazines stay in the shop," his wife, Twinkle, commanded. The house was hers, it seemed, and the garage was his. The two led divided lives in a number of ways.

Boone and Twinkle never had children, which might be why he always found time to talk to me, even while he worked. I'd puzzle through the *Popular Mechanics* magazines at the back of his shop, and he'd help me with them when I got stuck. When I asked about the scars on his chest and back, he agreed to talk about them, but only once.

"When the torpedo hit," he said, "the only part of the ship that decided to throw diesel fuel and explode happened to be the deck I was standing on. My shirt caught the diesel spray and lit up with me inside. I tried, but I couldn't strip it off in time."

Boone's skin looked like it had been melted rather than burned. As if cords of rubber had cooled into something other than skin. An especially thick band roped from his shoulder blade into his armpit. "Does it hurt?"

He reached around and slapped the scar like it was something normal. "Not anymore."

"Shouldn't burnt skin be black and crunchy like scorched toast?"

"It was black for a time. I stunk to high heaven, stunk like I was dead. I got fouler each day until they cut the black out." He touched the scar again, this time more gently. "These scars cover an old book best kept shut."

"What does dead smell like?"

For the first time that morning, his wrench stopped working. He stared at me, thinking. "You haven't ever smelled death?"

I shook my head, but that didn't worry me. Boone wouldn't expect me to have the right answer. Still, I tried to come up with one. I thought about our kitchen. Mother prepared dead things for supper: chicken, raw steak, liver and onions. "Does it smell like liver?"

"Even worse than liver," he laughed. "A hell of a lot worse!" He considered his words. "You've never walked by a dead animal on the side of the road?"

We'd driven past dead skunks and raccoons in the car, but had never stopped. I didn't think that was what he meant. "No," I said, wishing I could say yes.

For the first time since I'd known him, he looked at me as if I was from another world. "That's probably for the best," he said, taking up his wrench and going back to using it.

21

In addition to being a master mechanic, Boone Shaw was the Bucket of Blood's bouncer and manager. Only a few could remember back to when he got the job because the generations of men who frequented the roadhouse turned over every five or six years—the Bucket of Blood discouraged the old and overwhelmed the introspective.

"Hard men gave the roadhouse its name," Boone told me while he wrestled a leaky valve from the engine that drove our main saw, "but not in any legal sense. If you ask any lawyer, he'll likely tell you the place doesn't even have a name. But sure as hell, for two hundred dollars and a signature, he'd be happy to come up with one. That's what a sorry son-of-a-bitchin' lawyer would say."

Boone's huge hands rarely stopped working while he talked. When a bolt resisted his grip, he would reach to his workbench, and, without looking, select the wrench he needed, give the bolt a turn, and set the wrench back right where he had found it. "Hard men pay for things with their blood, and you ought to respect them for it," he continued. "The rest have the money, and that's fine. But then there's those who expect something for nothing, and that doesn't play."

I always tried to understand what Boone was saying because he talked to me like I was worth effort. I'd even replay his words after the fact. From what he was saying, I concluded that the men who walked into the Bucket of Blood did so to buy a reprieve. Some from the loneliness that seeped in through empty mine shafts and echoed in their heads like hammer blows. Others from fatigue and impossibly long days spent battling stands of timber, sawdust, and insects.

Young women, relieved to be away from their parents, met young men grateful for any interest. A few of the women hoped the Bucket's low door might open to a bigger world, a world they'd seen in the movies. For the rest, the roadhouse offered far less, yet it offered something. Perched on my stump at the back window, I'd watch the girls dance across the polished floor. I'd see them mingle at its borders. They always seemed to be filled with high spirits, talk, talk, talk, and the restless anticipation of meeting the right man.

The men who congregated at the Bucket of Blood didn't always get along, and that was part of the fun. Sawmill men didn't like miners because the miners were from Italy who believed that God was the Pope. The locals had it in for the pretty boys who drove up from the city to steal the girls. The loggers and sawmill men fought each other strictly on the basis of principle. "I never take sides," Boone said, "but I keep the peace."

Boone would lean on his elbows with his back against the bar. He had an uncanny sense for trouble. He would meet it at the door and review his commandments for anybody he thought needed it. A not so gentle giant with a short fuse and a club, Boone had earned near unanimous respect from everyone who met him. "Moses made a goddamn mistake in bringing down so many commandments," he'd state. "Ten's far too many to keep track of. Any halfwit can remember two." His were simple. "Number one: don't harass the musicians." He'd pause and check for signs of comprehension. "Number two: all disputes belong in the parking lot. No fights in the dancehall."

For the most part, Boone's system worked well. The hard-packed parking lot, its gravel surface rutted during the rainy season and worn flat in the dry, could handle any number of fights among the Ford, Chevrolet, Studebaker, and Dodge automobiles. Early arrivals, hoping to avoid a broken mirror or a dented fender, parked at the periphery. The fights were usually quick affairs, resulting in skinned knuckles, bruised lips or eyes, with just enough violence to reinforce the pecking order or occasionally rearrange it. When the fights were over, everyone moved inside, more relaxed and always thirsty.

One Saturday evening, near the end of August, after Dad had left for town, Mother and I again ate without him. After we finished, she poured a drink and took it to her bedroom.

"Don't stay out late," she called through her door.

"I won't," I promised, which was always safe since she never kept track of time.

The band was playing when I rolled my tree stump to the back window. I sat down on it and listened to a mix of music and voices. Since nobody else pushed through the brush behind the roadhouse, I felt safe from discovery. However, I always remembered to roll the stump away from the window when I left.

When the band stopped for a break, I looked in. Two smiling women, still breathless and flushed from dancing, were moving toward my window. I leaned away into the dark and held my breath. They were inches from me, fanning their faces.

"Feel the cool air," one of them said. Her face and her hair were shining. Dark curls stuck to her forehead. She brushed them back, and her fragrance found me. She didn't smell of flowers or sweetness, but of something dark and damp like the forest floor. I tried to breathe it in, again and again. "Let's go outside," she said. She turned and stepped away from my window. I watched her from behind. Her wavy hair was swept up and pinned in back, but several strands had drifted down. They fell against her neck and brushed the top of her dress. Beneath her dress, she had slender hips. My eyes followed her through the room until she disappeared out the door onto the porch.

Wattie Blue's voice boomed. "Everybody, let's start steppin'!"

Couples collected on the floor and waited for their cue. Wattie towered over them by a head, not because he was tall—he wasn't—but because he had climbed onto a narrow raised stand.

"Grab your partner and do-si-do!" he sang out. With Wattie on his harp and Twinkle squeezing her accordion, music filled the room. Twinkle only played chords, and people questioned her talent, but that didn't matter because she came with the bouncer.

The dancers twirled and passed by each other with shared smiles and a change of hands. Wattie danced with them, shifting across his pedestal in time with the music, his shoes sliding from one side to the other like they were home. As Wattie called out his moves, some easy, some challenging, his eyes caressed the dancers like a mother duck. He sized them up, considered their abilities, and called the dance accordingly.

"Change partners," Wattie sang out, and the dancers shifted as one. Wattie liked to pick out a couple and wonder about who they might be and what it was they wanted from this life. If a couple danced especially well, he'd reach out and pat them. Those who needed it, he'd gently instruct, and the rest, he'd laugh at when they needed that, too. Wattie could do all this and never leave the confines of his space next to the band. That's why Wattie was so good.

But the way he played his small harp…that was what made Wattie Blue great. Couples and singles alike would navigate a winding canyon road and press inside a ramshackle building that probably should have been condemned to hear Wattie play. When the time was right, and only Wattie knew when that was, he'd smile, wipe his face, and press the harp against his lips.

If you measure years by the color of a man's hair or by the depth of the creases that etch his face, Wattie was old. But he never looked it, not while his music played. Melodies rustled through Wattie like shifting breezes stir a willow. He bent and flexed with a harmony of movement his own.

I watched Boone drift from his spot beside the bar and casually walk to the front of the roadhouse. With his back to the room, he filled doorframe as he listened to two angry men. He let them have their say and then placed his open hand on a shoulder while he talked. The unformed fist rested between the men like a monument. They listened while Boone had his say, and then they left.

I searched the room for the girl with the brown, upswept hair, but couldn't find her. She had gone, too.

22

Mother turned to the calendar by the kitchen stove and flipped a page. "It's nearly September," she announced.

I felt a cloud pass over.

"Do you know what that means?" she asked.

It meant endless chores and impossible tasks. It meant school was only days away.

"You'll have a nice new teacher this year."

I'd been down that road before, and it had never mattered. From a safe distance—the first week of June—another school year never seemed quite so bad, but now, with the arrival of fall, a hundred hurdles separated me from happiness. When I looked in the mirror, the certainty of my failure stared back. If I could see it, who in the world couldn't?

"Hello, Mith Cherry."

Mother had me practicing so I wouldn't embarrass myself.

"Nythe to meet you."

"Daddy says Miss Cherry is young and pretty, and this is her first job. He thinks she'll be the ticket for you to learn to read."

Most of the men at the mill can't read, I thought. They're all grown, and they have good jobs. So why doesn't everyone leave me alone?

When Monday arrived, Mother offered to walk me to school, insisted on it, actually. We took the shortest way and followed the railroad tracks. Not my choice either.

"I am so looking forward to meeting your new teacher," she said, walking three steps ahead of me, moving faster than I preferred. Our shoes crunched over the dead cinders that lay between the rails. The gray ash from countless locomotives that had tattooed the cedar ties now coated the toes of our shoes. "I'm sure she'll want to know all about you."

I knew every inch of that stretch of tracks because it was the route I took to get to the Bucket of Blood *and* to our sunken locomotive. How our hidden locomotive got there, I can't say for sure, but most of us believed that an army had blown it up several hundred years earlier. Reportedly, the bridge, the locomotive, and its trailing cars—with soldiers shooting and cavalry galloping—had exploded and fallen into the river. As we passed the hidden train, where the river takes a bend, I tried to make out the wreckage, but I couldn't see it through the brush. Since the place was secret, Mother didn't even know to look; and I wasn't about to tell her.

If we had kept walking, the tracks we were following would have taken us on past the school and well past Wildwood Falls, the next point of interest. The falls, for which my school was named, swirled and tumbled over black basalt outcroppings. On quiet days with the windows open, I could hear its waters churn.

Mother and I were the first to arrive. Nobody, not one kid, was loitering on the playground or waiting by the door. "Since we're so early," Mother said with her nervous, reassuring smile, "we'll have plenty of time to visit with your new teacher."

She was at her desk at the back of the classroom. The black cast iron stove in the corner was silent, but once winter came, it would pop and crackle all day long. She looked up and smiled. Dad was right about her, she was pretty, but I'd already discovered that. My new teacher was the woman I had seen at the Bucket of Blood, the girl with the wavy brown hair, the woman who had smelled so good. I stared at her with my mouth open.

Mother nudged me.

"Good Morning, Mith Cherry," I said without thinking.

"And good morning to you," she said brightly. She looked into my eyes while she spoke, and after what seemed like forever, not nearly long enough for me, she turned to Mother, and they shook hands.

Mother and Miss Cherry huddled at her desk while I roamed the classroom. The new teacher had changed everything. Pictures of animals, tall stone buildings, even Egyptian pyramids covered one wall. The ABCs, with matching words and pictures, scrolled along another, and a box filled with readers sat on a low table. Our wooden desks had been cleaned and oiled to a shine. I wondered who could have done that.

"Each child will have a special job," I heard Miss Cherry say. "The first graders clean the blackboard and clap the erasers outside, the second graders sweep the classroom and entry porch, and the third graders keep the wood box full." She turned to me. "Teddy, do you think you'll be able to keep the room warm when winter comes?"

I nodded and walked to a window. I examined my favorite trees. They looked about the same.

"Learning to read has been hard for Teddy," I heard Mother say. I glanced over and found them looking kindly my way. Mother waved at me while she spoke. "He's a bright boy, though. I know he is."

"I can see he is," my new teacher said. "Teddy will learn to read, Mrs. Fraser, I promise. We have new methods. When my brother was little, he needed extra help, too. Now, he reads everything."

Mother beamed. "I'm so glad you understand."

"Teddy," Miss Cherry said, "you will be reading us stories by the end of the year."

23

Miss Cherry was seventeen years old, barely out of school herself, when her parents drove her to Culp Creek to be our teacher. She took a room with Guillaume and Françoise Voisine in a small frame house within walking distance of Wildwood School. Guillaume liked to say that he was French first and Canadian second, but he and Françoise were really Americans—Acadians from northern Maine.

Guillaume had been a logger all his life. Years, like wars, had left him with broken bones, dislocated joints, torn muscles, and a hundred other unnamed injuries. By the time Miss Cherry moved in, Guillaume was nearly too old and too crippled up to work in the woods…but not quite. *"Worry pas vos brains sur la,"* he'd say if someone so much as suggested he give it up. He and Françoise made ends meet by renting out a room at the back of their home. Françoise cooked and cleaned while Guillaume carved wooden Santas to sell at Christmas time. His

Santas didn't look at all like ours, but he had no trouble getting people to buy them during the holiday season.

When the weather was warm and the ends of his bones slid past each other without too much pain, Guillaume would straighten his spine and head out with the crew. He ran the steam donkey, used to pull the downed logs out of the forest. When the wet, cold weather arrived, he didn't stray far from his wood stove. He moved with small steps that shuffled and cussed easier than he took a breath. He'd eat his aspirin, drink his black cohosh tea, and whittle away with his carving tools. If anyone dared to shorten his name to Guy, he set them straight.

"J'etais Guillaume, GeeYome, you ba'tard!."

Guillaume was proud of being French, and he loved the French language. His second favorite word after *bâtard* was *merde.* He used both to describe the British bastards who had kicked his grandparents out of Nova Scotia. *"Le bâtard Laurence, e'je vas kicker his ass, un beau soir."* That was Guillaume's plan for the former British Governor once he tracked him down in hell.

Françoise's faith, coupled with his firewood, warmed their house. With her head lowered and her heart raised to the dead Jesus on their wall, Françoise prayed to *Le Bon Dieu* several times a day. Her long-sleeved dresses were plain and always ironed. Over them, she wore a black or brown sweater. With rosary beads looped through her fingers, she kept her opinions close to her breast, content to let Guillaume express them for her.

By late fall, Miss Cherry had me at their home every Saturday morning practicing my reading and working on my sounds. That was how I learned about rosary beads and Catholics. Miss Cherry was Catholic, too, but never while at school. She never mentioned the Pope to me or to anyone else outside the house. I don't know if she felt as strongly about her religion as Françoise did. She crossed herself in front of the dead Jesus and said grace before supper like Grandma Lulu, but quicker and more to the point.

"When I was much younger," I heard Françoise say, "we said the rosary in French with the bishop on the radio. Now that Guillaume and I have moved so far from Acadia, we have no bishop on the radio in any language, so the Holy Father and I have to manage on our own, and we do fine, *grace a Dieu*."

"Say-see-sigh-so-sou," Miss Cherry would start out my lisp lesson.

"Say-see-sigh-so-sou," I'd parrot.

"Assay-assee-assigh-asso-assou," she'd chant.

"Assay-assee-assigh-asso-assou," I'd follow.

Françoise would tat or work on a piece of lace while she listened to my lessons. She'd nod to herself and smile whenever I did something right. At the end, she'd point me to the kitchen table where I'd find a fruit tart and a glass of milk, and then she'd visit with Miss Cherry.

Miss Cherry marveled at the lace objects Françoise made. "Every piece is so delicate. Would you teach me?" By November, as soon as my lesson was over, the lace bobbins came out, and the two of them would go at it with Miss Cherry frowning in concentration and Françoise talking.

"The best thing for Guillaume's rheumatism and lumbago," Françoise said one day, "is tea made from the black cohosh root. You should try it, too."

Miss Cherry laughed. "I'm too young to have rheumatism."

Françoise lowered her voice, thinking I couldn't hear her from the kitchen. "You should take it during your monthly time for the cramping."

"Oh," Miss Cherry said in the same hushed voice.

"I keep a jar of it in the pantry for Guillaume. He thinks his fancy Bayer is better and says so, but I see him use both."

"Where do I buy it?" Miss Cherry asked.

"You don't buy it," Françoise clucked. "I make tincture of black cohosh." She looked over at her husband. "And unlike Guillaume, with his little white pills, I know what's in it." Françoise set her tatting on a chair and walked to the pantry. She retrieved a large, knotty root draped with slender fibers. "Smell it," she said, handing the root to Miss Cherry. "Boil two teaspoons of the root in a pint of water, and then take five to ten drops of the tincture every two to four hours when the pain is bad." Françoise rubbed her knuckles. "For rheumatism in the small joints, blue cohosh is better."

I finished my tart and milk and left the dishes on the table. As always, I said, "Thank you, Françoise." Then, I asked her if there was anything I could do to help. I offered only because Miss Cherry wanted me to. It was easy being on my best behavior for her.

"Teddy, when you come to visit Françoise and Guillaume," she said, "please try to look for ways to help them. It doesn't have to be much, but it would be a nice way to thank them for their hospitality. They won't ask, so you need to offer." This usually amounted to carrying in kindling and filling the wood box next to the kitchen stove.

Miss Cherry spent more time with me than she did with the other children, I was sure of that, but she also made some time for everyone. As she walked through the classroom, I would impatiently wait for my turn. I'd watch her stop and lean over a desk. She might whisper a kind word into a grateful ear or sound out a sentence had seemed impossible or place her hand around a clenched fist to guide wayward fingers as they struggled to advance a stubborn pencil across an indifferent page.

"Make the O a little rounder, like this," she would say. "Add a smart little tail at the end like so." And then she'd stand back and let the eager fingers work. "Beautiful." After a moment, she'd move to the next child.

I knew I was special to her, but so was every other child in that small classroom. The rest didn't matter, though, when my turn came around.

"You certainly have your own special way of doing things, Teddy. I can see that you are your own man."

With her standing behind me, watching, I'd will my hand to race across the paper, hoping she'd marvel at my dexterity. With her looking on, my pencil would glide and spin like a top.

"Take your time, and you'll do even better." She'd take my pencil. "Now, try this...that's better." She smelled of Ivory soap with some kind of flower hidden beneath it. "It is lavender," she told me when I asked about it.

Every year, children left the classroom because their families moved away. Others dropped out to find work to help feed their brothers and sisters. Miss Cherry worried about all of the children in her class, even those who had stopped coming. It discouraged her to think about their futures. And there were those who stopped coming because they no longer saw the point. I easily could have been one if Miss Cherry had allowed it. "We are all here to learn," she repeated, "especially me."

In December, she pulled me aside and introduced me to four narrow rows of books lining the wall behind her desk. "This is our little library," she said. "Now that you are a reader, you may check out one book at a time. Return it when you've finished and take another. These are our easiest readers," she said, pointing to the taller, brighter covers at the left of the shelf. "The more challenging books are on the right." She walked to the shelf and pulled down a brown reader and opened it. "Why don't you start with this one?" she said. "It's one of my favorites." Although the book she selected came from the left side of the library, I was pleased to see that it hadn't come from the very end. After that day, I spent more time at the library, always insisting that she help pick a new volume. In return, she'd ask me to teach her about what I had learned. I began to read carefully, so as not to disappoint her.

By the end of the year, with a new confidence, I began selecting books by myself. I played it safe, limiting my selections to the left side of the shelf until Miss Cherry remarked that I might find more interesting topics farther right. The larger volumes took more time and effort, so I resisted. However, with her encouragement, they began to bring me pleasure.

Whenever a new book found its way into the collection, she would hold it up in front of the class and tell us about it. I remember one book in particular about Greek philosophers. Miss Cherry called them wise men, even though they never appeared in the Bible. "They lived long before Jesus, if you can imagine that," she said. Up until then, based on all the information I had received, I would have argued that Jesus Christ's birth marked the original day of creation.

Miss Cherry opened the book and turned to the part about Diogenes, a grizzled philosopher who ate nothing but onions and lived in a barrel tipped on its side. Day after day, old Diogenes crawled from his barrel and shuffled through the marketplace with a lantern held above his head, searching for an honest man: he never found one. While she read, I thought about Uncle Normal in the wood shed and the men in the bunkhouse. They ate a lot better than Diogenes; yet, most of them hoped for better days. Diogenes lived in his barrel and ate onions because he wanted to. Uncle Normal and the men in the bunkhouse didn't have a choice in the matter.

Before I met Miss Cherry, I had known only two women, my mother and Grandma Lulu, so my experience was limited. As far as women were concerned, Boone wasn't much of an expert either, but he did have something to say about the subject. According to Boone, a man has three responsibilities toward women. "But too many sons of bitches shit-can their obligations before they're halfway through the deal," he added.

Why Boone chose to share this lesson with me, and why he felt so strongly about it, I can't be sure, but I have my suspicions.

"To his bride," Boone said, "a man makes a promise; to his wife, he owes his loyalty; and to the mother of his children, he incurs a debt he can never repay."

That was exactly how he said it. Then, he asked me if I understood. How could I understand? How many grown men even try?

He sat me down and started over. Boone could be strong in his convictions.

"When a man walks into a church and stands beside a young woman, he promises to be faithful for as long as he lives. That part's easy. Men will agree to just about anything, as long as it gets them where they want to go, but later on, the promises often wear thin. I'm the first to admit that people change with time."

I thought about Mother with my dad.

"By then, a second obligation should have grown to take its place. When the newness of marriage wears off, a man no longer has a bride; he has a *wife*: a mate who has slept beside him night after night, a nurse who has cared for him, a friend who has cheered him when things got bad. That woman has earned, if nothing else, his loyalty and his respect."

I thought about Grandma Lulu living alone. This didn't apply to her.

"Does that make sense?"

"Maybe."

"The third obligation," Boone said, "is to the mother of his children. He owes her more than can ever be repaid."

"You don't have any children so you don't owe that part."

"No I don't," Boone said, "and I am poorer for it."

If Miss Cherry had been my bride, I'd have carried out those obligations better than any other man. I'd have kept all my promises, and I'd have been loyal. I thought about telling her so. At my desk, with her at the front of the room, I dreamed about her. When staring out the window and watching the train pass by, or while forming my letters, the result was the same. I imagined a life with Miss Cherry—with Arlene. Dad had called her Arlene.

The week we studied sonnets, she read a poem about "lips like cherries." As she read, I watched her lips part and press and glisten. Round red lips that kissed and tasted Shakespeare's words, the same lips that had so softly shaped my sounds. I wondered how it might feel to sit with her at our mirror and watch those lips press and part and reach for the color she held in her hand. I wondered how it might feel to slide a brush through the warm tangle of her hair and search for treasure that she'd hide for me to find, me alone.

When the final bell of the school year sounded, Miss Cherry's parents drove up to take her away. She ran from the house and greeted them, first hugging her mother and then embracing her father just as warmly. With non-stop chatter and smiles the three together packed her things into the car. It was a celebration I couldn't begin to understand.

"Don't forget to practice your sounds and read every day," she said when they were about drive away. "Promise me?" She pulled me close and held me with an embrace I thought I understood. She and her mother thanked Françoise and Guillaume for opening their home and for treating her like a daughter. She hugged them, too, but not in the way she had hugged me. And then she left.

Even now, when I'm out walking in the evening, or at home alone with the Big Screen silent, I find myself mouthing her careful sounds, more for comfort these days than for improvement. I'm past that. Behind my closed lids, her lips are forever taut and round as they sculpt a perfect O. So that I can see and understand a wayward T, her tongue presses against her teeth, white and clean and pink within.

I have long since stopped trying to fathom the depth of those obligations Boone talked about, and like the other "sons of bitches," I have concluded that it's far safer and easier not to risk a hernia in trying too hard. But I do remember every drill Miss Cherry and I practiced at lunchtime, after school, and in the front room with Françoise looking on. The music of her voice continues to play through me, more so these later years. I close my lids and watch the lips that made the music. I follow the eyes that once were so determined I'd succeed.

If you see an old man talking to himself, he might not be a fool or crazy. He might be sharing a conversation with the past, warmed by a memory he need not reveal. Or, he simply might be practicing his 'S' sounds. My lisp finally worked itself out by the fifth grade. After that, unless I was tired, anyone would have to listen hard to hear it.

24

Saturdays were for maintenance work and for repairs that could wait. Dad worked at his desk Saturday mornings because people rarely came by to disturb his thinking. The millwright and the oilers dragged in around noon and began their make-ready for Monday: greasing chains, oiling rollers, filing saws, sharpening planer knives. If a repair was anything big, Boone would be on it long before Dad showed. As long as I kept out of the way, Saturday was the day I got to tag along.

The Saturday morning Sid Mackenzie chose to stroll over to our side of the river was a rare sunny affair. Mr. Mackenzie ran the Dolomite sawmill that had just been built in the big meadow. A five-minute walk was all that separated the two mill properties, but neither Dad nor Mr. Mackenzie had made the trip. I was skipping rocks in the pond and spotted him first. I had heard plenty about him at the dinner table. He sauntered onto the bridge, stopped and stared at the river, and then continued across the highway. He didn't seem to be in a hurry, but from everything I'd heard about Mr. Mackenzie, he was not a man to waste time. I ran inside.

"Dad, some man is coming over from the other mill."

Dad glanced toward the window and then he returned to his work. The inventory ledger and his slide rule were spread out in front of him. He was working through the manufacturing process, trying to come up with a new angle for saving money, constantly weighing the cost of shipping against the price of idle inventory. He glanced out the window a second time.

"I have to find a way to cut freight charges," he said to himself. I moved closer and stared over his shoulder. "How do you suppose we do that, Teddy?"

I shrugged.

"If you can't be a help, don't be a hindrance. Give me some space."

I took a chair by the window and silently watched the man's progress.

Dad stuck a pencil between his teeth and began pushing the slide rule's mechanisms back and forth, pausing every few minutes to scratch at the green tally sheet. New mechanical calculators were showing up in the big offices, but, according to Dad, they were noisy and expensive. He preferred, "the simple elegance of the slide rule," which allowed him to show off a skill that nobody else in the lumber business possessed.

Dad was on the phone when the office door rattled open. "Listen, Lenny," he was saying, "you know as well as I do that orders are picking up." He seemed surprised to see Mackenzie standing in his open doorway—our own men knocked first. Mr. Mackenzie didn't know the protocol.

Mackenzie was lean and stringy. He looked older than Dad and shorter. From our dinner conversations, I knew that he was a high school dropout, nowhere close to being a college graduate and an engineer like Dad. Dad called Mackenzie a living contradiction in that he liked his booze, but still had money in the bank. Respected by the town bankers during the week, Sid Mackenzie was disparaged by his wife, Billie, and her Pentecostal family on Sunday and the six days after.

Dad waved Mackenzie to a small chair opposite his desk, but our visitor instead chose to wander through the office.

"Lenny," Dad said a little more loudly, "I can't hold onto this cedar forever." He listened for another moment. "You can have it for twenty, not a cent less." Dad picked up his pencil and jotted some figures, cradling the phone against his ear while he wrote. Since the conversation wasn't real, I wondered when Dad planned to end it.

Mackenzie pulled a leather pouch from his pocket and dipped some snoose. He studied Dad's desk. Alongside the green tally sheet, there were pens and pencils, an electric clock, dirty ashtray, chipped coffee cup, the slide rule and case, and a barometer.

Dad let his pencil drop. "Lenny, if you find cedar at eighteen per thousand somewhere else, then God dammit, buy it. Or tell me where I can find it." Dad hung up the phone.

Mackenzie turned away from some artwork on the wall he'd been studying. It was one of my favorites, a calendar of a blonde in a red bathing suit, straddling a can of transmission fluid.

"No sense selling at a discount when business is so good," Dad said. "He'll call back." Dad waved Mackenzie to the chair by his desk.

Mackenzie took a seat this time without a word. The silence stretched out while he and Dad frowned at each other. Dad spoke first.

"What brings you over, Sid?"

Although Dad hadn't spoken to Mackenzie before that day, he had made it his business to uncover all he could about Mackenzie, especially when he learned that Dolomite Lumber was grabbing the land across the river. His sources told him that Mackenzie was hard working and smart. He had done extremely well over the years, first as a logger, and now as a lumberman. But there were cracks in Mackenzie's reputation. Boone had no use for the man and said as much, especially when Mackenzie put on his home-guard uniform and pranced around. Boone called Mackenzie a chocolate soldier wrapped in tin foil, and since Boone was a war hero, everyone knew who held the high ground there.

"I thought a visit was overdue," Mackenzie said. "We're neighbors, after all." He was holding onto his hat. Dad didn't offer to take it.

"Maybe so."

Mackenzie smiled broadly. "I must have missed the welcome wagon when it came by."

Dad didn't respond, but I knew the expression. During supper, Dad had called Mackenzie a crook and a crony. I could see him sifting through his words. The land and timber across the river should have been ours, not Mr. Mackenzie's.

"I suppose I should apologize for not dropping by," Dad said, "but I haven't felt particularly hospitable."

Mackenzie walked over to the coat rack and hung up his hat. "Who were you talking to?" he said, as if it were an afterthought.

Dad glanced at the phone. "Some guy looking for advice. I gave him a little."

"Just curious." Mackenzie walked to the far wall where Dad had tacked up several maps with multi-colored pins marking stands of timber. Mackenzie examined the maps and seemed impressed. "Looks like an engineering firm works here," he said.

Dad took it as a compliment.

Charts recording lumber production and market volume were tacked to another wall. Mackenzie seemed to admire those as well. "This is a sealskin office for a muskrat operation."

Dad's look of pleasure evaporated. "What is the deal here, Sid?" I half expected him to start off on Christopher Columbus, but he surprised me. "When does your new mill start cutting?" he continued in a more friendly tone.

"Soon," Mackenzie said, "but a problem has come up."

"Laddie," Dad said with the highland lilt he had grown up hearing. "Wha' problem can there be that two Scotsmen canna work out?"

Mackenzie smiled at the sound of it.

"I hope you know," Dad said with flint in his voice, "it's not easy to fool an old Scotsman."

"'Tis true!" Mackenzie said. "And I've been a Scotsman a good deal longer than you." His words sounded even harder than Dad's. "I now have control of the entire Polk and Chisholm holding: land, timber, equipment, all of it. I suppose this comes as no surprise."

"The surprise came and went months ago," Dad said, leaning forward, resting his hands on his desk.

"At full production," Mackenzie continued, "my new mill will cut sixty thousand board feet a day."

"Very impressive, but where do you intend to sell it?" Dad lowered his voice. "Between us girls, I can't move a stick right now."

"We think the market's about to turn," Mackenzie said. "We're banking on it."

"What if your Ouija board turns out to be overly optimistic? You could end up with a million excess board feet." Dad had studied the layout of the new Dolomite mill. The design hadn't made sense because there was nowhere to dry and store the lumber. "Where will you put it?"

"That's the problem I've come to discuss," Mackenzie said, appearing impressed with what Dad had said. "I don't have space for my finished lumber." He pointed at our railroad siding and loading dock. "That's why I need your side of the river."

Dad joined Mackenzie at the window. Dad was taller, but he didn't look any bigger. "Sorry to disappoint you, Sid, but the siding and dock are in use."

Mackenzie returned to his chair. "I'm offering to buy your mill, lumber, and trucks—all of it. You can walk away clear. You're all but broke."

"Why would I sell out to you?" Dad rubbed his forehead. "And why now?"

Mackenzie seemed ready for the question. "If you don't, you'll lose it anyway. You have no money, no credit, and now you have no water."

"I won't argue about the money and the credit, but what does this have to do with water?"

Mr. Mackenzie looked embarrassed. "You've been using my water to fill your log pond."

"What?"

"The water you're taking from Culp Creek belongs to me. You're piping it across my land without a right of way. That's trespassing."

Dad didn't say a word.

"I won't take legal action, but I will have to cut you off. There isn't enough for both of us."

"This is stupid," Dad said, grabbing his slide rule. "There's more than enough for both of us." He began manipulating the ivory mechanism.

"Jerk off all you want with that thing," Mackenzie fired back. "It won't change the fact that I own that water, and you don't!"

Dad's hands stopped moving.

"Let's be reasonable," Mackenzie said, regaining control. "I'm sure we can find an arrangement that makes sense."

"What arrangement would that be?"

"You're young. You've had a fair run here. We'll see to it that you turn a small profit."

"I don't feel young, *Sidney*. I sure as hell haven't been given a fair run, and how in hell did you ever get such a sweet deal on that land?" Dad waited for an answer, but none came. "Who is this 'we' you keep throwing at me? Do Wulf Gehring and Ennis Neet make up your royal '*we*'?"

"My deals don't concern you," Mackenzie said. "I was in the right place at the right time. That's all there was to it." He spoke as if the argument was over. "I'm offering you more than you'd get from anybody else."

"I may not have legal access to Culp Creek, but I do own the lease to this piece of ground. I'm not selling unless you make me the deal of the century."

"How much?"

"A hundred thousand dollars," Dad said. "No, make it a million."

"Without water, your mill isn't worth a hundred dollars. You paid four thousand. I'll give you three, and the offering price could go down without warning." Mackenzie got to his feet.

"My attorney will have something to say about this," Dad said.

Dad wouldn't give up without a fight. I knew that much.

"The law is funny," Mackenzie said, "unless you don't have a good lawyer."

"What is this really about?" Dad sounded like he had figured something out. "Is it about the railroad?"

"This is about business." Mackenzie's voice was stripped of any niceness.

"And that's the first honest thing you've said. More specifically, it's about *me* getting *the business*, and I'm not rolling over." Dad forced a smile. "Do you know what Mr. Clemens would say about our predicament?"

"Who?"

"He'd tell you that 'whiskey is for drinking and water's for fightin' over.'"

Mackenzie plucked his hat off the rack. "It doesn't have to be that way."

25

"Lucky for me the teeth had just been sharpened," Ray said straightaway, the day I asked about his cut-off arm. "If not, they'd have gnawed me like an old rat and pulled me in, up to the shoulder. Sharp as the teeth were, the saw roared through them two bones like I was young pine. I later thanked the mill-wright for seeing to his saws the way he did. I even offered to buy him a beer."

I stared at Ray's stump and compared it to the other stumps rotting on our property. "Did it smell like pine?"

"I can't say that, but it sure happened fast. My hand was on the deck, tipped up against my boot before I felt a thing. I reached down and picked the thing up by the wrist."

My eyes were glued to his remaining part. "Didn't it hurt?"

"Not at first. It felt like a quiet burn, more of a hum than anything, but red was spurting all over the planking, big gulps of it. Blood shot past my boots, farther out than most men can piss.

"Can I touch it?"

Ray rolled his sleeve above the elbow and pushed the stump toward me. Scars and folds of skin puckered like the belly of a starfish.

I pressed a finger against the pucker. The starfish wiggled. I glanced up at Ray, but he hadn't seen it. I touched the scar a second time and it jumped.

"By then," Ray said, acting like nothing had just happened, "the word was out, and our foreman came running. He pulled a lace from his boot and tied it around my arm. He pushed me in his car and drove me to town, which wasn't worth the time it took to get there. The damn doctor didn't even try to save my arm after I'd carried it on my lap the whole drive down."

"Why?"

"I carried it because I wasn't willing to give it up, and because nobody offered to take it from me."

"Why wouldn't the doctor save it?"

"The quack took one quick look and said, 'The thing's dead.' I tried to argue, but he shook his head. 'Ray, your arm is gone!' And that was that. We might as well have thrown it in a garbage can and saved ourselves a trip...or fed it to his hogs and done some good with it."

I opened and closed my fingers and watched the muscles in my arm slide under the skin.

"Once the stitches were out, I tried going back to work. I found the foreman. I could see that he had got his boot lace back because the two looked different. The one he'd used on me was darker and stiffer than the other, and while we talked, he stood with the one boot tucked back behind the other. After that, he'd kick at any dog that showed too much interest."

"Mackenzie let me go two weeks later. I had to fall back on doing odd jobs and being a night watchman. The pay was half what I had got running the trim saw, but it was a job. My wife and me got some help from Sid's wife, Billie. Crazy as she was, that woman came over every day. She taught my wife to change my bandages, and she sat with me during my fevers. She even brought us groceries. I got hurt working at her husband's mill, but she was under no obligation to help. When we tried to thank her, she hushed us, saying she was doing her Christian duty. But what she did went far beyond that."

Within a year of losing his arm and his job, Ray lost his wife and his kids. He didn't actually lose them. "They just had to leave," Ray said, because he couldn't feed them. That was when Ray moved into our bunkhouse with the single men.

"Add another stray to the pack," Dad told Mother and me at dinner the night he hired Ray.

Except for the young guys, all the men in the bunkhouse had been married at least once. Like Ray, each man carried a set of troubles.

"There isn't a soul on this earth without problems," Mother said. "Some troubles are more easily seen than others, but they all add up to the same thing."

"What's that?" I asked.

"We don't own their troubles," Dad said, ignoring my question. He tapped his fork against a glass to make sure I was listening. "If your new bunkhouse friends are at all interested in our troubles, invite them to come by. I'll give them an earful, but they won't be interested."

Dad walked out, and Mother began clearing the table. "Heartache," she said quietly. "That's what they add up to."

A month after Dad's meeting with Mr. Mackenzie, I was at the bunkhouse Sunday afternoon playing checkers with Ray. Alec was hooting over the funny papers.

"Christ on a crutch!" Alec hollered, laughing out loud, "That Maggie is all over Jigs today. He ought to keep his mouth shut so he won't get in so much trouble."

"Hank," Ray said to Dad's bookkeeper, "you've been around some. Have you ever kept books for Sid Mackenzie or Dolomite Lumber?"

"I might have," Hank said, "but I can't talk about it." Hank stayed at the bunkhouse once a month, even though he was married. The rest of the time, he lived with his wife in Cottage Grove. She drove him up to our mill each month so he could update Dad's business books. Hank couldn't walk or drive a car because his legs had been paralyzed from polio.

"I was just wondering," Ray said.

Hank was standing in his leg braces, cooking his special potato soup for lunch. "I make it for my girls when I'm home," he said. His crutches were always within reach. The braces were leather and steel with hinges at the knees to keep them from buckling. To walk, he'd have to lock the hinges and drag the back leg forward by twisting his body and putting all his weight on his arms through his crutches. For the next step, he'd do the same with the other leg. Hank had the biggest shoulders I'd ever seen, bigger even than Boone's, but they looked funny on him because his legs were so skinny.

"You have other jobs beside this one, don't you?" Ray asked.

Hank was pouring potato water into the small sink that emptied onto the ground below the bunkhouse. "I've got several jobs," he said. "Most are in Cottage Grove. This is the farthest I travel."

"Wouldn't it be easier if you drove yourself?" Ray asked.

Hank pointed to his legs. "I can steer and shift," he said, "but I can't manage the pedals."

I had watched Hank walk—if you can call it that—from the bunkhouse to Dad's office. It took him thirty minutes when I could do it in one. He would be sweating and breathing so hard, you'd think he had run five miles.

I thought it was kind of sad watching Hank struggle to get from one place to the next, but he told me not to feel that way. "Governor Roosevelt of New York has polio, too," he said, "and he's doing just fine. He might even be President someday."

"FDR drives his own car," Ray said. "The state police can hardly keep up with him."

Hank set the knife he'd been using to chop onions on the counter. He had a pained look on his face. "Ray, I'm not a Roosevelt. I don't have a million dollars. I have no way to buy a car that fits me." He picked up the knife and went back to chopping onions and bacon, concentrating hard.

"What if Boone and I fixed up your car so you could drive it with your hands instead of your feet?" Ray waved his stump. "People told me I'd never drive truck with this thing, but I'm figuring it out, and when I do, I'll get a better job. You could do the same."

Hank put the bacon and onions in a skillet and set the pan on the stove. "You'd do that?"

"I would for a fact," Ray said.

We had the most wonderful potato soup that afternoon. The bunkhouse never smelled so good, and I never before saw Hank smile so much. He passed the soup around twice and talked about his girls and his brother who worked at the foundry in Eugene.

"Hank," Ray said, finishing off his soup, "the first Dolomite mill started up in 1917 didn't it? Two years before the end of the war?"

"That's right," Hank said absently, still showing pictures of his daughters. "Early enough to get in on the war profit."

"Were Ennis Neet, Jackie Sagers, and Sid Mackenzie the owners then?"

"No, it was just Sagers, Neet, and Gehring. Mackenzie joined on later."

"How did the partnership work?" Ray asked.

Hank looked up.

Ray smiled.

Hank put his photos away and answered carefully. "Neet and his bank put up the money. Wulf Gehring brokered the deal, and Sagers engineered the mill. Mackenzie later signed on to supply logs, but he was never an owner. When they bought the mill in 1917, it was a piece of junk. Sagers turned it around on a shoe string."

"Help me understand this, Hank," Ray said, looking puzzled. "Neet, Sagers, and Wulf Gehring buy a rundown operation. They haywire it together with almost no money and hit a home run?"

"That's about right."

"I still don't get it," Ray continued. "Dolomite hires a crew in June and has to cover the payroll, but because of delays doesn't start cutting lumber until August. Nothing about that sounds profitable."

Hank nodded. "It was far from profitable. By July, Dolomite was out of money and out of credit.

"Dolomite won out in the end," Babe remarked. "How in hell did they do it?"

"Dolomite Lumber wins because it has always been lucky," Ray said. "In August 1917, the day Dolomite cut its first board, its chief competitor burned to the ground. Before the fire, Cascade Lumber had controlled the regional market."

Hank looked grim. I could see that he didn't want to talk about it.

"The fire torched a million board feet of inventory, destroyed the OP&E roundhouse, and cleared a path for Dolomite," Ray continued. "After the Cascade fire, everything changed, didn't it?"

Alec looked up from his funny papers. "Don't you have something better to talk about? That happened ten years ago."

"I'm trying to think things through, Alec," Ray said. "Give it a try sometime."

Alec scowled and pushed his nose back into the paper.

"A number of things about the recent Latham fire are reminiscent of Cascade fire of 1917," Ray said. "There's more to it than coincidence."

"Neet was part owner in Cascade Lumber," Babe said, "why would he burn down his own mill?"

"Can you help us understand it, Hank?" Ray said.

Hank's leg brace clanked against the table. "Neet didn't own Cascade Lumber when it burned," he said. "He'd sold his interest a week before the fire and traded it for an even larger position in the new Dolomite Company. Neet made a great deal of money out of the Cascade fire."

"One last thing, Hank," Ray said. "Who has ownership in our little railroad, and how does it work?"

"Where do you get this shit?" Babe interrupted.

Ray raised his stump. "I used to work for the bastards."

Shaking his head like he knew better, Hank answered the question. "A week before the Cascade fire, Sagers, Neet, and Wulf Gehring purchased controlling interest in the railroad, which seemed curious since the railroad was basically worthless.

The gold mine was closed, and no logs or lumber were being shipped down the Row. The railroad had no revenue. Expenses exceeded income four to one."

Ray interrupted. "Let me get this straight. In June 1917, Ennis, Gehring, and Sagers invest everything they have in the Dolomite mill, but nothing goes right, and when they're about to lose it all—"

"Cascade Lumber burns," Babe said.

"In a single day, Dolomite has more orders than it can meet. It has experienced men clamoring for jobs and desperate loggers looking for a mill partner. Their new railroad instantly has business, servicing the Dolomite mill, which sits halfway up the Row River valley."

"The railroad was profitable within a month," Hank said softly. "By the end of the year, revenues were up by a factor of ten."

Babe stared blankly at the bookkeeper.

"It means the railroad made a shit load of money," Ray said. "And all of it went to Sagers, Neet, and Gehring."

"What's this got to do with the Latham fire?" Babe asked, looking more confused.

"Everything," Ray said. "Same three players—Neet, Sagers, and Gehring—plus Mackenzie. After the Latham mill burned, Dolomite picked up timber rights for nothing; it built a new mill using salvaged Latham equipment and added shipping business to the railroad's freight revenue."

Babe had been pacing near the bunkhouse window. He pushed back the curtain. "Uh-oh," he said, hurrying to his chair by the stove.

Brittle knuckles rattled the bunkhouse door.

"It's for you, Alec," Babe said.

Alec ignored him. He was still working through the funnies.

The bony fist again peppered the door. This wasn't normal. Everybody else just walked in.

Alec aimed his Norwegian English at the door. "Ya, we are here!"

"Are you men decent?"

Nobody answered.

"Prepare yourselves. I am about to come inside." The voice wasn't getting any more pleasant.

"She hollers like a damn fool," Alec said, throwing down his funnies and stomping toward the door. As he reached for the door handle, the knuckles started up again. "Christ on a crutch!" he fumed, yanking open the door. "Hold on to your panties."

Babe covered his face with one of Boone's magazines.

The red-faced woman standing in the doorway didn't look any happier to see Alec than he was in greeting her. "You have no business taking the Lord's name in vain," she spat.

Ray recognized the face and stepped forward. "Hello, Billie," he said with a broad smile. He looked genuinely pleased to see her.

The skinny woman elbowed past Alec and marched inside. She surveyed the room without comment.

"We're all covered up," Ray said amiably. "Every man here is decent."

She sniffed. "That remains to be seen." She pointed to Ray's stump. "Is your arm any better?"

"Some," he said, "but the darn thing refuses to grow back no matter how hard I pray." He flapped an empty sleeve. "Even God has limits."

"God has no limits," she responded flatly. "As for your praying, Ray Luke, don't mock me."

That was when I figured out who this lady was—Billie Mackenzie—the bony woman on the train who had praised the sweet breath of Jesus. The same lady who had helped Ray when he lost his arm.

The woman's eyes shifted from Ray to the bookkeeper. "Hello, Henry," she said. That was Hank's real name. We just hadn't known it. "Are you working for Mr. Fraser, now?"

"Part time," he said, struggling to his feet along with the others, leaning heavily on his crutches.

"How are your girls? They must be getting big."

"They are," Hank said. "Thank you for asking."

"Can we help you with something, Billie?" Ray asked.

Billie began circling the bunkhouse; her eyes seemed to take in everything. When they fixed on Babe, who hadn't yet come out from behind the magazine, her nose twitched again.

"Billie," Ray said, trying to make conversation, "if you came looking for desperate men, you've found them."

A smile crossed her face. "Don't get me started, Ray, unless you're prepared to hear all of it."

Ray held up his stump in surrender. "I lost my head, Billie."

"If you keep losing parts, Ray Luke, there won't be anything left to save." She took hold of his arm and carefully rolled back the sleeve. "Praise, be," she said. "Has it finally quit draining?"

"For the most part," Ray said. "There's still something inside that needs to work its way out."

"Let the Lord take hold of it, Ray. He'll remove whatever festers in your arm as surely as he'll remove the sin that stains your soul."

"I know that, Billie. I'm just not ready."

"Corruption of the flesh pales next to corruption of the soul."

"I know that, too," Ray said quietly, unable to look at her.

Billie patted his arm before letting go. "All right," she said. "Enough of that for now, but we need to pray together soon." She turned to the rest of us. "I am looking for Sid Mackenzie. Have you men seen him?"

"He wouldn't come here," Ray said, perplexed. "Have you checked the Dolomite mill site and his cottage?"

"Of course."

"Maybe he went to town," Babe added lamely.

"Sidney's car is parked across the bridge," she said. Nobody had an answer to that. "I thought I might at least speak with Boone Shaw. I knocked on his door for five minutes, but no one answered."

"Boone left for his gold claim this morning," I stammered. "He won't be back until tomorrow."

She looked at me harder than I thought I deserved.

"And where is Mrs. Shaw?" she asked no one in particular.

The men shook their heads like mutes. Even Ray didn't have an answer.

"Twinkle's at home," I said.

She glowered at me. "Are you Teddy Fraser?" I hadn't done anything.

"Is my husband visiting with your father?"

"They don't talk to each other."

"Don't be silly," she said, turning to leave the bunkhouse.

We crowded around the window and watched her cross the highway. Ray let out a breath. "She doesn't deserve this."

"Yah, that Sid is something else," Alec said. "Twinkle, you know, is his housekeeper."

"Twinkle crosses the river and cleans his cabin, one day," Babe said. "The next day, he crosses over and rakes her nest."

"Does Boone know about it?" Ray asked.

"He hasn't said anything."

"True, he hasn't," Alec added. "But that Boone is no fool."

Ray looked at me, and I looked at my hands. I had no idea what they were talking about.

"She's dying," Ray said.

"Who is?"

Ray considered my question. "It's not as if it's a secret," he said. "Mrs. Mackenzie's kidneys are about wiped out. She's slowly poisoning herself."

I turned to the window and watched her slowly climb into her car. She didn't drive away. She sat there, looking too tired to drive.

"Billie may be a little different," Ray said, "but she has a heart as big as this room, unlike her husband."

"Guys I know, men who worked for Mackenzie when he was woods boss, said he liked to sneak around and spy on them," Babe said. "If he thought somebody wasn't working hard enough, he wrote the man's name in a notebook, but never said a word to his face. When it came time for the next paycheck, he'd have docked the guy for the day."

"Good thing he isn't in the woods anymore," Ray said. "Gust Backer runs Dolomite's logging operation now."

"And doing a damn fine job, from what I hear," Alec said. "I'd work for him in minute."

"The men respect Gust," Babe said, nodding toward Boone's house. "He's getting twice the work out of them with no sneaking around."

26

Nine out of every ten trees we cut were Douglas fir with scattered hemlock and cedar mixed in. Dad came across an unusually thick stand of cedar and bought it, thinking he could turn it into high priced siding. The wood turned out to be soft and pecky, too riddled with worm holes to use for siding, but that didn't stop him from trying to make a profit from it. "We have it, so we might as well use it." Dad tried for a year before finally selling some of it to a pencil factory. He sold the rest to Mr. Pingree as special order timbers.

About the same time, we got a new dog, and since he was covered with spots like that cedar, we named him Pecky. Pecky wasn't my dog, or Mom's or Dad's dog, he was the camp's dog, at least in the beginning. In the end, he belonged to Ray.

Food smells must have brought him in; I saw him first. He was small and skinny and slinking toward the bunkhouse porch. Brown spots the size of dimes flowed across his white back and sides. After three days of rain that had turned the haul road into a black stew, I thought it was mud speckling him. He stopped and sniffed the air. He placed a tentative paw onto the haul road and followed it with a second paw. As he pushed forward, the road came with him, coating his legs and underbelly. A few minutes later, he climbed onto the porch and shook twice. When he saw me staring through the window, he turned his head away. For the longest time, neither of us moved. Still refusing to look my way, he began to edge toward a dry spot next to the bunkhouse wall, where he curled up with his spine pressed against the rough siding, his nose tucked into the warmth of his flank. That first night, he received no food from anybody.

In the days that followed, the small spotted dog was all over the mill site. When the sun came out, he lazed in the grass. At night, or when it rained, he wriggled into a cozy nest he had dug for himself under the bunkhouse. When the back door banged open, we'd see him peek out and sniff.

Stray dogs always left sooner or later. Nobody, dogs or people, expected anything more. If the stray didn't find a reliable handout, he moved on. Ray Luke was the first to say it. "I suppose he needs a name." Ray started out calling him Peckywood because the brown spots looked like worm holes and because of the way he had wormed his way into the camp's good graces. "And because you're not worth a damn," Ray said, blowing in his nose and causing him to snort.

Peckywood, Peckerwood, or Peckerhead, as the rest of the crew called him, made regular rounds among the men, but he always went back to Ray. Wiggling and wagging, he'd scamper through Ray's legs and then around and around them. I wanted him to do that with me. I tried petting him, and he nosed me once or twice, but then made it clear he wasn't interested.

I clapped my hands and called to him like Ray did, but in Pecky's mind, I wasn't worth the effort.

"Carry a bit of food in your pocket," Uncle Normal said when I asked him about it. "It doesn't take much to win a dog's love. A scrap of toast from breakfast will buy a good deal of affection. A bone is worth even more." Uncle Normal patted his hip pocket. "Slip the treat in and forget about it. He'll find it soon enough."

Before the day was out, Pecky came up to me, wagging his tail. After a week, he went out of his way to find me. He began following me to the pond and under the loading dock, where we'd sit together. When I called, he'd come running with his tail up and his ears flapping.

Pecky didn't like muskrats any more than Dad. He'd dash after them, howling, and would thrust his nose into their burrow and dig like mad. When I baited the muskrat traps, the smell of the bait interested him as much as it did the muskrats, but the traps were strong and sharp, heavy enough to mangle a dog's paw or snout.

"No, Pecky. Bad dog!" I'd yell whenever his nose approached an open trap. I couldn't make him stay away from the traps, and I stopped putting them out, which Dad noticed right off.

"Get those traps set before the muskrats get bad again," he said. I told him about Pecky, but that didn't faze him. "He'll have to learn the hard way."

I didn't want that.

"When he gets close, snap the trap at him," Uncle Normal advised me. "He'll back off. If he comes back, snap it again."

The second time I snapped the trap, Pecky yelped and ran away like he'd been hurt. I jumped, too, thinking I'd caught him in the trap, but I hadn't. Uncle Normal had stung Pecky in the ribs with a rock from his slingshot. After that, Pecky stayed well back from the trap. He eyed me like I'd been the one who had done it, but Uncle Normal had been right.

"Pecky's a smart dog," Uncle Normal said afterward.

When Ray lost his arm, even though he was still strong, he couldn't lift timbers because they were too heavy. He couldn't shovel sawdust because that required two hands, and he wasn't able to work as a mechanic for the same reason. Ray was reduced to being a watchman and doing odd jobs, but he refused to accept that as being the end of his story. In spite of all advice to the contrary, he decided to teach himself to drive a logging truck. It wasn't easy. He had to reach across the steering wheel with his left hand to shift gears, all the while steering with what remained of his right arm. The best he could do to turn the wheel was to push or pull against the spokes with the crook of his cut off elbow. Since there was no power steering, he had to twist his body and throw his shoulder against the weight of the truck to get leverage, each time smacking his stump, often blistering it raw. The bulb end of his arm would be so sore by the end of the day he could barely touch it. Even so, he kept at it because he refused to spend the rest of his life 'sitting on one good hand.'

Ray developed a callus where the steering wheel rubbed, which helped. What helped him even more was a leather sock that Boone sewed out of an old edger apron. When it came time to drive, Ray would slip the leather sock over the end of his stump and away he'd go with Pecky in the cab beside him. You'd see the two of them bouncing down the road with both windows open, Ray's good arm hanging out one side and Pecky's head out the other, his pink tongue tasting the breeze.

Ray and Boone often did favors like that for each other. Boone borrowed a surveyor's transit and taught Ray to shoot road grade because that was another thing Ray could do with one hand. In return, Ray helped Boone truck mining equipment up to his claim on Dolomite Mountain. Each spring, as soon as the mountain road was clear of snow, before anyone else dared to go, Boone would pack up his cook stove and start out for that claim. Once there, he'd set up his tent for the season, revive his steam engine, and lay out his mining equipment.

One June weekend in 1932, Boone decided to ferry a load of galvanized pipe to the claim while Dad was away. Since work was slow, he enlisted Ray to drive him up, and they invited me to ride along. Mother didn't object. Ray took the wheel, Boone got the other window, and Pecky and I shared the middle with the gear shift that angled up from the floor.

Ray started the engine and looked over to me. "Can I get you to shift gears for me?"

The question surprised me. "I don't know how."

"Well, it's time you learned." He pointed to the black knob on top of the gearshift." When I push in the clutch, you wiggle the knob and push it toward the number two."

I looked at the knob, trying to fathom what he meant, afraid I'd mess up, certain they'd decide not to take me.

Ray revved the engine and pressed down the clutch. "Shift her into second. Quick, now."

The gear shifter wouldn't budge.

"Try with two hands."

I grunted and pushed until my arms shook.

Ray released the clutch.

"I need to grow more," I said, pulling my hands away.

"Try it again," Boone said. "You'll get it."

"No I won't."

I placed my hands on the knob. One of Boone's hands covered my two. "I'll just help you guide it," he said. "You do the rest."

Ray revved the engine. And like magic, we were in second gear and moving forward.

"That a boy!" both men said together.

Ray turned left onto the highway and headed upstream. Picking up speed, we passed the old railroad bridge that crossed over to the big meadow and the new Dolomite mill. Pecky bounced from lap to lap and stuck his head out either window. Within minutes, we passed my school, then the Bucket of Blood, and finally Wildwood Falls.

I turned to Boone. "I guess you won't be working at the Bucket of Blood tomorrow night."

"Hell yes, I'll be there," he said. "The place couldn't survive without me. We'll unload tonight and start down first thing in the morning. We'll be back in plenty of time, as long as the truck doesn't break down."

"You're the mechanic," Ray said.

Boone was staring up into the trees. "I'd like to pick up two hunting dogs and go after lion," he said. "The state's paying twenty-five dollars a scalp."

This sounded like a lot of money to me—far more than I could get for muskrat tails. "Pecky is a good hunting dog," I reminded them.

"Have you been this way before, Teddy?" Ray asked.

"We rode the train to the end of the tracks and back once, but we didn't get to the gold mines."

"That's because the train doesn't go that far," Boone said. "Early on, the builders wanted to push the tracks all the way up, but they gave up on the idea." He pointed down the road. "We parallel the train tracks for another ten miles before turning off the highway at Brice Creek. That's where the real climb starts."

"How much gold do you think I'll find?"

"Don't set your hopes too high. Gold's not easy to come by." Boone must have seen my disappointment. "You can keep any of it you find. The first lucky bastard filled a gunnysack with nuggets."

"Where exactly was that?" Ray asked. He was smoking a cigarette, holding it with his good hand and driving with his stump.

"Why don't you drive with your good hand and smoke with the stump," Boone said. "I'd like to stay out of the river."

"And risk dropping a good cigarette?"

At Brice Creek, Ray bumped off the highway onto the mining road and began zigzagging between holes and boulders. "This road isn't worth a shit," he said.

"Careful, it's all we've got."

The road was slowly splitting away from the mountain. Parts had already dropped off. Above us, slabs the size of our truck, teetered out from the canyon wall.

"Engineering geniuses blasted this road from the canyon wall thirty years ago," Boone said. "They did a good job of it, but nothing's been done to maintain the road since." He chuckled. "And to think they wanted to push the railroad up here. Teddy, you are in for one hell of a ride."

The road narrowed to five feet in places where the outer half had dropped a thousand feet to the creek. Ferns and moss grew along the base of the wall on our left. On the right, nothing at all marked the edge. Ray's eyes were fixed on the road. He hugged the steering wheel with his hand and a half.

"Want a cigarette?" Boone said, lighting one of his own.

At the tree line, we began switching back and forth across an even steeper rock face. The road surface was slick with green moss and spring runoff. Boulders released by the snowmelt had battered the surface and had left behind rubble and gaping holes.

"The place will be crawling with prospectors and miners once the road is clear," Boone said. "It's nice to get a head start."

At the top of the climb, we stopped in front of a shattered granite wall that looked like a castle with a drawbridge in the middle. A wild stream had once tumbled from a natural split at the base of the wall. In its place, water now squeezed beneath an iron door that blocked the opening to a caved-in tunnel. The door smelled of creosote, and the tunnel door had the look of a dungeon. A solid sheet of orange rust, much of it flaking into the water, had welded the door hinges shut, probably forever.

"That was the Orphan Boy claim until the tunnel flooded," Boone said. "The miners did real well until they drowned."

The stream that flowed from Orphan Boy's shuttered tunnel had to pick its way through rocky rubble and tailings, broken machines, and rotting timbers. At the end of the gauntlet, the water swirled through a mix of colors that settled at the bottom of a shallow pond.

Fifty yards on past Orphan Boy, we reached Boone's claim. Three heavy timbers and a cobweb of roots framed the tunnel entrance. A hand painted sign over the black hole was all that marked it. In front of the tunnel, a rusted ore cart sat on rails set in the dirt. Machinery, hitching rails, and a canvas tent that sat on a wooden floor formed a semi-circle around the toothless opening. The sign above the tunnel entrance read, *Paradise*.

"I didn't name it," Boone said, "but I believe in it."

Below Boone's camp, at the bottom of a wooded slope, a second creek, a spring really, wound through a stand of birch. Boone filled a bucket and carried it up from the creek. He ladled the clear, spring water into a cup. "This water is better than the other," he said. "You'll like it." Without sitting down once, he began offloading the heavy pipe. He carried two lengths at a time across the campsite and stacked them outside the tunnel entrance.

Boone fixed beef stew with biscuits for supper on his camp stove. Afterward, Ray scraped leftovers back into the stew pot and added warm water. "There's a good dog mess," he said, making sure the pot wasn't hot before setting it on the ground. Pecky's head disappeared inside, his entire body wagging gratitude.

Boone put me to bed on a cot inside the tent. It was cold in the mountains, like winter in town. I could see my breath, but I was warm under all the blankets Boone piled on top of me.

"I don't usually have company," he said, tucking in the corners around me. He pulled a single gray blanket from a wooden trunk and spread it over his cot, next to mine, and then he reached for the lantern. He was about to join Ray outside.

"Boone, when you were a little boy, did your mother put lots of blankets on your bed?" I had been thinking about the winter nights in my bedroom when the cold crept in through the thin wallboards and caused me to wake up shivering.

"You bet she did."

Ray stirred the fire outside our tent and clanked a pan.

"If you woke up cold in the middle of the night, could you have asked for more?"

"I suppose I could have. I don't know that I ever did."

"Because you wanted to learn to be tough, so you could be a better soldier?"

"It wasn't anything like that. My mother piled on so many covers I had to push them off to keep from sweltering."

"Wouldn't you have been a better soldier if she hadn't done that?" As soon as I said it, I realized how foolish it must have sounded because Boone couldn't have turned out any tougher. He had to have been the best soldier any general ever had.

"You ask the damndest questions." He set the lantern on the floor and sat at the foot of my bed. "I'm hard pressed to understand how that would affect a man being a soldier, one way or the other."

"Some fathers worry about those things," I said slowly. "It was something I heard when I was supposed to be asleep."

"What was it you heard these fathers say?"

I hoped I wasn't going too far, but I needed to know. If anybody could help me, it was a navy mechanic and champion wrestler. "One night," I said, "after I was in bed, Mother peeked in and asked if I was cold. I wasn't shivering cold, but I wasn't warm either, so I said yes. I shouldn't have. She went to get another blanket and left my door partly open. Dad sounded really unhappy with her. 'You can't keep giving him so many blankets.'

"'It's only one,' she said.

"Dad said she was ruining me. He said they needed to toughen me up for when I go into the service. 'You're growing a hothouse pansy in that room.'

"A few minutes later, the bedroom door pushed open, and a narrow shaft of light fell across my bed. Mother was standing in the doorway with a blanket in her arms. She tucked it around my feet and pushed it up under my chin. 'You are still a little boy,' was all she said.

"I remember lying under the blanket, feeling the warmth grow around me. It was warmest where she had tucked and patted. The next morning, the first thing I did was kick that blanket onto the floor."

The lamp hissed softly with Boone at the foot of my cot. "For the most part, I agree with your mother," he said evenly. "You are a boy, but not so little anymore, not at all by the looks of you."

I liked that.

"Parents know best, and I'm not one, so I don't mean to take anything away from your dad. If you were my boy, I'd give you as many blankets as you needed. At the same time, I'd hope you wouldn't ask for something you didn't need."

"I would never do that," I promised.

"I sure as hell wouldn't hurry you off to any war. Life will regiment you soon enough without going out and looking for it. Being a soldier's not an easy thing." He walked over to the chipped basin next to the door. "The best soldiers do what's required without thinking about it, with no need for drums or bugles." He dipped his hands into the water and began scrubbing the black lines that etched his knuckles. "Some men are good at it. Others are better talking about it."

"Talking about what?" I asked.

Boone reached for a towel beside the basin. "About soldiering," he said.

"My dad and Mr. Mackenzie were soldiers," I said. I'd seen Mr. Mackenzie wear his reserve guard uniform while driving around in his car, and I had admired the framed picture of Dad in his ROTC uniform that sat in his office.

"I can't speak for your dad," Boone said. "Mr. Mackenzie is the type of soldier who likes the look of being one, but that's about as far as it goes. You've seen those chocolate soldiers dressed in shiny uniforms? They stand about so high." He made a gap between his thumb and forefinger. "Chocolate soldiers look real pretty in their red and gold foil until it gets warm, but with any heat at all, they turn into brown puddles. A uniform doesn't make a man a soldier any more than an extra blanket keeps a boy from being one."

"Girls like men in uniform," I said. That's what Dad had told me when he found me looking at his framed picture.

"That may be true," Boone said, moving toward the door. "And these may be lessons you'll have to learn for yourself. For your sake, let's hope the price of the schooling isn't too steep."

Boone left the tent. I heard him pour a cup of coffee and take a seat by the fire. I smelled cigarette smoke before either of them spoke.

"That was quite a conversation," Ray said.

"That it was," Boone replied in a soft voice. "Let's give him a minute to get to sleep."

They sat in chairs that creaked when they leaned forward to stir the fire. I did fall asleep, but only for a while. I can't say for how long. The murmur of men's voices or maybe the hoot of an owl woke me. Pecky was curled in the crook of my knees.

"I'll be up a creek if Fraser goes under," Ray said.

"You'll do fine. You'd get hired on with somebody else."

"Doing what? Not many outfits want a one-armed driver. I'll say that for Fraser, he treats his men better than most, gives us the benefit of the doubt."

"Everybody but that boy of his," Boone said.

"It could be worse," Ray said. "He is the boss's kid, and he gets three squares a day. I'd take it and feel like I was on Easy Street."

"You'd want to be in his shoes?"

"Only partway."

"The boy was just telling me what war heroes Mackenzie and his dad are because they wore uniforms."

Ray choked on his coffee. "Sid Mackenzie wore a uniform all right, but he didn't get any closer to a battle than you and me are right now. He cut lumber for the Frogs; that was it. The army didn't even issue him a gun. For that, the brass gives him command of a coastal artillery battery. With Sid protecting our shores, we'd be better off in Iowa."

"When I meet a man for the first time," Boone said, "I don't automatically dislike him. However, I do expect the worst from him. After that, I step back and wait to see if he'll prove me wrong. That way, I'm rarely disappointed. Sid Mackenzie has never disappointed me."

I rolled over. Pecky didn't like the new arrangement and jumped off. I slid into his warm spot and heard Ray murmur a friendly greeting, and then I fell asleep for good.

Boone was right when he talked about the high price of an education. Mine was plenty steep, but not as steep as it was for some of the others—at least I'm still around to talk about it. I learned that it is far better to be at home, near the girls and making money, than it is rotting in a trench, picking lice from your head, and wondering what's going to get you next—even if it's nothing more than boredom. That might be what Boone was trying to tell me, but I can't be sure since he had been a great soldier. I do know that Zane Gray got it right in The Day of the Beast. *Life is a fatalistic crapshoot, so you'd better be lucky or smart. Since I wasn't overly smart, I must have been lucky.*

27

Mother slept naked and rarely considered getting dressed until she'd had a cup of coffee and a good look out the window. With a mug in her hand, she'd pad from one room to the other in her bare feet. If she'd had her way, she'd never have worn shoes. If somebody unexpected knocked on the door, she'd scramble for the bedroom to grab her robe and yell, "Teddy, see who it is," or "I'll be right there." If it was somebody "we didn't really need to talk to," she and I would rush toward her bedroom bent over and crouching, where we'd whisper and hide like little mice.

She might slide into her robe and slippers before coffee when it was particularly cold, but many mornings, with the air so cold I could see my breath, I'd find her standing beside the stove with her hands wrapped around the steaming cup, dressed only in her goose bumps. That's just how she was at five in the morning in July when she looked out our kitchen window and screamed.

"Fire!!" The first panicked cry didn't register with me, but when her feet pounded through the kitchen and tattooed across the porch, I was jerked upright.

She was onto the haul road, sprinting and waving her arms before I got to the kitchen window. I watched her scramble on all fours up the pond wall. At the top, she stopped to again sound the alarm. "The mill's on fire!"

Men erupted from the bunkhouse; Mother's voice was soon lost in theirs. I hunted down my shoes and stumbled after her. I found her standing at the edge of the fire. Her chest was heaving, and her hands were at her face. Tears were streaming through her fingers, and sweat moistened the skin across her shoulders. The fire's red glow reflected off her thick braid, but its light was lost in the shadow between her legs.

Most of the men were in their underwear, many without boots, all fighting to keep the fire from spreading. Boone and Ray threw bucket after bucket of water on the flames closest to the mill, but even with that, the heat grew and pushed them back to the edge of the pond. Alec ran by, carrying a bucket. "Christ on a crutch," he muttered, "this one's bad." He was drenched with sweat or water, trying his hardest to keep the contents of his bucket from sloshing out.

"Can they save it?" Mother asked me.

Uncle Normal was first to the gasoline engine that ran the pump. He pulled and pulled on the cord, but couldn't get the engine to start, not even to sputter. He looked up, as if asking for help.

Sharpe, the lead sawyer, pushed Uncle Normal out of the way. "You flooded the son of a bitch, you idiot!" He bent over the carburetor, blew on it, and yanked on the cord. "Son of a bitch," he yelled, "Son of a goddamn bitch!"

Uncle Normal, I remembered, had always had trouble with gas engines. I had seen him struggle with the chain saw for hours. He just didn't know how to start engines.

After several long minutes, with Sharpe swearing and flailing against the starter cord, the pump's engine coughed. Sharpe dragged the canvas hose closer to the fire, but gave up on the finished lumber. He began spraying the dock and the mill. "Concentrate on the structure!" he commanded. "There's no way to save the lumber."

Our entire lumber yard was reduced to charcoal that morning; it smoldered the rest of the day, but the men had saved the saw mill. Before it was over, Boone's wife, Twinkle, wrapped Mother in a blanket and walked her back to the house. Babe Ashman drove down the canyon to find Dad.

"When the lumber yard caught fire, it was like burning money in the bank," Dad later said, but he hadn't been there to see it. He had been away on business.

Rod Mohl, the watchman on duty, hadn't spotted the fire while it was small for good reason. He hadn't been anywhere near it. He'd spent the night across the river, partying with the Dolomite crew. When the flames jumped from the planer shavings onto the finished lumber, Mohl was drinking beer and drawing cards.

Dad wanted to fire Mohl that day, but angry as he was, he couldn't keep the mill running without an experienced millwright.

"It was an innocent mistake," Mohl said. "No way could I have known there'd be fire. It won't ever happen again."

Dad was about to give in when Boone stepped up.

"Get rid of the little bastard, now," Boone said. "I'll take care of the saws until you find somebody permanent."

With that assurance, Dad let Mohl go, and Boone walked him off the property. Dad squarely blamed Mohl for the fire, and Mohl never forgave Boone for costing him his job.

"Timber and relationships are fragile," Dad said. "All it takes is one spark to destroy either of them." That was why Dad preferred to buy the rights to someone else's timber rather than own timber outright. In the aftermath of our fire, and the giant Tillamook burn later that year, I began see why he felt that way.

Speaking of fragile relationships, I might as well mention the two friends I had at Culp Creek. First was Leo Snodgrass, the ranger's son. Everybody called him *Snotgrass* naturally, me included. Snotgrass had permission to use his dad's ranger pony; he rode double with me a few times. I also played with Lenny, who lived three miles downstream. To get to Lenny's house, I had to walk along the gravel highway and dodge logging trucks, or else follow the railroad tracks in mountain lion country and worry about getting jumped by a cougar—it wasn't much of a choice. The three of us sometimes rode our bikes together, and I saw them at school. So I did have friends.

I was down at the river with Lenny and Snotgrass a week after the fire. Since it was a hot July day, we decided to cool off at our secret spot beside the old train wreck. The place was secret because it was hidden behind a ten-foot high wall of blackberry bushes that grew along the riverbank. Nobody could see past the thorny tangle or push through it without injury. A hard to find tunnel, sized for us and not for grownups, was the only way in. We had to get on our hands and knees to fit through.

The main attraction behind the brush was an old steam locomotive and coal car that sat rusting in the middle of the river. The coal car lay on its side with its spine broken; the engine was still upright. Orange rust had bubbled away much of the locomotive's black paint, but had spared the white block letters on its side that spelled, *TEXAS*. Green moss and spidery plants grew throughout the wreckage, providing food and shelter for the world's biggest crawdads.

Lenny, Snotgrass, and I were relaxing in the shade, fishing for those monsters when no-good Marvin Ellis showed up. We didn't know much about Marvin, except that we didn't like him. No-good Marvin and his family had moved in during Easter vacation, which made him the new kid. Lenny's mother told us to be charitable. She even suggested we include Marvin, although we had no choice in the matter, pushy as he was. Lenny and Snotgrass swore they never told Marvin about the secret spot, however somebody obviously had.

When he crawled out of the bushes, I didn't say anything, and neither did the others. No-good Marvin didn't need an invitation to take over.

"Texas is the biggest state in the union," he announced, pointing at the locomotive, "and that's a fact!" In three short months, we had learned that Marvin was from Abilene and that he was privy to all the world's facts.

"Flapping mouths are the only things of any size in Texas," Snotgrass said. I knew it would take more than that to shut no-good Marvin up.

"Texas was also the first state in the union," Marvin added, not bothering to consider the excellent point Snotgrass had just made.

"Horseshit!" Lenny said.

It wasn't just me. Nobody liked Marvin.

No-good Marvin faced us with his arms crossed. "Texas was, too, the first state! I friggin' guarantee it! That's why they call it the Lone Star State."

Where did he get this stuff?

"Not even close," Lenny smirked. "New York was first state." Lenny was quick, the kind of friend you wanted around at times like this. "That's why the President gave New York City the Statue of Liberty."

"Who told you that?" Marvin laughed. "One of your Wop friends from the mines?" He never gave up. "Just because some Wop floated by the Statue of Liberty on his way here from Wopland, doesn't mean he knows shit about it."

"Boone Shaw told me," Lenny said.

Lenny might have been lying about this particular fact, but with Boone's name in the mix, the conversation took on an added level of respect.

No-good Marvin changed the subject. "They blew up this train during the War of Northern Aggression," he said.

The three of us scanned the sunken locomotive, searching for evidence we could use to disprove Marvin's claim.

"Confederate soldiers killed a hundred thousand Yankees that day," he continued. I could hear his confidence building. "But that wasn't nearly enough because Yankees breed faster than rabbits. God committed a goddamn sin when he created more Yankees than he did bullets."

"Who says?" I chipped in. Normally, I wasn't one to argue because I was way too slow with my comebacks, too much like Uncle Normal in that way. I needed time to think things through before knowing where I sat on an issue. But Marvin was the first Texan I had ever met, and his lies were so outrageous that I found myself halfway believing them.

"My grandma told me. She lived through the War of Yankee Aggression."

"This train wasn't in any war," Lenny said with a sneer that promised superior information. "Buster Keeton used the train to make an old movie. I read about it. He ran it off the logging trestle."

Another good thing about having Lenny on your side was that he would lie to make his point. Since Marvin had no right to make such an outrageous claim, Lenny had every right to lie to his face.

Tired of the conversation, Snotgrass decided to wade out to the locomotive and climb up one side. At the top, he pulled a wrapper from his shirt pocket and revealed a cache of raw bacon, undoubtedly stolen from his mother's ice box.

"I've got the perfect bait," he grinned.

Bacon wasn't easy to come by during the depression, certainly not purchased to feed crawdads, but it did work the best. The scent alone drew snappers from their holes like mice to cheese. Snotgrass tore off a piece with his teeth. He chewed with his mouth wide open to prove that he had really done it. Then he swallowed! He tore off a second bite, but pushed it onto an open safety pin attached to a string.

"You'll get worms doing that," no-good Marvin said, obviously impressed.

"Not me," Snotgrass said. "The best bait in the world for catching grandpa crawdaddies is raw bacon. And now, my farts will bring them to the surface." Snotgrass emitted a blast so loud it might have come from the locomotive. "They'll smell that one a mile away," he said with some pride.

The part about smelling it a mile away was no lie.

I felt a tug on my string. "I got one!" I yelled, happy to be first. I had dropped my hook in an eddy behind a large boulder because crawdads like quiet pools where the dead stuff settles out. Slowly, I began to retrieve my string. It takes nerves of steel to pull in a big crawdad. If you hurry or jerk the line at all, the crawdad lets go, and gravity carries him back to the silt. You don't hook a crawdad like you do a fish; rather, the crawdad catches you. It takes hold of the bait with its pinchers, and you play its greed against its instinct to survive. One or the other wins out. Which would it be?

When the crawdad was an inch below the surface, I grabbed him high on the back, behind the pinchers. He reached for me at the same time. I was still working to imprison the crawdad in a cloth bag when I heard men's voices downstream. I didn't see anyone, just the bridge that connected our side of the river with Mr. Mackenzie's side. Its heavy timbers crossed ten feet above the stream with a low railing on each side. The pipe we had used to siphon water to our pond still ran underneath. With the high brush around us, we could have waded all the way to the bridge and never have been seen.

Footsteps crashed through brush above us. We still couldn't see anyone, but they couldn't see us either. "I want you to start the new waterline high enough upstream to get a decent head of pressure for the pond," Dad said.

"Easy enough to do," Boone answered, "We'll have to follow the railroad right of way. Do we have a permit?"

"Slow and Easy won't be a problem," Dad said. "Neet and his shareholders care more about the revenue my mill generates for the railroad than they do about a pipe running along their easement."

"This has nothing to do with water," Boone said. "Mackenzie wants your rail site. He'll do whatever it takes to get it."

"Piss on Mackenzie," Dad said. "With gravity and four-inch galvanized pipe, we will be fine.

"Was that your old man?" no-good Marvin asked after they had left. "What's he up to?"

"I don't know much about his business," I said.

"Everybody else does. Your dad will be out of business and you'll be gone by next summer."

"You don't know anything, Marvin!"

"When you go, ask your daddy to leave your mother's burning bush behind." He snickered at Lenny and Snotgrass, and they smiled. "My dad says he'd start another fire, just to watch your mommy put it out."

"You stay away from our mill, and stay from my mother!"

Marvin poked a finger in and out of his open fist like he was pretending to *do it*.

I wadded my string and safety pin together and stuffed them into my pocket. "You have no right to be here."

Lenny didn't move, didn't offer one word of support. I looked at him and then started running up the path. A thorn bit my cheek and another caught my shirt. I pulled against it until the fabric ripped.

"I'd come to watch your momma, too," no-good Marvin yelled loud enough for the whole world to hear.

Dad was more right than wrong when he said, "Relationships are fragile." He actually put my feelings into words. At the time, I believed that good behavior produced love, but that love was always at risk. By doing what Mother wanted, I had the power to manufacture love. With the just right moves, I could guarantee it. Dad described business transactions as tit for tat relationships. Why, I thought, would love be any different? On the surface, this made so much sense that I believed it. I needed to believe it. The transaction with Mother failed only because I didn't know how to be good enough.

I had to look past my family to understand that there are different types of relationships, and that some of them can be strong. Boone was a case in point. No matter what I said or did, he remained my friend. He also stayed close to Wattie and Ray after the events that follow. Boone even forgave Twinkle for what she did. In his eyes, loyalty rendered a relationship nearly unbreakable. My relationship with Miss Cherry was unbreakable, too. It could have been timeless. No one, but my father, had the power to destroy it.

28

A carpet of bark, bottle glass, and tobacco spit was all that remained of the empty log pond. Lugged tracks were churning through the muck, fouling the air, as the steam shovel swiveled between pond and idling dump truck, digging and dropping and deepening the hole. Inside the battered cab, with barely enough room for legs and levers, a solitary man sat on a raised seat. His body bounced, and his head snapped each time the shovel lurched. In anticipation of the shocks, he kept one knee braced against the cab's frame, never changing expression.

"That could rattle a man's brains by day's end," Dad said.

"It sure does stink," Sharpe responded.

Broad leaf ferns and cattails marked the pond's inner bank. With the water gone, they seemed out of place. Dry brush and thistle covered the outer wall. A family of otters sniffed both sides of the bank and looked confused.

Each time the toothed bucket swiveled, Dad, Boone, and Mr. Sharpe turned as one, following its progress. Two roaring dump trucks shuttled between the pond and the river, flattening our blackberry bushes and spilling their loads down the riverbank. The black contents covered the river rock and dammed the flow until the current built up enough force to push the debris downstream.

"To get the pressure you'll need," Boone said, "we'll have to drop the pond three feet and run the line from the top of Wildwood Falls."

"It's only money," Dad said.

"How is this going to work?" Mr. Sharpe said. He was a first-rate sawyer, but that didn't make him an engineer.

"It's a simple gravity feed downhill," Dad said. "With enough pipe, there really isn't much to it." He pointed toward the Dolomite mill site. "Our first pond was perfect, three hundred feet across, five and half feet deep. Now we get to do it all over again because we're being blackmailed."

"Did you look into getting a right of way?" Boone asked. "We don't need trouble with the railroad."

"You run the line," Dad said. "I'll worry about the railroad."

The shovel operator climbed down from the cab. He began to stoke the boiler and grease the cables.

Dad silently shook his head. He looked as if he were having an argument with someone we couldn't see. "God laced these mountains with timber and gold," he said, staring at the surrounding hills. "If you made it here first, you got it all. If you were smart, you kept most of it."

At the turn of the century, endless stands of Douglas fir, many trees bigger in diameter than a man was tall, crashed into spongy soil. Enterprising men pushed steel rails and steam donkeys up hillsides, higher than gravity and physics should have permitted. It had been an engineer's dream, but Dad had missed it by twenty years.

Dad turned his back on the pond and stared at his mill. The idling, clanking shovel couldn't begin to smother the silence that surrounded him. Stacks of un-sold lumber swamped his loading dock, more of it covered the dirt yard at the far end of the mill, but that wasn't what caught Dad's attention. He fixed his gaze on the two by three foot handmade sign that he had nailed above the main saw, the day he bought the mill. On the front, he had printed the name of his new mill: *Fraser Lumber Co.* On the back, he had penciled his vision: 'Big things begin with humble origins.'

If you were to hand me a photograph from that time, I could tell you exactly when it was taken by the way Dad looked. With each passing year, the gray skin covering his face drew tighter around the bones, and the expression grew harder. Lack of sleep and worry wore him down, but that alone couldn't explain what photos would capture. Like Napoleon on Elba, Dad was swallowing arsenic. Within a year of buying the mill, he began to poison himself with the fear that he wouldn't measure up.

"If things don't get better, soon," Dad said, "that faded sign will be all that's left of me." Dad hadn't been lucky enough to get to the good timber first. All that remained for him, and the others like him, were leftovers. But Dad still meant to find a way.

"When the gold mine reopens," he said, turning back to Boone, "who plans to quit the mill?"

"There's no way of knowing until Champion starts hiring," Boone said. "With the price of gold up, Champion can afford to pay top dollar."

"What about you?"

"I don't see myself leaving for another salary," Boone said slowly. He was making Dad wait for his answer. "But when I hit the mother lode, get the hell out of my way!"

"You've got gold fever no different than the rest of them."

"Worse," Boone said. "But I'm different, too. I like to eat, and that requires a steady job." He tilted his head toward the small house behind his machine shop. "Twinkle doesn't do too well when I'm away. So, for the time being, I'm destined to stay a part-time prospector and full-time machinist."

29

With orders for lumber growing sparser than trees in the eastern half of the state, Dad began to rethink his approach to business. In August, when Rex Pingree called saying the Klan was holding a public meeting at the new armory, Dad agreed to go.

"The speaker will be a man worth listening to," was all Pingree said when Dad asked for details.

Dad met Pingree at the armory's entrance. To hear Dad later describe it, you'd have thought it was the last place on earth he ever wanted to be, but just as Gust had observed at the first Klan meeting, nobody forced him to go. "Necessity might be the mother of invention," Dad said, "but she spawns a number of other bastards as well."

Colonel Sid Mackenzie's new two-story armory was freshly painted. WWI artillery pieces, polished to the point of newness, guarded the entrance. Inside the drill hall, several hundred voices echoed and mixed with the harsh tinsel sounds of folding chairs scraping against waxed concrete.

"We hold all our big meetings here," Pingree said with pride. "We need the room, *and* we have the access. Tonight's speaker is Reverend Sawyer from Portland. You've heard of him, I'll bet."

Reverend Sawyer filled the front of the room, chatting and glad-handing his admirers. Dad easily recalled Reverend Sawyer's performance from eight years earlier—the one he and Gust had attended at the request of their Latin professor. The Reverend looked like the same man, except that there was so much more of him; and yet, there appeared to be less. His girth had doubled in eight years, but the circus trappings that had accompanied the first show were nowhere to be seen.

"You'll see that we're more of a fraternal group these days, brothers helping brothers," Pingree said. "We're a big part of God's plan."

"I'd love to see the blueprint," Dad said.

Pingree laughed at the joke and slapped Dad on the shoulder. "Wouldn't we all!" Pingree pointed to the opposite side of the room. "Look over there," he said. "That's Sid Mackenzie, the unit commander. Sitting next to him is Gust Backer, Ennis Neet, and Wulf Gehring." Gust was chatting with Neet and Gehring like they were great friends. "Looks like you took the job, after all," Dad said to himself.

"Gust is an old friend," Dad said out loud. "Does he work for Mackenzie, now?"

"Gust is Dolomite's new woods boss on Sharps Creek. He'll be supplying logs for the new mill."

At the front of the hall, Reverend Sawyer glanced at his watch. At seven o'clock, he squeezed a final set of fingers and lumbered to the podium. He cleared his throat and set several chins in motion.

"The great question tonight," he boomed, "is whether we stand for one hundred percent Americanism or for Rome." Dad glanced sideways. He watched the tired phrase flow through the audience. The seats around him were packed, their occupants tightly tuned to the message. Dad felt like a voyeur.

The old reverend still spoke with authority. He seemed perfectly suited to the itinerant life he had led for so many years, summoning demons from behind the podium and casting them forward. His new message mirrored the old, but had been molded to fit a new set of villains. There also was a change in tone and direction. The new words carried less of an edge and a more limited political message. Nothing was being said about a "rising flood of color." In its place, the reverend warned about "alien influences".

Dad had little use for politics and none for religion. He concluded that nothing worthwhile would be gained from the exercise, but with Pingree rapt at his side, he did his best to appear engaged. While he listened, he recalled fragments and phrases from the old speech. At the time, sterilization had been considered a necessary component of any moral purification process. He remembered the reverend's call for castration of the socially unfit, a concept that had caused his nuts to ache at the time.

Pingree dipped his shoulder toward Dad. "If more people would pay attention to this man, we'd get our country back on track."

Dad pursed his lips and nodded. He reached down and gave his goods a tug.

"Don't you think so?" Pingree asked, encouraged.

"He does have a lot to say," Dad said, keeping his eyes riveted on the front of the room.

"Our homes, schools, and churches are the three pillars upon which this nation rests," the reverend intoned. "The American school bill, soon to go before the legislature, will abolish private and parochial schooling. It symbolizes a battle of humanity against sects, classes, combinations, and rings. This bill is against entrenched privilege and secret machinations of a favored few. We intend to protect the less favored many."

Pingree leaned in again. "When the bill passes, it means the end of Catholic teachers in public schools. The papists will have to find employment at the Vatican."

Dad said nothing.

"Ever been to a Catholic ceremony?" Pingree said. "I hear they speak in tongues."

"You mean Latin?"

"Which nobody understands but Satan himself. The high priest jabbers away while the sheep slobber and stare at our savior hanging on the wall, as if his crucifixion was entertainment."

"I think it's the Pentecostals who speak in tongues," Dad said.

"With the Pentecostals," Pingree countered, "the Holy Spirit speaks through *His* chosen vessels. With the Catholics, the Pope—or worse—speaks through black-robed minions. Effigies, gold, smoke, and blood speak of hell, not of God. A Papal ceremony has nothing to do with the Holy Spirit."

"I never took you for being religious, Rex."

"I'm not," Pingree said harshly, "but this Catholic thing has got me in an uproar. Catholics steal Protestant children and convert them in monasteries and nunneries."

Dad turned back to the speaker.

"Don't misunderstand me," Reverend Sawyer was saying. "We respect the law, and those who say otherwise do not understand us. Or they fear us and choose dark lies in hopes of defeating us. We serve the laws of the land, especially those that make up the United States Constitution." He raised up an open palm toward God. *"Like God's own commandments, laws of a higher moral order must guide the creation of the rest.* After a few years, people will not regard the Klan as a menace, but rather as their savior."

Reverend Sawyer paused. The gravity of his bearing pulled all eyes toward him. "The great state of Oregon must be kept free of all alien influences, Papal and Bolshevik! We oppose control of American public affairs by aliens and so-called Americans whose primary allegiance is to a foreign power!"

The audience clapped but didn't cheer like they had eight years before. A few spectators immediately rose to leave, but Reverend Sawyer appeared satisfied with the response.

Pingree's face was shining. "What did you think?"

Dad didn't know how to respond.

He and Pingree were being carried toward the door by the pressure of the crowd when Pingree abruptly turned against the current. "There's somebody I want you to meet."

Since he had no choice, Dad followed Pingree toward the podium. Reverend Sawyer was speaking with Ennis Neet and a man Dad didn't recognize.

"The American School Bill is about to go before the full legislature," Reverend Sawyer was saying. "Your support is critical."

"He's telling you to pull out your checkbook, Ennis."

Neet and Reverend Sawyer glanced at the new arrivals. The reverend welcomed the comment with an indulgent smile. "The Lord works wonders when we all work with him."

Pingree placed a hand on the banker's slight shoulder. "Ennis, did you know that money and fish are brain food? Fresh dollars, like fresh fish, improve the thinking process. With enough dollars, a soft-headed moron can be turned into a god-damn genius. Don't you agree, Reverend?"

"The words wouldn't be mine," the reverend said, "but I share the sentiment. Our Savior did have a fondness for fish." Reverend Sawyer turned back to the man he'd been speaking with. "This is the perfect time for a favorable editorial in the *Morning Register*," he said.

"There can't be any mention of the Klan," the man said. "I'll only discuss the education bill, and it will have to be subtle."

"Probably for the best," the reverend said. "No sense muddying the waters."

The newspaperman pulled a notebook from his pocket, slipped off the rubber band that held a pencil stub, and started jotting. "What points do you want to stress in the piece?"

"Mostly the truth, as I've laid it out," the reverend said. His fleshy fingers began to tick off the points. "Tell them we believe in compulsory education in public schools, but *in the real sense*. Emphasize that point."

The reporter stopped writing and looked up.

"Compulsory public education means that no child is to be educated at any *private* school. If the federal government refuses to support public education in the form our founders intended, then the great state of Oregon will have to do it. We intend to regulate all curriculums in private and parochial schools, and in sectarian colleges. No religious garb will be worn by teachers anywhere."

"So, no more penguins," the writer said, scratching away with his pencil.

"Not a feather. This is America, not St. Peter's Square."

The newspaperman reviewed his notes. "Is that it?"

"Not quite. There are two more items. We will require a loyalty oath for teachers and college professors."

As he scribbled, the reporter mouthed the words "loyalty oath."

"If teachers are unwilling to make that simple gesture," the reverend said, "how can we entrust our children to them?"

"And the other thing?" the reporter said.

Reverend Sawyer lowered his voice. "Here, we have to be a little careful, so don't come on too strong. Think of it as firing a shot across the bow. You figure out how to say it, that's your job. We need to let the school boards know, and we intend to be as direct as we need to be…"

"About what?" the reporter said with a hint of impatience.

"About the fact that Catholic schools don't belong anywhere in America, and that Catholic teachers have no business being in front of American children, for any reason. We are taking this message to every school board in the state. Since school boards hire and fire, and we intend to see to it that they do their jobs. We've already had success in Eugene."

"I heard about that," Pingree said, trying to jump into the conversation. "Patterson and Brigham, both members of the Eugene Klan, just got elected to the school board. Right after that, the board voted to fire three women teachers, all of them Roman Catholic."

"Mr. Patterson and Mr. Brigham campaigned on a promise to purge Catholic teachers from the public schools," Reverend Sawyer said. "After the election, the school board finally understood its obligation."

"One board member argued pretty strongly against the firings and almost won out," Pingree said. "What was his name?"

"Arnold, and he won't be reelected," the reverend said. "We've found a candidate to replace him."

The reporter flipped a page. "What about Portland?" he said. "You can't budge the state without moving Portland."

"Portland is a leftist cesspool. We'll clean out Portland later."

Pingree walked Dad to his car. Staring back at the new two-story building, Dad felt as if he'd been bypassed on a number of fronts. "This armory must have cost a million dollars to build," he said softly. "Does Mackenzie really control all the funds?"

"The lion's share. He assigns bids and approves new recruits. The officers and NCOs are all Dolomite men. It wouldn't hurt you to know Sid a little better. I'll introduce you if you want."

"We've already met," Dad said, choosing not to delve into the details of their meeting. "It looks like it's going to be Roosevelt in November," he said, moving on to a more neutral topic.

"A dog catcher could beat Herbert Hoover right now, and it's too damn bad," Pingree said. "Hoover's from the West, he's an engineer, and he's all for business. Unless the economy turns around, Herbert's had it. Roosevelt talks about a new deal for Americans. It's going to be a raw deal for any working American who pays taxes. The crippled son of a bitch will bankrupt the country!"

"Hoover says the worst of the depression is over."

30

Miss Cherry returned in the fall with enough books to double the size of our tiny school library. That was why she had been so excited about leaving at the end of the school year. During the summer, with the help of her congregation, she had spent days knocking on doors, scouring basements and attics, searching for derelicts and discards. Most of her finds were in tatters and without covers.

"They just need a little fixing up," she said, as she unpacked the boxes. "It will be a wonderful art project for the class."

While she had been away, I worked hard on my reading, but instead of rewarding me for the effort, she punished me. As a result of my new competence, Miss Cherry spent less time with me and more of it with the younger children.

A month into the school year, she decided to teach us about the Three Sisters of Fate. "Day after day, minute by minute," she explained, "life moves forward for everyone until it ends. There are no exceptions to this rule."

She stepped up to the new blackboard that my dad had paid for. When Dad bought blackboard, he did it out of civic duty, he said, but like with everything else he undertook, he expected it would provide him with leverage when he needed it.

"Even though there can be no exceptions," Miss Cherry said, continuing her lesson, "there are important differences. Some of us live longer than others, but none of us knows for how long." Her eyes touched on every child. "Why don't we know how long we'll live?" she asked.

I raised my hand. "Yes, Teddy?"

"Because it's a secret?"

She smiled. "That is indeed the problem." She took up the chalk and sketched a pair of scissors, and then she sketched a ball of yarn. "When we are born, each of us is given a piece of yarn, except the lengths are unequal." She tapped the yarn with her fingernail. "If the lives of everyone in this room were rolled into an enormous ball of yarn, which length of yarn would each of us receive?"

I looked around. I didn't have any idea, but neither did anyone else.

No-good Marvin Ellis snickered at the back of the room. I *hated* the sound of his voice,

Miss Cherry walked to her desk and picked up real scissors and a real ball of yarn. She cut two pieces: the first, an inch long; the second, a foot in length. She turned to no-good Marvin.

"Marvin," she said, "you seem to have something to say." She held up the two pieces of yarn so we could see them. "Which would you prefer?"

Marvin surveyed the classroom, smirking. "I already got the long one, Miss Cherry," he said, grinning at her. Two older boys snorted. He never would have dared to say that to Mrs. Ames.

Miss Cherry's face turned bright red. She dropped her eyes. "I'm sorry, Marvin," she stuttered. "You must have misunderstood. I was talking about the length of our lives." She turned to a young girl at the back of the room. "Myrna, if it were up to you, and one of these strings represented your life, which would you choose?"

"The long string," Myrna said hopefully.

"As I think we all would," Miss Cherry said, avoiding Marvin's gaze. "But there's a problem with that."

"There is?" Myrna said, looking fearful.

"I'm afraid we don't get to choose. Wishing for a long life doesn't make it happen. The Three Sisters of Fate decide for us." She returned to her drawings. "The first sister always cuts the yarn short," she said, raising that string before us. "The second sister cuts it a middle length." She held up the second strand. "And the third sister," she said, holding up a length a yard long, "cuts the yarn generously."

As Miss Cherry described the process, I put more effort into trying to see the sisters than I did in trying to understand the point of the discussion. What kind of woman, I wondered, would cut a boy's life in half, or snip it down to a third?

"How big are the scissors?" I asked.

"As big as they need to be," she said.

I also wanted to know whether the sisters managed to cut all that yarn with one hand or if they needed two. If one got behind, did the others help out; how pretty were they, and what did they wear? Were they like the women the mill hands wanted to be with on Saturday night, women with bare necks and knees and dark places in between? Or were they more like the women who parceled out cookies in the church foyer, the ladies who accused you of taking more than what they considered to be your share?

"Don't worry about what they wear or what they look like," Miss Cherry said not unkindly, never unkindly. "Think about what the idea means to you and how you might want to live your life."

Since the sisters got to cut the yarn, did they also choose the color? Why would they influence the substance of a life any less than they did its length? I didn't get to choose my parents— was that the sisters' doing, too? As for the things I've done, maybe I had no choice in that matter, either.

Miss Cherry didn't mention a fourth sister that day, probably because she hadn't yet had to face her. The fourth sister, still hiding in the shadows, represented a choice Miss Cherry would have to make, but that day at school, she only spoke of the three.

A week before Easter, somebody threw a rock through the schoolhouse window, shattering the glass. I jumped out of my desk, and little Myrna screamed. Miss Cherry ran to the window in time to see a car roar away. She stared for a long moment and then walked over to the rock. Brown paper and knotted twine wrapped it like a parcel. She struggled to untie the knots, before cutting through them with her scissors.

"What does it say?" we all asked.

She put the note in her pocket and began to sweep the glass from the floor.

"Tell us what it says."

"It's a nasty message written by sick people," she finally answered. She didn't let us go outside for recess that afternoon. At the end of the day, she told us to go straight home and to be careful.

When Miss Cherry's second year of teaching came to an end, she didn't leave like she had done the year before. Even so, her parents drove up and hugged her. They brought a cake and wished her happy birthday because she had just turned eighteen. I was ten years old by then. Her mother took away her winter things for cleaning and left her with a box of folded summer clothes.

Miss Cherry had decided to stay in Culp Creek over the summer to help Françoise and Guillaume since they had become second parents to her. In exchange, Françoise promised to teach her about herbs and teas. Like Siamese twins—one bent, one straight—they tramped through the woods together, foraging, digging, talking, and filling bags. They compared spots on mushrooms and examined the undersides of leaves. They pinched buds and plucked pods. On their hands and knees, they grubbed for roots. By midsummer, Miss Cherry began to go out on her own, disappearing for hours and not returning in the evening.

Although she continued to help me with my reading and with my sounds, the effort didn't amount to much more than mild encouragement. If I needed a new book, she would unlock the schoolhouse door and make me choose on my own. I was reading well enough to easily tackle the middle rows. I could have selected much harder texts, but I didn't see any reason to push it. By then, neither did she.

"Why don't you go to the dances anymore?" I asked her one evening while we were with Françoise and Guillaume. I thought it was an innocent question.

"What dances do you mean?"

"The Saturday night dances at the Bucket of Blood."

"I never go to the Bucket of Blood."

"You did once."

"Have people been talking about me?"

"No," I said. "I saw you there."

"How could you have seen me?"

I didn't want to answer. I hesitated, but then told her about my window at the back of the roadhouse.

"That's not nice, peeping at people from the dark and spying on them."

"Isn't that what windows are for, looking in and looking out?"

"Not when other people can't see you."

I thought about all the days I'd spent looking out the windows of my house, watching the men and machines work—nobody saw me then.

That conversation proved to be a turning point for us. My private lessons abruptly ended. If she caught me staring at her, she glanced away, and she began to make excuses for everything. She rarely had time to help me look for new books. When we did go into the schoolhouse, we grabbed any old cover and hurried right out.

But that didn't stop me; it had the opposite effect. I began stopping by daily, offering to fill the wood box—since it was summer, it required little effort on my part. Françoise thought I came for her cakes, but that wasn't it. I only wanted to be with Miss Cherry; and just like her, I learned to make excuses, endless excuses to stay and visit. When she wasn't looking, I'd gaze at her from across the room. Any time she passed by, I'd lean in to rekindle the memory of her scent. If she felt my presence, she didn't show it. Until then, she had been so pretty, her hair perfectly brushed and pulled back, her green eyes always sparkling. Until then, hers had been a face without a mask.

Miss Cherry continued to hum while she sewed. She smiled at Françoise and Guillaume when she greeted them, but the music and smiles evaporated whenever, if ever, she looked at me. Dad began to take fewer trips to Eugene, preferring, it seemed, to attend to business closer to home. By midsummer, when she began to disappear inside the schoolhouse with him, I understood that my time with her had become his, and from what I saw through the schoolroom window, he spent the summer leveraging his blackboard and banging more than the erasers. With her skirt pushed up and her pale bottom scouring the floor beneath him, I watched my father foul something that didn't belong to him. Some might say that it didn't belong to me either, but that's not how I saw it.

The second time I found them together, I picked up a rock the size of my fist. I didn't throw it because I was too afraid. I simply stood and watched them through the window. When they finished, I slipped the rock in my pocket and slid away. I carried the rock for days, its cold weight against my thigh, a reminder. At night, I hid the rock under my bed and considered all the ways I might use it. After a week of carrying the rock and hiding it under my bed, I woke up one morning, knowing what I needed to do.

I rummaged through the kitchen for brown paper and string. I wrapped the paper around the rock and secured it with a knotted string. I wanted to write her a nasty note, like the one on the other rock, but I didn't know what to say, so I said nothing.

When they entered the school, I hurried to the window and watched. I waited for them to drop down. When they began to churn on the floor next to Myrna's desk, I hurled the rock with its blank wrapping paper. As soon as the window shattered, I started running, hoping the glass would cut my father so that he could never do that with her again.

31

When Herbert Hoover announced that the Depression was over, he couldn't have been more wrong, and that wasn't his only mistake. His pledge of a balanced budget during the campaign hadn't stood a chance. In the year that followed his lost election, Dad saw business go from bad to worse. The theorists and communists who had sabotaged Hoover's administration took over and began subverting all laws of nature. By August 1933, anybody who paid taxes or had a modicum of sense could only stand back and wonder, *What next?*

The National Recovery Act (NRA) created a minimum wage and a maximum work week, which Dad could have tolerated had it stopped there. According to Dad, "the government screwed the pooch by adding production controls and price caps based on some technocrat's idea of future consumption, and by hiring auditors, inspectors, and stool-pigeons to police it."

Dad hated the NRA. He considered its emblem—a royal blue eagle—to be a "pornographic perversion of our country's national symbol." The NRA lit a bonfire under labor unions by promising higher wages and a shorter workweek. Within months of passage, union organizers showed up in Cottage Grove, promising to raise wages from seventy-five cents a day to a dollar twelve.

"New Deal, my ass," Dad remarked to anyone who would listen. FDR's New Deal amounted to high taxes, federal debt, and backbreaking welfare programs. Thinking people tried to resist the legislation, but FDR was always a step ahead. He even stacked the Supreme Court to get what he wanted. Dad never forgave Roosevelt or the Democrats for what they did. When he died of prostate cancer forty years later, he died still hating them. Relegated to a nursing home and marinating in a leaky diaper, he hadn't forgotten. "The worst thing that ever happened to this country," he said, "was FDR!"

At the time, Dad wasn't one to let personal philosophy get in the way of survival. In spite of his objections to the Recovery Act, he saw no reason not to take advantage of it. He hired a photographer to shoot scenes of the mill in full production, with steam rising from the boilers, and all the men working. He stacked the yard with lumber and parked five boxcars on our railroad siding. He did all this and more because "illusions print money."

Dad planned to beat FDR at his own game by applying for a federally backed, interest free loan. He called it his share of the New Deal. In the application, he inflated his production and employee numbers because that was how the game was played. With federal money, Dad intended to pay off his expansion costs, dredge the pond, put in a new water pump, and finally get out from under Wulf Gehring. Problem was he had to go through Ennis Neet's bank to get the money.

A week after Dad submitted the loan papers, Wulf Gehring, Jackie Sagers, and Neet made a special trip up the canyon to see him. Sagers climbed out of the Cadillac and offered a warm greeting. "Happy days are here again."

"It'll be a happy day when I receive *my* first welfare check," Dad said.

"There will be no check for you, Merle," Sagers said, "unless you write it to yourself. You are not a member of the *favored proletariat*."

"Neet tells us you've put in for a federal loan," Wulf said, getting to the point of their visit.

Dad stared at the banker, but the bloodless face revealed nothing. "That's right," he said.

"It's a smart move," Wulf continued. "Easy money with good rates, why not go for it?" Wulf raised a casual thumb toward Neet. "Judging from the figures you put on the application, you've been cutting more lumber a month than the rest of us put together."

"I thought banking was private matter," Dad said.

Sagers laughed. "With all your men in a fever to go hunting, you couldn't cut that much lumber in three months." He slyly winked at Dad. "I have to hand it to you, brother, the photos were sheer genius. You ever consider a career in Hollywood?"

Dad needed ten thousand dollars. Without it, he'd be bankrupt within weeks. "Everything on the application is accurate," he began to argue.

Wulf put a hand up. "Nobody here holds it against you. I'm sure your loan will be passed on to the feds. You'll get your money, and the government takes the risk. Isn't that right, Ennis?"

"Mr. Fraser's loan hasn't been approved," Neet said stonily. "There are still details to resolve."

"I forgot about the details," Wulf said.

Dad started to argue, but Wulf stopped him. "We're all friends here," he said. "You're talking to the loan committee." He looked thoughtfully at Neet. "We see no reason not to pass your loan along. Your photos, production numbers, and assets are bound to snow the bureaucrats in San Francisco. The feds will buy your loan, and nobody will be the wiser."

Wulf slipped a rolled photograph from his briefcase and opened it. It showed the mill with stacks of lumber swamping the dock alongside twenty-five hardworking men. "Do you know what the Democrats are buying with these loans?" Wulf said, studying the photo.

Dad shook his head.

"FDR and the Democrats will look at this photo and count heads. With your loan, the NRA will buy them twenty-five grateful votes." Wulf rolled the photo and placed it inside his briefcase. "I'll be sure to get this back to you once the committee has finished processing your loan. It is a beauty."

Dad smiled in spite of himself.

"Let me ask you this," Wulf said. "As a businessman, what's your take on the new quotas and this labor union business?"

"My men can't feed their families on a thirty hour work week, and with the production quotas, I can't cut enough lumber to cover the higher labor costs. It makes no sense."

"FDR has built an army of technocrats, trained to browbeat us into complying with his quotas," Wulf said, "but the actual law provides *no penalty* for breaking it. Technically, we can do anything we want. The worst the feds can do is not like us."

"What does this have to do with me?"

"We'd like you to stand with us against the unions. By mandating a thirty-hour workweek, the union figures we'll hire more men rather than pay overtime. We don't see it that way."

"If they come to me with those demands, I'll lay them off," Dad said. "With thirteen million men out of work, there are plenty of pebbles to choose from."

"It won't be that easy," Wulf said. "Last summer, the Sawmill Workers Union struck Seattle and Portland and shut down half the mills in the Northwest."

"Now, they're in a froth because we pay thirty cents below the Portland wage," Sagers said. "They're threatening to strike the Cottage Grove mills."

"That doesn't affect me," Dad said. "But why this change all of a sudden? I thought union radicals were a thing of the past."

"They were until FDR stirred them up," Wulf said.

"The three of us, and a few others, have agreed to work together," Sagers said. "We've sworn to close all our mills, the minute one of us receives a union demand. There won't be an hour of work for any of the men until the unions leave."

"Dolomite Lumber, too?" Dad said. "Mackenzie isn't much of a team player."

"Sid has had problems in the past understanding the needs of the group," Wulf said, "but he's on board with this."

"When the union backs down and the agitators leave," Sagers said, "we'll increase the minimum wage. The men will see that they can get what they want without any union."

"What's to keep someone from cheating?" Dad asked. He had learned that there was no honor among these thieves.

"A number of things, including long term self-interest," Wulf said.

"We intend to go ahead with this, regardless of what you do," Sagers said, "but we'd like to have you on board."

"I'll consider it," Merle said.

"And while you do," Wulf responded, "the loan committee will consider your application."

32

Miss Cherry had always blushed easily. In the winter, after recess, her cheeks glowed red with the cold, but this was summer. She rarely chatted with Françoise, and when she did speak, it was only in response to the older woman's questions.

Hot as the days were, Guillaume was having a terrible time with his lumbago. Because of it, he found more for me to do. One afternoon, as I watched them silently go about their work, Françoise at her tatting, Guillaume whittling a Santa, and Miss Cherry painting another Christmas face, the old man waved me over.

"Teddy," he said, *"help-moi chercher right more wood a` travailler."* He wanted a certain shape of driftwood to carve, but it was nearly impossible for him to dig through the woodshed pile. He still used the old language, he said, to remind him of home and to let everyone else know who he really was.

"*J'viens* right back," I said, teasing him.

On my way to the shed, I passed the huge double-bladed axe he kept near his chair. Guillaume no longer cut trees with it, but he still used it to split wood and hadn't forgotten how to swing it. He sharpened and oiled the twin blades each week, and like the old language he still spoke, he kept the axe at his side as a reminder of *what* he had been. "*Le bâtard* keeps getting heavier," he'd say whenever he picked it up.

I stopped to heft the big axe. I had to use two hands to lift it.

Guillaume let me struggle for a minute, and then he helped me raise it above my head.

"That axe belongs to the best damn logger in the north country," he said. "I hope you know that?"

"*Oui*," I said, pretending to take a swing.

Without looking up from her work, Françoise clucked, "Don't swear in front of the boy."

"*Merde*," he responded, smiling. He took the axe from me and set it in its place. "When I was a man, I could take down a tree in minutes."

"You are still a man," Françoise said. It was her turn to smile. "Who knows better?"

They were both smiling at each other.

Guillaume took the gnarled piece of driftwood I'd found. He turned it in his hands.

"This will make a fine Kris Kringle. Or maybe St. Nicholas."

"Aren't they the same?"

"*Ah non*. St. Nicholas is a good Catholic bishop and French. For him, judging the deeds of children is serious business. That is why my St. Nicholas never smiles. Since his work is such serious *travail*," he tapped a finger as gnarled as driftwood against his forehead, "my St. Nicholas must think and see clearly. I give him a lantern to carry, so he can better see."

Thinking of old Diogenes in his barrel, I said. "Is your St. Nicholas searching for an honest man, too?"

Guillaume scratched an ear with the misshapen finger. "St. Nicholas looks for good men and good children—honest and good—are they so different? St. Nicholas is a bishop, so he must always wear red." He reached for a bearded figure painted dark green. This one carried a small Christmas tree, but no lantern. "This Santa," Guillaume said, "has no business in red. He is Protestant and called *Christ Kindle*, little Christ child, but look at him. Does he look like the Christ Child? *Ah, non! Les Protestants et les Allemands, ce sont fous, tous les deux.* Protestants and Germans, both are crazy!"

I heard a clatter. Something hit the floor and broke. Miss Cherry gasped.

"It slipped from my hands!" she said, reaching down for Father Christmas. An arm had broken off, and black streaked his eye. She cradled the injured figure in the hollow of her lap and hid her face behind her hands. "What is wrong with me?"

"*Worry pas sur la*," Guillaume said, looking embarrassed. "*Je le fixe.*"

Reaching across her needlework, Françoise took Miss Cherry's hand. I didn't know what to do.

"You go home now, Teddy," Guillaume commanded.

Which was unfair since I hadn't done anything wrong.

Pecky was waiting for me when I walked onto the porch. He yipped a greeting and started wagging.

"Shush, Pecky!" I didn't feel like playing with him.

He barked louder, smiling and nosing my pocket.

"I don't have anything for you." I pulled out my pockets to prove it.

Pecky had gotten into the habit of following me whenever Ray couldn't take him to work. He especially liked visiting Guillaume who always had a treat.

"This little Pecky, he is the first dog I ever liked," Guillaume said. "He should come live *chenou*—with us."

Pecky felt the same way about Guillaume, but not enough to trade away Ray. Pecky had become a one-man dog, but if anything ever happened to Ray, Guillaume would be next in line for his affection...certainly not me.

Pecky and I took the tracks home. We were at the edge of the mill clearing when Pecky lifted his ears. I stopped and listened, too. In the distance, I heard the rumble of Ray's log truck as he downshifted and turned onto our property. Pecky was off, head down with his legs stretched out, racing toward the truck turnaround by the pond. I did my best to chase after him.

Ray's good arm was dangling outside the cab window, his hand slapping the steel door in time to some song he was singing.

Pecky lifted his head and slowed to a trot, intently watching the loaded truck as it ground toward him along the haul road. He must have heard Ray singing because he started wagging and began trotting faster straight toward the oncoming truck.

Ray didn't stop or even try to turn. Maybe he didn't see Pecky, or maybe he couldn't spin the wheel fast enough with only one good arm. Ray never said. He hit brakes as soon as it happened, so he must have known something, but that was after Pecky had been run over by the rear wheels of the trailer.

Ray was slow to get out. He sat unmoving with his head lowered against the steering wheel. When he did climb down from the cab, he stood motionless beside the idling truck, his arms loose at his sides. Pecky's stomach was open and bleeding and his back didn't look right. His blue tongue lay in the dirt with wood chips stuck all over it.

Ray bent down and brushed the dirt off Pecky's tongue. He stroked the small white head. "I'm sorry, little dog." Pecky didn't even try to wag. "I am so sorry." Ray picked Pecky off the haul road and held him in the crook of his elbows. He carried Pecky to the tool shed behind the mill where he picked up a shovel. Ray and his dog disappeared into the woods, with the truck still idling in the road.

"Trucks are tough on dogs," Dad said, explaining the situation to me.

But there was more to it than that, something bigger had occurred. Like Miss Cherry's ball of yarn, our lives began to unravel the day Ray buried Pecky in the woods.

33

"Supper's almost ready," Mother said.

In Yamhill County, autumn worms into the bruised end of the year. It quietly bores through the spent earth, slipping unseen among roots and bulbs. No quick frost in Yamhill County, no burst of color to mark its arrival.

"Your uncle didn't show for work this morning." Dad said, folding his paper. "Have you seen him?"

"I was at school."

Evergreens stand tall above the cooling earth, seemingly unaware of changes unfolding at their feet. Ferns die back with brown at their edges, but no reds or yellows. In the valley, the orchards drop their leaves—filberts and hazelnuts—but do so without pretense. Pods shrivel and dry around their kernels, littering the ground and filling the gutters.

"Time we had him here for supper," Mother said. "It's been too long."

"It has barely been a week."

"Your Uncle Normal might not be feeling well, Teddy. Run over and tell him supper's ready."

"Free food—it's the one thing that might get Normal moving," Dad said.

I jumped down the steps, happy to have something to do. When I reached Uncle Normal's shed behind the slab heap, the door was closed.

"Uncle Normal," I called through the wall, but no sound returned, not even his snoring. I tried again, pushing against the door, but it wouldn't open. I pushed a second time, harder, and then I ran to his window and stretched up on my toes to look. The door was blocked. One end of a board was wedged beneath the door handle and the other end caught a crack in the floor.

"You can't keep a good man down," Dad liked to say. "A good man keeps at it until he rises to the top and wins. And then there are those who choose to quit."

Or maybe, after they lose so many times, they understand that they were never meant to win.

"Your Uncle Normal has been sad for a long time," Mother once said. "He lost his wife and family."

I squinted and looked deeper into the room. His bed was made, but the picture he kept of his wife and children had been turned down on the small table beside his pillow. I opened the window and crawled through. As always, the bottles were hidden away, except for the one beside his bed.

In a lonely room, behind a locked door, the headless horseman had finally caught up with my uncle. Uncle Normal's arms were dangling loose at his sides, and his hands were open, no longer grasping for things he'd never hold. Where his weight and the knotted rope joined it, the rafter above me creaked. Work boots with broken and knotted laces drifted above the floor boards. Uncle Normal's head was ripe and round like a harvest pumpkin, but not orange. It was purple with red eyes that bulged and stared past me. With his rope tight around my uncle's neck, the horseman had claimed the trophy he'd chased for so long. I reached out and lightly touched his boot. The rafter above us creaked, and I felt my uncle swing away.

On the table beside his carefully made bed, he had left a short note and had weighted it down with an empty bottle—two monuments that did not fairly represent his life. The only thing Uncle Normal asked from us was that we bury him at Newberg, in Yamhill County, so he could be near his children.

"I have not been a good father to them," he had written, "and they might not want to see me even if I am close by, but I hope to watch them now, just the same."

The men removed the rope from Uncle Normal and laid him on top of his bed. Nobody saw any sense in hauling his body to the undertaker in Cottage Grove. Mr. Mulberger built a coffin without needing to take a measurement since he had known Uncle Normal in life. He used our own lumber, which Dad said would be best.

"Since Normal helped cut it, he ought to feel at home resting in it," Dad said. "No sense buying what we already have."

Uncle Normal didn't have a suit to be buried in, but he had two sets of work clothes that Mother always had washed for him. Even though one set of clothes lay clean in the drawer beside his bed, she took them away and rewashed them. And then she ironed them.

"I can do that much for my brother."

They put Uncle Normal in Mr. Mulberger's coffin and left him in the small room behind the slab pile because he was most at home there.

Since it had been his wish, Mother insisted on burying him in Yamhill County. She knew the place. "We'll take him to a little cemetery with a black iron fence around it," she said.

Dad couldn't get away to attend the funeral, so we planned to take the train. The afternoon before Mother and I were set to leave, Boone came by the house and told us that he and Wattie would drive us to the cemetery. "You'll need help with the coffin," Boone said. He had arranged to borrow Gust Backer's flatbed truck.

When Gust's old Packard rumbled up to our house the next morning, Uncle Normal's coffin was already in back. Boone was at the wheel with Wattie on the seat beside him.

"If it's too cramped in front," Mother said, "Teddy can ride in back."

I looked at the coffin and hesitated.

"It's way too cold for that," Boone said. "We'll all be fine in front." Boone drove, of course. I got the middle by the gear shift with Mother next to me. Wattie took the other window.

After we had been on the road for a few minutes, Mother spoke so softly that I could barely hear her over the engine noise. "You didn't have to do this. We could have taken the train."

"Normal was our friend, too," Boone said.

"For sure, he deserved a better send off than what 'Slow and Easy' could do for him," Wattie said.

Boone had the headlights on, even though it wasn't dark, "out of respect for the dead."

"Gust wanted us to tell you," Boone said in a voice that also was hard to hear "that he's sorry for your loss."

"Burying a brother just might be harder than burying a parent," Wattie said.

Mother nodded.

After a mile or two, Mother said, "Please tell Gust thank you."

It was early afternoon when we reached the cemetery gate. The sky was blue, but the air felt raw. A fresh hole gaped open in a far corner of the cemetery. As we climbed down from the truck, a man in overalls, carrying a shovel, walked up. He pointed to the hole and told Boone where to back the truck. With the man's help, Boone and Wattie slipped ropes around the coffin and lowered Uncle Normal into the ground.

Two old gray people were standing near the black fence watching us. I didn't know them, but Mother did. She walked over. They were grim and wordless.

"I'm sorry," Mother said, sounding as if something about this was her fault.

"With what he's done, your brother is lost forever. You should know that, Mary."

"Normal has been lost for some time," Mother said, "but he never gave up hope, not until, I don't know." She started crying, but nobody moved to put an arm around her.

"Normal is damned. We will never see him again," the other gray person said.

Mother looked away. "Where is the minister?" she said.

"We never asked him to come. It would do no good."

As the man with the shovel began his work, Mother stood at the edge of Uncle Normal's grave. Boone, Wattie, and I stood with her, saying our own goodbyes. The two gray people left without another word.

That afternoon, as the shovel completed its work, as the black earth covered Uncle Normal, the clear sky above us also passed away. Autumn arrives like that in Yamhill County, the blue ebbs away and the gray flows in nearly unnoticed.

"Normal," Wattie's voice rose beside me, "as you pass to the other side, we are here to see you off. We don't intend for you to walk through an empty room on your way out."

At the sound of Wattie's voice, Mother sighed.

"Go now and find your reward." Wattie's head was bowed down and so was Mother's. "You may have to look hard for it. We pray to God the road you've chosen takes you there, but before you go, we hope to give you something to hold on to— that being the knowledge that God loves all us sinners." Wattie took something from his pocket. He covered it with his two hands. "Since it's time to lay you down, I thought you might want some music to rest your head on. Praise be to God. Amen."

"Amen," Mother added.

Wattie put the harp to his lips and began to play with a hurt we all could hear. Like no way I'd heard him play before— with a sound I can't forget and don't ever expect to hear again. As if unsure of their direction, the notes wavered when they left Wattie's hands, but I like to think they found Uncle Normal's soul. I knew the melody; I had heard it before, but never so slow and never so sad. When Mother sang it at home, it had been a happy tune.

In Yamhill County, autumn slides in thin like a poor man's soup. Over days and weeks, it simmers, and as it does, clouds darken and thicken. When the winter rains start, they do so furtively, and then they don't stop. As Wattie played his music, the cold mist of winter brushed across my cheek.

The harp fell away from Wattie's mouth, but he hadn't finished saying his goodbye. He pointed to heaven—to Uncle Normal—I hoped. At first humming, then singing, he called out a single question: "What kind of shoes you goin' to wear?"

Looking to the sky for an answer and shaking his head when he didn't get one, Wattie pressed the silver harp against his lips and played the same aching refrain. Again, he called out his question: "I said, what kind of shoes you goin' to wear?"

This time, Wattie answered for Uncle Normal with words and a melody I'd heard at home, but so different now. "Golden slippers, I'm bound to wear." And he began singing.

"Golden slippers!

To outshine the glittering sun,

Oh, yes, yes, yes my Lord,

I'm going to join the Heavenly choir.

Yes, yes, yes my Lord,

Soldier of the cross."

Wattie played through his chorus. Once again, he called to Uncle Normal: "What kind of dress you goin' to wear?"

"A long white robe I'm bound to wear."

Mother began singing, too, her strong voice mixing with Wattie's. As Wattie played the final chorus, his melody mixed with Mother's tears so that the one became the other.

"What kind of crown you goin' to wear?

A starry crown I'm bound to wear.

A starry crown!

To outshine the glittering sun."

Among the chipped and leaning headstones, autumn's leaves covered the mounded earth and marble slabs. I held a single leaf up toward the graying light and then another. The veins that branched and ran from stem to tip were dry. At my feet, the leaves and the pods, the small kernels inside, littered the ground and waited for winter's rain to stir them through the mud.

34

"Aren't these sweet?"

Wattie and I were sitting together at the Bucket of Blood, not long after Uncle Normal died. The place was empty except for us.

"What?" I asked.

He pointed to a white vase on the table between us. "Why these pretty little flowers, of course. My mama would smile at them, broad from her heart, and say, 'Aren't...these...sweet?'" Wattie tasted each of his mama's words before moving on to the next. "I have never seen a woman since so crazy about violets. She couldn't keep from touching their petals. They were love magnets to her fingers. She'd turn a blossom over like so to show me and say, 'Look at this cute little face.'"

I was grateful that Wattie's gaze was fixed on the pink and purple flowers and not on my weepy eyes and runny nose.

"Mama liked pansies, too, but an African violet was as precious as baby Jesus himself. She dedicated an entire window to them. I asked her one day where they grew best."

"'In the east, for certain, always in a window facing east. If they so much as peek at the afternoon sun, they shrivel up and die.' The thought alone caused her to wring her hands. 'I don't mean to speak for the Good Lord,' she said, 'but as sure as He is good, He would find that troubling.'"

Wattie laughed and pressed his sore eyes with his thumbs, which he was apt to do. "That wasn't at all what I'd meant when I asked," he said," so I tried again. 'Where in *Africa* do these flowers grow best? African violets must come from some place in Africa.'

"'Lordy,' Mama said, considering the question like I'd taken it from the Bible. While she went about her considering, she reached and turned a plant so that it faced the light just so, and then did the same with a second plant. When she had no more plants to arrange, she said, 'They must be from the east side of Africa. That way they'll always get the morning sun.'"

How his mama's purple flower got to Missouri all the way from Africa, Wattie never did figure out, and what the circumstances of their journey might have been, he could only guess.

"We all lose something," Wattie said finally. "These violets lose their tiny petals, which might not seem like much to us. You lost your Uncle Normal, and that is a real shame."

I nodded because it *was* a shame.

"Mr. Ray lost his arm to a trim saw, and your daddy near lost his sawmill to that big fire." Wattie stopped as if not wanting to speak the next thought that had come up inside him.

I tried to guess. "And you lost your mama?"

Wattie caught a blossom and gently turned its face toward me. "No," he said. "My mama is right here. But I wasn't so lucky as you. I had to share my mama with eleven brothers and sisters. You have your mama and daddy all to yourself. That's what I call lucky."

Or ducky, I thought. That's how life was for Wattie...always ducky.

"Yes, sir, young Teddy. We all lose things. Your Uncle Normal lost plenty himself before he left us."

"He did?" Uncle Normal had rarely talked about himself.

"He kept on losing until it added up to a burden more powerful than he could bear. After that, I believe he lost faith." Wattie considered his words while I considered my shoes. "At some point, he decided he had nothing left to live for and nothing left to lose."

I pictured Uncle Normal's small room in the lean-to shed he had built, the narrow cot and the bedside table with two drawers. I thought about me. All that amounted to something.

"Your uncle lost his little brother in the war. Did you know that?"

"He told me," I said

"After that, he lost his wife, his family, and finally his self-respect."

I started to cry. "I should have tried to make him happier."

Wattie reached into his back pocket and offered a folded handkerchief. "You had nothing to do with this, young Teddy. Once your uncle started losing faith in his self, the rest of him got lost at the bottom of a bottle." Wattie shook his head sadly. "I suppose you know he was a drinker?"

"No," I said. I knew about the empty bottles he kept hidden behind his bed, but I didn't know he was a drinker. "Did that matter so much?"

"Some will say it was his ruination, but the drink wasn't the cause. When he lost faith, the rest of him followed along."

"What is faith?"

"That, young Teddy, is a question for the ages." He considered it. "Mighty hard to say." He thought some more. "You might could find it in a dictionary. But the truth is, you don't find faith in a big book...or in a bottle neither." As we sat side-by-side, Wattie's warmth reached out to me. "Not even the Encyclopedia Britannica has got the answer to that one."

My head felt too small for what he was pouring in. Wattie rested a hand on my knee, the same gentle touch he had used with his mama's violet. His voice so quiet, it made me listen.

"What I am trying to say is not for you to understand today. It is for those times when you find yourself alone, and it is way too dark to see." He spread open his palm like he had something to show, but the hand was empty.

Seeing only the chocolate lines that etched the breadth of his skin, I said, "What?"

"Faith has to find you. You can't go looking for it. Faith is not big, and I don't believe it is ever as strong as some would say. Faith can always be injured."

Side by side, we stared into his open hand.

"Do you know your Bible?" he asked.

"I know the twenty-third Psalm and the Lord's Prayer," I said. Grandma Lulu had drilled me on their contents every night before supper so I'd be in a proper frame of mind when she said grace.

"In Psalms, the Bible tells us to trust in the Lord and be like Mount Zion, which cannot be moved and abides forever." Wattie scratched his head. "That's what the Bible says, so it must be true." He glanced up and added, as if it were an apology, "From what I've seen in *this* world, faith ain't a rock in the ocean. It is more like that ship your daddy talks about."

"The Santa Maria?"

"The Santa Maria," Wattie echoed. "A right good name for a vessel built of faith." Wattie seemed to be resting easier in his thoughts, back to smiling. "Old Mr. Columbus, he sailed through his dark waters with no real compass, just a magical rock that floated on water."

"He did?"

"Faith carries you from what you do know, to what you hope to know. If it's built strong enough, you make it through. If the belief ain't real, and you got no port to look toward, you sail in circles until you drift off the face of the earth."

"Is that what Dad meant when he said Uncle Normal was on a Christopher Columbus expedition?"

"I can't rightly say what your daddy had in his mind, but I truly believe your good uncle is safe today, sailing in the arms of the Lord. He was too good a man not to be cared for."

"Even though he sinned and took his own life?"

"Even so."

Wattie sounded so strong in what he was saying, I almost believed him. I now wonder who he was really trying to convince, him or me. It didn't change the fact that Uncle Normal was gone.

35

"Teddy," I heard her call through the bedroom door. "I need you."

It was almost dark. I hadn't seen her in more than a day. I had listened for her music, but hadn't heard it, and she hadn't come to the kitchen. She needed time alone to think about her dead brother. That was how Dad explained it.

I left the front window and knocked on her door.

"Come in."

She was sitting at her dressing table, staring into the mirror. At the corner of the table, a small candle flickered in a glass cup. She patted the seat cushion and, without looking at me, inched forward. "Brush my hair, Teddy." She was holding a small white jar with rouge coloring.

I didn't want to do that anymore. I stood in the doorway. I didn't like being in her room.

The small jar slammed against the table. "Don't make me ask again!"

I climbed onto the chair behind her, my legs astraddle her naked hips, my spine pressed against the hard wooden back of the chair. She smelled of alcohol and an odor I thought I had forgotten—Grandma Lulu. I cringed. A bottle of gin sat in the middle of the table, its silhouette framed by the mirror, its neck and shoulders streaked with red. A second bottle lay empty at her feet.

She stared at me through the mirror. "I have something very special for you, but you have to work for it."

I took her hair in my hands. There was no braid. The strands were gnarled, and the color was dark, not because the hair was wet, but because the oils and skin from her unwashed scalp had altered it. I picked up the brush and began.

"You are...my little best man."

Powders and color were spilled and clotted on the table's surface, and she was painted everywhere. Her lips were bright red like always, but so were her cheeks and the line of her jaw. The pink circles that danced at the front of her breasts were ringed in red.

She pushed a finger inside the rouge jar and then tried to find her cheek with it, but missed and smeared red inside her ear. "Your father says you can't paint rough-cut lumber," she said. "He taught me that lesson when I asked him to paint this shack. 'Rough-cut lumber,' he so clearly explained, 'soaks up paint like a sponge without improving the appearance. It's not worth it.' Bet you didn't know that about paint and lumber."

I shook my head.

"That's how he treats me. Like old...rotten...lumber. You wouldn't do that, would you, Teddy?"

She dabbed at the rouge again, but didn't take it to her cheek. Instead, she rubbed it over her breast. She caked red onto a nipple and left it there for me to see.

"Rub it in if you want," she said. "That's what men do."

I gripped the brush more firmly and lowered my eyes.

"Don't you like to paint, Teddy?"

"No."

"Do you remember the first time we climbed the steps to this house? It was nothing more than boards and batten without a future, but I tried to make it a home. I did try. I just couldn't mold my heart to fit a home meant to be torn down the day it was built. I planted marigold seeds around that stump in back when I wanted roses, red blooms that return year after year. I wanted to cover our little home with roses...and clean white paint...and be like other people...people with paint and red roses." She shifted her breasts just enough for me to notice. "Do you like these roses, Teddy?"

"Will you wear the gold hoops today?" I wanted us to go back to the way things used to be.

She smiled at the thought and reached for the earring box. She leaned toward the mirror and tilted her head one way and then the other as she slipped the hoops through her lobes. "Your wonderful father likes to call himself a lumberman," she said. "He thinks he's virile, chasing his virgin timber, but he's no different than the other woodsmen-in-rut. They're all eunuchs. They strip the forests and plant no seed."

She straightened her back and pressed it against me. She pushed her hips into my lap. "Put the brush down."

I did as she said and let my hands fall to her waist.

"I so wanted to be a mother," she said, picking up my hands and kissing them. "But I killed the one honest chance I'll ever have." She cupped her hands around mine and placed my palms against her red, sticky breasts. "This is what men like to do. Don't you like it?"

Caught between her spine and the back of the chair, I couldn't move.

"You are not my son, Teddy. Didn't you know that?" She released my hands, but I held on to her. Love and longing overwhelmed me, with neither surrendering to the other. "I will never have a son." I closed my eyes and pushed my face into the nape of her neck.

She picked up the half empty bottle and swallowed deeply, emptying it. "I have a little story I saved for only you. That's your surprise. It isn't a bedtime story, and I won't tell it again. But it is the truth."

My hand slipped from her breast. She took it up, kissed it, and replaced it over her nipple. Her heart was beating faster than mine. "You have been the best little boy. Did I ever tell you that?"

"Yes."

"I have two dead brothers. There is nothing I could have done to change that. But why did I throw away the babies I might have had?" She pressed her palm against the mirror. "This is where they live. I see them all, but I never get to hold them. If I had been able to have at least one baby, I might have forgotten the one I let them take, but I got no second chance. When I agreed to lie down that one time and suffer 'a small insult,' I threw away a life and buried a family."

I searched the mirror for her face. In the dark, she wasn't there. I took up the brush for what would be the last time.

"I like it when you press the bristles against my scalp," she said. I moved the brush up. "You are such a good boy."

I couldn't speak, and I couldn't make the brush travel through the tangle of her hair.

"As punishment, God gave me a bastard for a husband, and then added a bastard son. But it's not your fault. You came to us without parents, and you'll leave with none." She blew out the candle and stood. "I can't do this anymore."

I followed her shadow across the room and watched her open the closet door. She pulled out her robe. "I haven't finished brushing your hair."

"Go play now," she said, slipping on the robe. "We're finished here."

Mother changed after that evening. I never again saw her naked. When Dad was out, she went through his business files and copied every document, deed, account number, address, and invoice she could find, and she used his fountain pen to do it.

36

I'm the first to admit that I don't know how to treat women. They all want something in return for love, and it's never the same with any of them. If there really is a difference between a mother and a whore, I haven't seen it yet. A straightforward business transaction as the foundation for a relationship seems to work best. It's the easiest to consummate, and it does fill the gaps.

Then again, Rita might be different. I said she was "Hot! Hot." And she is, but that by itself doesn't capture who she is. Rita is no beauty, I'll confess that—I mean, she has scars on her face from acne— but she is a good person. She surprises me with small gifts and holds my hand in the movies. She makes room for me and for her grandchildren, and she doesn't want anything from me other than to enjoy my company. But how do I know if that's true or not?

When Rita first asked me to take her dancing, I agreed because I didn't think it was asking too much. We went to the Elks Club with her friends and danced to a live band in the basement. I had forgotten what a good dancer I am! Last Saturday, we drove to the coast and stayed overnight at the Adobe Resort in Yachats. It's a hilly, eighty-five mile drive to get there, but it was worth it. We stayed in a suite with an electric fireplace, and we soaked in the Jacuzzi together. I didn't want to leave after brunch, but she had to get back for her lunch-room job. I wish she would make more time for me, but she likes serving kids their lunch, and she has all her grandchildren to see.

37

Saturday afternoon, two weeks after we buried Uncle Normal, I was at the Bucket of Blood watching Wattie and Twinkle get ready for the evening dance. Wattie had his harp out, wanting to try a new key. He'd play a note, then a bar, and Twinkle would do her best to match it on the accordion. When she got it right, they'd start into the song, trying to make it come together.

"That ain't it, Twinkle," Wattie said, stopping partway through when she should have played a flat or a sharp or something in between. But Wattie didn't get mad. He just laughed and waved his hands and made them start over.

I didn't laugh. I didn't have the heart to do anything more than watch other people and wonder why Uncle Normal chose to leave the way he did, especially without telling me good-bye. I thought he had been my friend, and the more I thought and wondered, the more uncertain I became of just about everything.

"You look like a boy with a thirst," Boone said, setting a Coca-Cola on the table in front of me. That was not something he did. He kept the bottles in the icebox behind the bar next to his trench-slayer shotgun, but they were strictly for customers.

I sipped from the icy bottle while Wattie and Twinkle started and stopped. After a dozen attempts, Wattie said it was a time for a break. He picked out a Coca-Cola for himself and joined me.

"I sure enough do like these," he said, slipping the opener over the metal cap. He took a long swallow and gasped. "Yes, sir, I do."

Boone sat down, too, except he had a beer in his hand. Across the room, Twinkle started putting her things away. She couldn't stay.

"I remember the day I tasted my first Coca-Cola," Wattie said. "It was at the World Fair in the middle of White City." He grinned. "That's what people called the Chicago fairgrounds. Every building was painted white and built with columns like Rome itself." He paused. "You ever get to the World Fair, Boone?"

"Never did."

"Seemed to me like the whole world was there. From the top of Mr. Ferris' big wheel, you could see the lake, the whole city of Chicago and most of the state, I believe." He smiled, this time to himself. "Chicago was where I learned to play my music."

"Is that where you were born?" I said. "Chicago?"

"Mercy, no, but I lived there a good long time. You might could say I was *reborn* in Chicago, but not in a Christian way. I never needed help in that department because Mama saw to my soul even before I could crawl. Just the same, I was reborn in that big happening city." He sat quiet for a moment, staring at the small harp, resting in his lap.

"Wattie—" I started to say, but he headed me off.

He raised the red and silver instrument more out of habit, it seemed, than desire. "I don't dwell much on my time before Chicago." His knuckles were about to press the instrument against his mouth, but they stopped. His tongue flickered across his lips to wet them. "I'm a little dry." He took a deep breath and sighed into his closed hands. A blue chord rumbled out like smoke from the bowl of an old man's pipe. The hazy sound coiled around him. More chords were pushed out, drawn back, and begrudgingly freed, but they didn't warm the room. They banged against one another. These notes had no business playing in Wattie's music. Wattie's chest began to shake.

"That is no way for a man to leave this world, and no boy should ever have to see it." He looked at me. "They shouldn't have done it."

Reflected in his eyes, behind the pain, I saw Uncle Normal at the end of the frayed rope he'd used to drag himself to another place. I was confused. Uncle Normal's death had been done at the direction of his own hand. I didn't know who Wattie was talking about. "They...who shouldn't have?" I asked.

"I was born in Alabama," Wattie said quietly, "just off the Alabama and Georgia line." His hands lay in his lap, loosely folded around the empty instrument. "Daddy had heard life was better up North, so we moved in that direction, all the way to Missouri. Daddy sharecropped—believing he'd be able to save up for his own place. But what he got was babies. I was sixth in a passel of twelve, but I never got to see the others grow big. I left home way too young."

"Why would you do that?" I said.

"I was just fourteen years old, but Mama said, 'You are almost a man. You'll be fine on your own.' When she said it, I grabbed on to her, but she pushed me away like she was done with me. Soon as she'd done it, she pulled me back and held on like it would have to do until forever, the rise and fall of her big bosom saying goodbye over and over. 'Lord, there can be nothing right in taking these good boys for no reason.' I had never before heard her rail at the Lord like that. When she pushed me away a second time, I knew there would never be no third."

The door clicked shut behind Twinkle as she stepped out, but none of us looked up.

"Mama was all business after that," Wattie said, "talking and making plans like she was sending me off to visit Aunt Jenny in the next county. 'Promise you'll send a card. Don't feel you have to put much on it, just a word. That way, I'll know where to direct my prayers. I'll know right where God is watching over you.'"

"If leaving made you so sad, why did you go away?"

"Because I didn't have one thing to say about it," he said, sliding the heel of his hand across his cheek.

"Weren't you afraid?"

"I still am afraid." He turned his wet eyes away and shook his head, embarrassed. "Now, you tell me? Why am I talking about this now, and why to the two of you?"

I didn't want to hear anymore. It wasn't right for Wattie to be sad. Things were supposed to be ducky with him.

"I suspect the Lord is involved, so it must be time. Too much has been locked up for too long, like some spook that got buried in the wrong grave, now scrabbling to get out. Scratchin' at me until I'm bleeding."

Wattie set his harp on the table and folded his hands alongside it. "I was fourteen, like I said. I had no choice in the matter, and neither did Jessie. Me and Jessie were big enough to help in the fields, so there wasn't any school for us. When we weren't doing odd chores or working with Daddy in the fields, we ran the countryside, hunting squirrel, rabbit, and possum for the meat and the skins. The skins, we'd bundle together and hike them to town, to the back side of the Excelsior Springs general store. We'd knock on the door, only once, find some shade, and wait until Mr. Stanley had time for us. He'd buy our best skins for a few pennies, and as a special favor, he'd take the poor quality skins off our hands for nothing, so we could be done with them. We knew what he was doing, but we didn't mind. It was the easiest money we ever earned. Once he brought out the big amber jar he kept on the store counter next to the cash register and gave us each a piece of penny candy."

Boone leaned back in his chair like he was ready to listen for some time. I so wanted to leave, but I couldn't.

"When we weren't hunting," Wattie said, "we fished for big catfish. Jessie taught me to hand fish. Once you get the hang of it, you don't need nothin but ten willing fingers. Ever see the likes of that, Teddy?"

"I've hand fished on several occasions," Boone said, "with a stick of dynamite tied to a rock. Ba-Boom! It saves a whole lot of effort."

"No sport in that," Wattie said. "You should be ashamed."

Boone didn't look ashamed.

"To catch them fish, we'd slither to the riverbank on our bellies. We'd inch one arm into the water and then follow with the other, slide one palm under the fat underbelly, and slip the other along the tail. Before long, you're stroking one happy tabby, paralyzing him with delight. Old tabby won't move a whisker, afraid you might stop pleasuring him. That's when you grab him with both fists and fling him far as you can up on the bank. He'll flop in the grass, mad enough to snap a sapling."

"When was it that you were you in Missouri?" Boone asked.

"That might take some figuring," Wattie said. "I was born in 1878, and Jessie one year before me, and I was fourteen at the time. Let me see," he said, searching inward, "so this would have happened in…" I could see him trying to stretch his brain around the numbers.

"1892," I said.

Wattie brightened. "I suppose that's right. Nobody had a car at the time, and Daddy didn't have a mule. People were still angry about Mr. Lincoln's war. It was all some of them could talk about, what with it ruining their lives and Yankees stealing their rightful property. We knew to stay far away from that talk."

"Hadn't it been a long time since that war was over?"

"Not for some. They'd look at Jessie and me like we was to blame."

"Were you?"

Wattie looked at me, surprised and then not.

"Isn't that what started it, you wanting to be free?"

"Jessie and I didn't have one thing to do with it," Wattie said flatly. "Jessie told them so over and over, but they wouldn't listen, none of them would, not to him." Wattie shut his eyes tight. "And they never heard a word from me because I said nothin." Wattie was holding onto himself. "There was no why to it. We was in the wrong place at the wrong time, and the Lord chose to look the other way.

"Them white men came up behind Jessie while he was on his belly working a catfish. I was back in the woods relieving myself. 'That fish belong to you, boy?' Startled out of his wits, Jessie sat right up. 'No, sir, it ain't mine,' he said, polite like we'd been taught. 'That must mean you're stealing because this here is private property.' 'I didn't know. I'm sorry.' 'It's way too late for sorry, boy.'

"I laid in the brush, stupid like a stunned catfish, and watched Jessie's party. That's what they had called it. Like no party I'll agree to see again." Wattie spoke as if it were a promise. "Jessie was dead a day before they finished with him, but even with him gone, that didn't stop them from slipping a hanging rope over his head, didn't stop the laughing and whooping. 'Let's see if this nigger can fly!' They hoisted him up and snubbed the rope around a tree. Jessie's feet hung loose, like Sunday's chicken. I just kept watching them two feet, praying for a sign, one little flicker, so I'd know he was still there.

"Jessie kicked and screamed plenty before they killed him. He begged them over and over to stop. From my hole in the brush, I covered my ears and prayed for him to stop, and he finally did. It was the barbed wire and the horse that killed him. They stung the horse on its rump and made it gallop from one end of the field to the other. Then they turned the horse and stung him again. The horse ran back and forth until the rocks were black with the wet of Jessie's blood and the barbs on the wire had worn away.

"The next day, you'd have thought it was Easter Sunday the way people turned out, people talking and looking, some eating, everybody pointing—like Jessie was an animal in the Chicago zoo.

"Mr. Stanley, the store owner who bought our skins and gave us candy, spoke up. 'Where do you suppose that brother of his might be?' He had brought the rope from his store. 'Those two boys are usually joined at the hip.' He and another man tied packing twine around Jessie's wrists and pulled. Jessie's arms spread out from his sides like eagle wings.

"'Wheeeeeee,' Mr. Stanley said. 'I told you this nigger could fly!'

"At dark, they took a final picture and rode away, leaving Jessie hanging. Even then, I kept watching his feet. In the flickering light of a dying bonfire, Jessie's feet finally came to life, and he danced with the shadows, but I knew that was no good. I ran to tell Mama and everybody at home what had happened to Jessie.

"Five men on horses showed up at our place just as dawn was just beginning to gray away the night. They circled their horses through our crops before settling in a line facing the porch. All of them held torches and two carried rifles.

"'Washington Buford,' one white spook called out, 'you better get out here, boy.'

"Daddy walked out to the porch. The spook told him I'd killed my own brother and that I was wanted for murder. He promised to burn us out if Daddy didn't give me up.

"Daddy was shaking like he had a fever. 'We ain't seen him or his brother for two days.'

"'Your boy is a damned murderer,' the man said. 'What he did was like Cain killing Abel.'

"'My boy could never do what you say.'

"'You calling *me* a liar?'

"'No, sir.'

"The spooks didn't burn the place, only because it wasn't ours—we were just tenant farmers—but they sure tore it up. Threw our things in the dirt, rode their horses through all that we owned, but they never did find me. Mama had hid me in the muck at the bottom of our outhouse. I fought her when she pushed me in. I held my nose with one hand and pressed the other as tight as I could over my mouth. When I climbed out, covered in foulness, what I remember seeing was the pink and purple honeysuckle vines that climbed the sides of the out-house. Mama had planted them to hide the broken boards and cover the raw smells.

"My eyes burned for days afterward. The sunlight hurt so much, I was afraid of the day, but I was even more scared of the night. I did my best to rinse the pus away with clean water. With time, the infection cleared, but it affects me still. I see good enough to play my music, but I don't see much far away."

Wattie rubbed his eyes, trying to wipe away the moisture. "After all these years, it still stings."

38

With Halloween a week away, I woke up early, shivering. I pushed a hand out from under the covers and touched my nose, the only part of me sticking out. It felt like an icicle. The bedroom was cold from ceiling to floor. Since the door to my room was closed, I was cut off from the rest of the house and the heat.

A piece of wood banged against the kitchen stove. The dry hinge on the stove's door creaked, and the door clanked shut.

Fall had come.

After breakfast, I dug through a drawer for my gloves and the wool hat with ear flaps. I found my heavy coat in the closet, and then I tromped out. The morning was crisp and clear, and so quiet. Best of all, it was Saturday. The ice on the puddles was thick enough to skip rocks across, but not strong enough to prevent my boots from breaking through. With a series of resounding hollow cracks, I shattered the ice around the house, in the ditches along the haul road, and then finished up with the ice along the edge of the mill pond. With the sun warming up and prime ice breaking time ebbing away, I moved upstream in search of fresh kill.

Across the highway, four strange men were blocking the entrance to the plank bridge that led onto Mackenzie's property. They must have arrived awfully early because they were in their places, stamping their feet and swinging their arms, long before any of us had gotten up. I didn't know them; not one of the men worked for my dad or for Dolomite. I waved when I walked by, but didn't get a thing in return.

Smoke was curling from Boone and Twinkle's chimney. I angled in that direction and thought about stopping, but decided instead to break more ice. Crunching over the familiar cinders, I followed the railroad bed toward the Bucket of Blood. A solitary squirrel ran down a tree trunk, hit the ground, and shot back up the next. The brittle note of a hidden bird was the only sound to pierce the trees.

With the change in temperature, the season had turned, but something else about the day was different. The men at the bunkhouse had been speaking of change and a new deal. They had argued about a labor union in Cottage Grove and the need for a strike. These conversations may have been the source of what I was feeling, but that wasn't all. Mom and Dad rarely spoke to each other, and Miss Cherry didn't speak at all.

Since it was so cold, I figured Guillaume would want help filling his wood box. I still visited Françoise and Guillaume, although it had little to do with them and everything to do with Miss Cherry. I didn't believe that our time together had come to an end. I refused to understand what had happened, and I knew who to blame.

No one answered my knock at the front door, but smoke was rising from the metal chimney. I walked around back and pushed the kitchen door open, expecting to find Françoise at the stove.

Miss Cherry jumped away from the stove and dropped her spoon. "You scared me!" she nearly shrieked. Her hair was straggly and hanging down, and she had on a dirty apron. She gazed at me without expression—her eyes had lost their understanding. "There is no lesson today, Teddy. You know that."

"I've been breaking ice," I said.

Blotches filled the places where she used to blush, and the gaze hardened into anger. "Why can you not understand the simple fact that I no longer teach you on Saturday?" She looked worse than tired.

I pointed to the empty box beside the stove. "I thought Guillaume might need help."

She looked at the box, and her face softened. "I'm sorry," she said. "He does need help." She turned toward the stove and two boiling pots. "When you finish, just go home."

I propped the door open and went out to get kindling. I made extra noise when I returned with my first armload. I stomped my feet and dropped the wood in the box, hoping she'd look up. Finally, I asked, "Where are Françoise and Guillaume?"

"Out."

She was cutting up black cohosh. I knew the root well because Françoise boiled it down for Guillaume's arthritis medicine. I didn't know the herb in the other pot. I hadn't seen it in the kitchen before.

"Are you making medicine for Guillaume?"

For the second time that morning, she looked startled. "No," she said. "I mean, yes." The dress she was wearing was wrinkled and loose fitting, as if she had slept in it. "I would hate for him to run out of medicine," she said finally, "and I have time."

I returned with another armload. "Is Guillaume working today?"

She ignored my question. Her hands were busy at the cutting board, mincing the purple root and seed, cutting away greenish white flowers.

I deposited the last load and silently watched. As she sliced through the unusual plant time and again, each pass reduced it to finer and finer pieces. Sap from the stem emitted a peculiar, not altogether unpleasant, odor that filled the kitchen. It smelled sweet.

"What is that plant?" I asked.

She gathered the pieces together, placed them in the boiling water, and covered the pot. She wiped her hands on the dirty apron.

"This is Guillaume's last day in the woods before winter," she said. "Françoise is out harvesting plants. There is no telling when either of them will be home." She glanced at the wood box. Seeing it filled, she added, "I'll let them know you came by. They are sure to be pleased." She turned back to her pots, peeked under a lid, and stirred the contents. "Teddy," she said without looking up, "please go home."

I returned Guillaume's axe to its place by the stove and pushed through the back door. I stopped at the woodshed and closed the latch. Miss Cherry had never talked to me like that. She had never sent me away. She had always wanted me. I crouched behind the woodshed, unsure of what to do or where to go, but I didn't cry. Tears were of no use unless someone saw them.

When I started back, I took the little used path that veered into the forest. I didn't want to see anyone, but within minutes I met up with Françoise. She was carrying two bulging burlap bags looped over one shoulder, and she seemed delighted to see me.

"I didn't expect to see you today," she said. She knew my lessons with Miss Cherry had ended.

"I filled your wood box," I said, not wanting her to think I'd had come over by mistake.

"And I wasn't there to feed you cake," she said with an apologetic smile. "I'll make it up to you next time." She opened one of the bags and displayed its contents: leaves, flowers, roots, and mushrooms of varying colors and sizes. "What a fall harvest, I've had! I'll be home hours early." She seemed so delighted with her great successes.

"That's good," I said, not interested.

She started down the trail. "Come by anytime for cake," she called back. "We all miss you."

I watched her go. Françoise didn't walk like an old lady. She moved like a young girl, and the way the bags bounced against her hip, they might have been filled with air. She was almost skipping. I considered her offer of cake. I thought about Miss Cherry. I turned and followed, but stayed far enough back not to be seen.

When I reached the house, I slipped around back, making sure to crouch below the window sill. The back door was still partly open, the way I had left it. I slid onto my stomach like I was hand fishing and peeked in. Françoise was at the stove. Her two bags were on the floor.

"What are these decoctions, Arlene?" I heard her ask. A remnant of the black cohosh root sat on the counter, but all trace of the other plant was gone.

"I'm making Guillaume more medicine," Miss Cherry said.

Françoise sniffed. "What is that smell? It's much too sweet for cohosh." She lifted the first lid and then the second. "The first is black cohosh, but the second certainly isn't." She pushed her nose into the steam. "This has to be Angelica." She looked at Miss Cherry, as if trying to understand. "Guillaume has no need for a stimulant or carminative aid."

Miss Cherry said nothing.

Françoise pondered the expressionless face. She replaced the lid and reached her hand out. She hesitated and then placed it against Miss Cherry's stomach.

Miss Cherry gasped and leaped away, as if the hand meant to harm her. She covered her face.

Françoise wrapped Miss Cherry in her arms and guided her to a chair. "I know, I know," she murmured, letting Miss Cherry sob. "I know, I know." Without further words, they sat next to each other for the longest time.

"Are you to take both syrups until the bleeding starts?" Françoise asked.

Miss Cherry nodded, her face still hidden behind her hands. "How often?"

Miss Cherry let her hands fall, but she refused look at Françoise. Her eyes were swollen. The red blotches I'd seen earlier had grown larger. "If I drink a cup of each every four hours, the bleeding should start in two days."

"It sounds as if you received good advice," Françoise said. She rose painfully from her chair. Gone was the girl I'd seen on the path. She crossed the kitchen and busied herself at the stove, lifting lids and stirring, adjusting the fire. "Both tinctures need to simmer on low heat for least twenty minutes," she said, sliding one pan off the heat. "Too hot and the medicine loses its potency." She spoke as if she were teaching Miss Cherry to bake a cake.

Miss Cherry raised her eyes enough to follow the activity, but she didn't move from the chair.

Françoise filtered the potions through a cloth and filled two stoppered bottles. She left them cooling beside the stove. The contents of one bottle was yellow, the other dark brown, nearly black. Pointing to the darker liquid, she said, "You will want a teaspoon of sugar with the Angelica." She began to wipe off the counter, and then she stopped. Struggling to find words, she said, "What has happened to you is not your sin. The sin is his."

Miss Cherry's hands writhed in her lap.

Françoise moved from the counter and sat beside her. "In this, you are not blameless, but you are also very young. The Virgin understands and forgives." Her voice hardened. "But for a grown man like Mr. Fraser, with a wife and child, there can be no shelter." She reached toward Miss Cherry's lap. With her stained claw, she settled the two young hands. "What you are about to do, Arlene, is a grave sin that you will carry for eternity. There is no way to shed such a sin."

Miss Cherry bowed her head. "I don't know what to do, Françoise. I am so guilty."

Françoise lifted Miss Cherry's chin. "You are guilty of being a woman, nothing more." Inches separated the two. "There are far worse sins than being a woman," Françoise said, smiling. "About that, I'm certain."

"I prayed to God for guidance, but he doesn't answer."

"Pray to the Virgin," Françoise said. "She will comfort any woman who opens her heart."

"Please tell me what to do."

Françoise shook her head. "I am a sinner, but the Virgin is blameless. Let her take your hand." Françoise stood and touched Miss Cherry on the shoulder. "A sin can be a blessing," she said. She picked up the two bottles and moved them to the windowsill. "Let the tinctures cool over night, and then take them only if you must. If they remain untouched after two days, I will use them to water my plants, and nothing more will be said." She hesitated, considering her words. "If I find the medicine gone," she said, troubled, "nothing ever will be said about that, either." Françoise hugged Miss Cherry before she left. "The decision is yours, but I will pray for you every day." Miss Cherry didn't follow her out. She remained seated at the kitchen table with a hand against her belly.

I had to get away. I ran for home, not by the forest path this time, but by way of the railroad tracks, letting my feet find their way. I was not seeing. I was thinking about Miss Cherry, trying to understand what Dad had done, wondering why he had to take everything for himself.

I remembered Wattie and what he had said about faith—it being a small ship looking to find a way across the ocean. If faith really could get me to wherever it was I was meant to go, how would I know when I got there? What would keep me from being like Christopher Columbus—never knowing, always wondering?

Françoise spoke of sin as if it might be something forgivable, but I knew better. I had learned about sin from Grandma Lulu: sin wasn't like fresh cut lumber. It couldn't be graded into clears or checks—some bad, some not so bad, some worse than peckerwood. Sin adds to sin. Each new blemish darkens the stain that came before it.

I had utmost faith in enduring sin. It was the one compass I could believe in.

39

I am floundering. I don't know what I have been saving myself for since Mimi preceded me, and now, there's nobody left to take care of me. Rita's cancer came back in her leg bone. In a rib and her brain, too, I think. I told her the leg is easy to get at, but she started crying anyway. I don't know about the rest. Oh God, I can't believe it. They gave her six months to live.

She'll get MRI scans and chemotherapy. On Monday, she has radiation for her brain tumor. To do it, they take a picture of her brain and then punch holes in a metal helmet for the radiation waves to enter. Medical treatment is great, fantastic even. She says she feels pretty good, right now; if that means frisky, I might have to go over and see if I can score.

40

While I was out breaking ice, Dad stationed himself at the office window and tried to figure out what the union men were up to. For several hours, there wasn't much to see. The strikers shed their jackets when the morning sun reached the bridge, and then they leaned against the bridge railing as if they were picnicking rather than picketing. One of the four made a pretense of picketing, ambling back and forth with a stenciled sign on his shoulder: *Strike Conditions Prevail by Order of the A.F. of L.* The others remained perched on the guardrail as if they didn't have a care in the world.

The men were young and fit, and looked as if they could handle themselves. Dad watched them cache baseball bats in the weeds behind the guardrail and figured they were outside agitators. At that moment, and for years to come, Dad blamed FDR and the Democrats for the fact that those men were there in the first place. He blamed FDR and his cronies for unions, price controls, poor sales, and for his inability to get a break.

But as bad as this was, Dad acknowledged that the situation could have been far worse: the lazy bastards hadn't struck *his* mill. If the truth were told, he'd have had to admit that he was taking great joy in watching the union men rake Mackenzie, Neet, and the others over the coals. Being a small fish finally had an advantage; the unions were leaving him alone. On top of that, he had received his NRA loan. For the first time in months, the world appeared almost rosy.

Dad was at his desk, not even pretending to work, when he saw the men jump to their feet and grab their signs. Dad stood up. Before he could move to the window, three cars were skidding to a stop at the bridge entrance, forming a steel semi-circle around the agitators. Two of the three cars looked official: the first contained Cottage Grove police; the second was filled with state troopers. Eight officers of assorted heights and girths spilled from the two cars. The third vehicle was anything but official; it had to be Wulf Gehring's burgundy Cadillac. The strikers didn't take one step back. They moved closer together and stood shoulder to shoulder.

Dad grabbed his hat and hurried out. When he reached the bridge, the cops were donning their own hats, tucking shirts into tight-legged riding breeches, and slipping bully clubs into leather holsters. All eight wore knee high riding boots, even though there wasn't a horse in sight. When the state bulls had their Smoky Bear hats in place, and the Cottage Grove officers, their flattop military caps, a single state trooper stepped forward. The other officers closed ranks behind him and formed their own wall. All eight clubs were out. Since Dad had no interest in getting brained, he stayed on our side of the road.

The lead officer took a moment to size things up. In a voice made to sound deeper than it probably was, he said, "Where you boys from?"

A thin slouching union man stepped toward him. "We have as much right to be here as you do," the thin man said. His hands were pushed deep inside his pants pockets and his hat was tipped forward, hiding his eyes. He looked like any other mill hand, but Dad worried that the hidden hands held a weapon. "The law gives us that right." The sloucher's voice was steady.

"Your rights don't include vagrancy and destruction of private property," the trooper said.

"No need to worry about that," the sloucher said, pulling one hand from his pocket and gesturing toward his companions. "We are peaceful men engaged in public assembly, exercising a protected right of free expression."

No mill worker speaks the King's English like that, Dad thought. Any local mill hand would be pissing himself at the sight of two police cars and eight bully clubs. The sloucher had to be an outside agitator.

Dad smelled kerosene, just a whiff. He scanned the bridge and the far bank for a can or rags, but didn't see anything obvious, just two stains on the planking where something had been spilled.

By then, three civilians had climbed out of the burgundy Cadillac, and like Dad, they were choosing to stay well back. Wulf Gehring was closest, leaning against the driver's door. Ennis Neet and Sagers were hovering near the back bumper. Wulf waved Dad over.

"What's this about?" Dad asked.

Sagers rubbed a hand across his beard. He hadn't shaved in several days. "The damn union has eight hundred men out on strike."

"The situation is about to blow up," Wulf said. "Last night, two communists approached the night watchmen at Sagers' Cottage Grove plant."

"The red assholes offered to burn my property for ten measly dollars," Sagers said. "Can you believe that shit?"

For the first time that morning, Dad felt afraid. "They didn't really do it, did they?" This was becoming a game he no longer wanted to play.

"Didn't get the chance." Sagers' voice sounded tired. "The local union sent men to guard my mill. Neet's plant, too."

"Not everybody's crazy," Wulf said. "Not yet. Most of *our* men still see the value of having jobs to come back to once the strike is over. If the mills burn, so do the jobs."

"Would they ever go that far?" Dad asked. He was contemplating the kerosene fumes and the stains on the bridge, weighing risks and benefits. If Dolomite's bridge burned, Mackenzie wouldn't really be hurt, but he would have to shut down to rebuild the bridge. That would translate into more orders for Dad and might prove to be an answer to his prayers.

"The out-of-town organizers are getting frustrated," Wulf said. "When they convinced the men to strike Sagers place, we locked them out. That wasn't what they wanted."

"What's good for the goose is good for the gander," Neet chimed in. "Nobody works until we're allowed to operate our businesses at some profit for ourselves."

"The four of us are on the same page with this," Sagers said. "Me, Ennis here, Wulf, and Mackenzie. We'd be a lot stronger if every owner in the region joined in."

"We shouldn't have to fight them on our own," Neet whined. "Everyone needs to make a sacrifice."

"Maybe so," Dad said, still calculating how the lockout might work in his favor. He had no interest in making a commitment that wouldn't directly help him. A few good months without competition just might clear his inventory, and what had these pricks ever done for him?

"If the union beats us, you'll be next," Wulf said, in a more reasonable tone. "And you did get your bank loan."

"I'm not so sure that Mackenzie is on board with this," Dad replied, ignoring the comment. "I've watched him ship lumber every day for the past two weeks."

"We know about that," Sagers said, tight-lipped.

"Why isn't he here? You'd think he'd want to see this," Dad said. "Is he too busy screwing someone else's wife?"

"Sid is in the woods with his logging crew," Wulf said. "Once we see how this turns out, we'll have a talk with him. He'll come around." Wulf paused to watch the action on the bridge. "From the looks of things, there won't be trouble here."

"Mackenzie's been shipping lumber behind your back all along," Dad said. "We know he hasn't been supporting the lockout, so why would the union strike his place? What sense does that make?"

"We think Mackenzie made a deal with the union and later decided to change it," Wulf said. "Knowing Sid, he tried to sweeten the pot. The union undoubtedly sent these boys over to make a point. We're here to see that it doesn't go too far."

The sloucher was gesturing toward the burgundy Cadillac. He began yelling at them through the wall of policemen. "We are not asking for much! Fifty cents the hour. What's that to you?"

Dad stepped away from the Cadillac.

"We demand a forty hour week," a second man heckled.

The policemen stood straighter and tightened their line. Neet, of all people, slid around the officers and marched toward the strikers. Shaking his small fist, he shouted, "We will run our businesses any way we see fit. If you don't like it, find another job!"

One striker edged toward the hidden bats. A second man picked up a rock. Dad took three steps away from the Cadillac.

"You are thieves and grafters!" the man with the rock yelled. "Working men everywhere are getting a raw deal."

"You should thank us for any jobs we give you," Neet sneered back. He pointed a bony finger at the sloucher. "I'll see to it that you never work here, ever."

The man lunged at Neet, and a rock sailed over the police barrier, striking the Cadillac's windshield. A second rock struck the hood, chipping the burgundy paint. "For Christ's sake," Wulf said, surveying his damaged car.

All four strikers ran for their bats. The policemen raised their clubs and took a disciplined step forward. In a panic, Neet scrambled behind them and then shouted, "Arrest these criminals!"

The sloucher pulled a steel bolt from his pocket and pitched it at Neet's head, narrowly missing. Neet crouched down as the enraged police charged. The strikers broke ranks and fled onto Dolomite land, not stopping until they were well away from the flailing clubs.

"That's private property," the state bull yelled. "We'll take you in for trespassing as well as rioting."

A well aimed rock struck a cop in the face and dropped him to his knees. The lead trooper unsnapped the cover to his side arm, raised the pistol, and fired.

Nobody moved.

"This has to stop!" the trooper said. He leveled his weapon at the strikers. "You men stay where you are." He turned to Merle and the others. "Get that goddamn car out of here!"

"We're not the criminals," Neet said. Still on his hands and knees, he pointed across the bridge. "They are."

The trooper pulled Neet to his feet and punched a stout finger into the banker's chest. "You are making things worse." The trooper turned toward Sagers and Gehring. "Get this little prick out of here before I club him."

Another salvo of rocks dented chrome and chipped more paint. Wulf and Sagers ignored the trooper's request and dove inside the auto. Dad followed, using his hat to brush broken glass from the seat. When Neet realized that they were about to leave without him, he threw himself headfirst into the back, slicing his hand on the shattered glass.

41

The battle was just starting when I returned to the mill clearing. Men were clutching bats and pitching rocks. A home run flew through Mr. Gehring's car window, and a double bounced off his hood. You'd have thought it was the World Series. Not wanting to miss any of it, I ran toward the bridge to get a better look, but a fat policeman blocked the way.

"Get on home!" the red-faced bully hollered. "This is no place for you." He was so out of breath, he could barely get the words out. He was struggling to loosen the heavy belt around his big belly as if that would help. I didn't think he could catch me, so I started edging around him.

"I'm not fooling, you little bastard!"

That didn't faze me. I angled around him, trying to see what was happening on the bridge, edging closer for a better view.

A black rage took control of his face, as if I were the cause of his problems. "If you make me chase you down, I'll paddle your skinny butt blue." That got my attention. He raised a meaty hand and showed me the flat of his palm. He spread the bulky sausages and demonstrated how big they were.

I stopped, but I didn't turn and run.

"Get home. Now!" The fat man's voice was raw. He took two surprisingly quick steps toward me and closed the distance between us. That was when I ran. I didn't stop running until I reached the loading dock where I hid behind a stack of six by eight timbers. I looked back. The officer was bent over, with his hands on his knees. He had chased me half way before giving up. On the bridge behind him, the rest of the policemen were waving clubs and pointing. But that was all I could see.

Then I heard the gunshot. I knew that I had to get closer or miss everything. I raced around the back of the mill and along the firebreak, hoping to get to the bridge without being seen. I ducked into the blackberry thicket, wriggled through the secret path, and scrambled down the bank. From the locomotive, I waded knee-deep through the stream toward the bridge. Nobody could see me through the bushes, or get to me even if they did. I hoped they wouldn't shoot me, either.

When I reached the bridge, it wasn't voices that initially caught my attention. It was the ropes. Two were dangling from the bridge with their upper ends knotted around spikes driven into the supporting timbers. Two dented metal cans swung from the lower ends. The cans were invisible to anyone standing on the bridge or walking along the road.

I waded out and took hold of one. It was completely full, and so was the second. I twisted off a cap and sniffed. On the bridge above me, the policemen were still running back and forth and shouting. One officer said he had a shotgun in his car.

I replaced the metal cap and gave the can a push, watching it swing out on its rope. When it returned, I pushed again, thinking about nothing in particular, unable to make sense out of what was happening. When the can returned a second time, I decided to steal it—it wasn't very heavy. I easily could carry a two-gallon can, and nobody would ever know it was me who took it.

As soon as I decided to steal the kerosene, I started worrying that I might be seen. I struggled to untie the knot, but I couldn't get it to budge. I clenched the kerosene-soaked knot between my teeth and pulled, gagging on the oily hemp. I tried to spit the taste out. When that didn't help, I rinsed my mouth with river water. That didn't improve things, either. Continuing to gag and pull with my teeth, I finally succeeded in getting the knot loose. As soon as I did, I carried the can under the bridge, where I sat for some time, studying my new treasure and enjoying the riot above me.

I was sitting under the bridge with my can of kerosene when Dad sped away in Mr. Gehring's Cadillac. I listened, as he and the others drove onto our haul road and parked behind the office. Dad later told me what went on there.

Dad was angry, most likely scared, convinced that the strikers' were about to hit our mill next. When the car stopped, he got out and walked around to Wulf's open window. "What's to keep these lunatics from torching *my* place?"

Wulf hadn't moved from behind the wheel. He ignored Dad and appeared lost in another world, blindly staring ahead and tapping his fingertips against the steering wheel. Sagers showed some life. He rubbed a hand across the stubble on his chin, but he didn't have a thing to say either. Neet was totally occupied with his cut hand and no help at all.

Dad put his head inside the driver's window and tried again. "Wulf, you know better than anyone. Are they planning to take me out?" When he got no answer, he turned to Sagers. "Jackie?"

"You're not in anybody's crosshairs right now," Sagers said. "But *we* sure as hell are."

Wulf snapped his fingers and looked at Dad. "I've got it!" he said. "I just figured out who the hothead on the bridge is. Mike Dugan. Wherever there's been union trouble, Tacoma, Seattle, Portland, he's been nearby. Dugan is not a patient man. He'll be back to finish up. My bet is tonight."

"I'll see to it that he's arrested," Neet said.

"Dugan won't run," Wulf said. "Sid is in for trouble, and we have an investment in this mill, too." Wulf glanced at Dad. "You're probably okay."

Ennis laid his injured hand on the seatback between Wulf and Sagers. He had it wrapped in a handkerchief. "I need stitches."

Wulf pushed the hand away. "Get that bloody thing off my leather seat, or I'll take it off at the wrist!"

"I could get an infection!"

Sagers turned in his seat. "Let me see it." He unwound the handkerchief and turned Neet's hand over.

Neet winced.

"For Christ's sake, Ennis," Sagers scowled. "It can wait."

Neet slouched back in his seat and rewrapped the hand. He elevated it above his heart and tried to slow down his breathing.

Sagers leaned across Gehring so he could see Dad. "If you talk to Mackenzie before we find him, tell him to get his ass down to the legion hall. He needs to round up his Klan buddies and get them here before dark. This job is perfect for them. Reds killed four legionnaires in Centralia not too long ago, and the reservists haven't forgotten."

"We'll watch your back tonight, Merle," Wulf said, "but we'll expect you to return the favor."

42

The sun had barely dipped behind the ridge when I heard engines. I was home from the bridge by then and had changed out of my wet clothes. Five cars slowed across from Mackenzie's bridge and parked single file along the highway. I'm not sure how many men slipped onto the bridge. In the twilight, there were too many to count.

Dad walked over and stood behind me. He stared out, too. "Who are they?" I asked.

"Mr. Mackenzie's friends from town. I suppose they're here to protect his mill, but all I see is trouble." Dad picked his hat off the rack. I heard the door close behind me and then watched his shadow cross the porch and disappear in the direction of the highway. I reached for my coat and hat and walked over to Mother's closed door.

"I'll be on the porch," I said to her door. I grabbed my rubber boots, but didn't put them on. I didn't stay on the porch, and I didn't follow Dad to the bridge. I went the opposite way, clutching the boots and running as fast as I dared in the dark. I felt for the secret path and crawled to the water's edge where I changed into my boots.

Two lanterns glowed on the bridge ahead of me. Wading tight against the brush, I was invisible. The remaining can of kerosene was still hanging on its rope. I brushed by it in the dark, but didn't stop there. I continued wading until I was directly beneath the hissing lanterns. Four silhouettes were gathered around the glow: two were leaning against the bridge railing; the others looked to be a step or two back. I couldn't see faces, but I recognized the voices.

"Maybe they've run off," Gust Backer was saying. Gust was second in command and in charge of the mill whenever Mr. Mackenzie was away.

"I guess these Reds are a bunch of chicken shits," Mackenzie said. "What a waste of time this turned out to be."

"They might still come back," Gust said. "Let's give it more time."

"I've got three men with shotguns waiting for them at the mill," Mackenzie said. "If the Reds try anything, we'll blow a hole in the union movement the size of Moscow. I, for one, have had enough of this wild goose chase."

It was cold under the bridge, much colder than I thought it would be. I turned my collar up and tugged on my earflaps.

"If you take off now, you'll leave the bridge unprotected." That was Dad's voice.

"Fraser," Mackenzie said, "you can stand in the cold as long as you want, but it doesn't appeal to me."

I wrapped my arms around my body and clamped my teeth together to keep from chattering.

"If this bridge burns," Dad argued, "sparks could set off either one of our mills."

"I'm going to the Bucket of Blood for a drink." Mackenzie said. "Sure you don't want to come along, Gust?"

"You go ahead," Gust said. "I'll stay here a bit longer. We've all got a lot to lose."

"Suit yourself, but I'm taking the rest of the boys with me. They drove up for a party, and I feel obligated to give them one. Since this didn't work out, we might have to say hello to the Catholic schoolteacher."

"Leave her alone," Gust said. "All the kids like her."

"We'll just have a little fun," Mackenzie said. "God knows, she's been asking for it."

"Forget about her," Gust said.

Ten shadows were now gathered around the lantern. It was impossible to make out individual shapes.

"Merle, you're president of the school board," Mackenzie said in a louder voice. "Why do we have a Catholic bitch teaching our kids?"

"She won't be back next year."

"It's barely October. That leaves her a year to spread her poison."

"I'll talk to her on Monday," Dad said.

"Sid, let school board handle it," Gust said. "This is not something we want to be a part of."

"I'll be part of anything I choose," Mackenzie said. "If you keep this up, Gust, you might talk yourself out of a job."

Mackenzie's shadow disappeared from the railing, but he hadn't finished talking. He started up again, sounding as if he was giving a speech.

"Gentlemen," he shouted, "the Reds aren't coming back tonight. They know better. It's time for a drink, and I'm buying!"

"About time we got something out of this!" It was Mohl's voice.

"That makes it unanimous," Mackenzie said. "Let's go find a drink."

"The hell with that!" Mohl said. "I'm not stopping at one."

The men laughed, and every shadow but one faded from the lantern's light. Car doors slammed and auto engines started. Headlights paraded toward the Bucket of Blood. Within moments, the bridge was as empty as I suddenly felt.

My feet were numb from standing in the water. I was shivering with no hope of quieting my teeth. All I could think about was Miss Cherry—I was so afraid of what they might do to her. I tried running along the streambed, but it wasn't easy fighting the current in the dark; I slipped on the river rock and fell in twice. I had to get to Boone and warn him. He was the only man I knew brave enough to stop them.

When I reached the highway, I stopped only long enough to catch my breath. A cigarette's pinpoint glow marked a solitary presence on the bridge. I guessed it was Gust. I didn't know if Dad had gone back home or if he had taken off with the others—it didn't matter. I had to find Boone.

In my rush at the riverbank, I had forgotten to change from the rubber boots into my shoes. I tried running in the boots, but they sloshed and wouldn't stay on. I took them off and tried running in my socks, but the gravel and cinders cut through. I tried balancing on the steel rail, but my wet feet slipped off time and again. I was taking way too long. I wasn't going to reach Boone in time.

The parking lot was full of men when I finally got to the Bucket of Blood. Boone was standing alone in the center of headlight beams, gripping his club. He had just thrown two men out the door. One of them had tripped and fallen. The other was holding his head.

"You'll pay for this," the upright man said. I knew that voice—no-good Marvin Ellis from Texas, but this wasn't Marvin. This man was grown. He had to be no-good Marvin's dad. "You'll goddamn pay for this," he repeated.

"If that's so," Boone said, "come on over and collect." Boone stared at no-good Marvin's dad and calmly waited. His arms were loose at his sides. One hand gripped his club; the other was ready to become a piston—I had seen it before.

Marvin's dad didn't even twitch.

Boone turned to face ten other men who were standing in a half circle around him. "You all know the rules," he said. "If anyone else wants to spit on my friend, save yourself a step and spit on me first."

I looked toward the Bucket. Wattie was standing in the doorway with a handkerchief against his face.

Mr. Mackenzie spoke up. "Boone, we're only here for a drink. Give us one, and we'll be off."

"You didn't come for a drink," Boone said, watching the ten men carefully. "You came looking for trouble. Now that you found it, you better go home."

Mackenzie shook his head. "Not until we've had our drink."

"No one is coming inside tonight," Boone said. He glanced at no-good Marvin's dad. "As for you, Ellis, don't ever come back."

I don't know what I saw. I thought it was a shadow. That's why I didn't say anything when it slid behind Boone—I didn't think it was real, I swear it. I honestly didn't know what it was until it was too late. Boone never saw it at all.

Mohl swung down with both hands. The crowbar struck Boone just above his ear, and something inside his head broke.

I couldn't believe it: Boone didn't even try to fight. He fell forward like he had no bones and landed with his face in the gravel. Mohl swung the steel bar a second time and broke Boone's arm above his wrist, causing it to bend back on itself. Mohl hit the arm again, tearing away skin and muscle, uncovering pinkish, white bone.

Mohl rotated the crowbar and turned the claws out. "This'll pretty him up," he said. Blood was pooling around Boone's face and arm. Mohl took aim at Boone's head.

Two men grabbed his arm. "You'll kill him," they said.

Mohl shrugged like it didn't matter and turned toward the roadhouse. "Anybody else want to tell me I can't have a drink?" He spat on Boone's face as he walked by, and then so did Ellis.

"He's not so tough," Ellis said, following Mohl toward the roadhouse. "Where's my beer? More important, where is that skinny nigger?"

I glanced toward the roadhouse. Wattie was no longer in the doorway.

"Hold it right there, Mohl," Mackenzie said. "You too, Ellis."

Mohl turned on Mackenzie and raised the crowbar.

Mackenzie held up his hands. "You can do whatever you want, but I have an idea you might like even better."

Mohl waited.

"You know that little teacher at Wildwood School, the pretty one?"

"I've seen her around," Mohl said.

Mackenzie spoke up so all the men could hear. "We've got a Catholic school teacher here who insists on polluting our kids. We've tried to reason with her, but the papist bitch won't leave. The legislature wants her gone, and so does the school board. I think it's time we educate her."

Most of the men listening weren't from Culp Creek. They had driven up from Cottage Grove and they didn't know anything about her. Even though these were lies, I could see that they didn't like what they were hearing.

"We've told her leave our children alone, but she insists on staying. What do you suppose her motives are?" Mackenzie pointed toward my dad. "The school board president is standing here. Let's ask him."

Dad stiffened. He could have told them what a good teacher she was. He could have explained how she taught me to read and how much she used the new blackboard. He might have mentioned the books she brought us. He had his chance; there was so much that he could have said, but Dad didn't offer one word to stop the lies. He mumbled something and looked at the ground.

"Speak up," Mackenzie said.

"I think she's trying." That was it. That was all he could say about her.

"She's a papist, isn't she?" Mackenzie asked.

"She's Catholic," Dad said, almost to himself.

"In this country," Mackenzie roared, "we decide who teaches our children, not some Italian Pope. If we don't protect our children, then God help us." He turned to Mohl. "How would you like a date with a Catholic schoolmarm?"

Mohl dropped the crowbar.

"I didn't think you'd want to miss the fun."

"Not that kind of fun."

43

Only three cars eased off the road this time. Half the Klansmen had decided to return home after the violence at the Bucket of Blood. The remaining three doused their headlights out of sight of the isolated house. Dad saw a glow through the trees and hoped that Guillaume, not Miss Cherry, was sitting on the other side of the window. Right from the very beginning, Dad hadn't wanted any part of it, he later told me.

Dad recognized a few of the men as belonging to Mackenzie. The rest were managers and business owners from Cottage Grove. For the most part, they were hard working, respectable men, doing what they thought was right, but as they pulled on their robes and hoods and spoke in hushed voices, there were giggles and some clowning around. Dad didn't think much would come of it. He suspected the whole thing would turn out to be more bluff than anything else.

Mackenzie reached into the trunk of his car and retrieved a large wooden cross that had been wrapped with cotton rags. He passed it off to a robed figure and dug deeper for a can of kerosene. He pulled out a dozen tree branches, similarly wrapped with layers of cotton. Dad began to lose track of who was who.

"Dip the torches," Mackenzie said. "Pour what's left of the kerosene on the cross. We'll light things up when we get to the house."

Pete Ellis took charge of dipping the torches. "When we're finished here," he said, "I'm going back for the nigger. I don't know where he went, but I'll find him." He flashed the butt end of a pistol that he had tucked inside his belt.

"You won't need that," Mackenzie said.

"Maybe I will," Ellis said, straightening up. He towered six inches above Mackenzie.

Mackenzie slipped on his hood and adjusted the eye holes. He surveyed the Klansmen and then noticed that Dad hadn't changed his clothes. "Where's your stuff, Fraser?"

"I didn't bring it." Dad couldn't see a face. It made him uneasy.

This party isn't black tie optional."

"I don't think I want any part of it."

Mackenzie silently appraised Dad. So there could be no misunderstanding between them, he pulled his hood off. "You already are a part of this, Fraser. Don't think you're not!" When Dad didn't respond, he continued. "We'll deal with you later. Be here when we get back." He snatched a torch from Ellis and set off toward the Frenchman's house.

As the other ghosts slid past, an unseen elbow struck Dad in the ribs. The butt end of a torch caught him on the back of the head and knocked him down. By the time he got to his feet, his fellow Klansmen had faded into the gathering night. He began following from a safe distance.

A dozen torches flared ahead of him. They illuminated the small house, the yard, and steps. Flames rising from the kerosene-soaked cross filled the night and attracted every eye.

"Pretty, ain't it?" Ellis said.

"Voisine," Mackenzie called out, his voice sounding strange and muffled as he tried to disguise it behind the hood. "We've come to talk to you."

Still hidden in the shadows, Dad edged forward. He felt compelled to watch, but he had no intention of interfering. He recalled what he had told her. He had warned her of the danger, more than once. All this was her fault because she had chosen not to listen to his advice. She was "a stupid, stupid bitch."

Old Guillaume appeared in the doorway. He gripped his axe in one hand and steadied himself against the doorframe with the other. His spine was so stiff and bent forward that he had to straighten his body through the hips just to see the Klansmen. He pointed his axe at the white silhouettes. "Get away from my house, *putins* of the devil!"

Ellis laughed. "Go back to Canada where you belong, Frenchie." Ellis was standing beside Mackenzie at the front of the group. He sounded drunk. "You don't belong in this country any more than she does." Mimicking Guillaume, he pointed his torch at the old man. "We're not here to burn your shack down, but we'll do it if you don't send the bitch out."

Guillaume spat. *"Tu manges du merde!"*

A Klansman behind Ellis snorted. "The old man says you eat shit."

"Listen to reason, Voisine," Mackenzie said. "We just want to talk to girl. She has no business perverting our children."

"Miss Cherry is a good teacher," Guillaume said. "The state, he gives Miss Cherry the right to teach these children."

"God and the State of Oregon have taken that right away."

"You are not God. You are nobody."

"Tonight, we are whoever we want to be."

Dad pulled the brim of his hat low, nearly covering his eyes, willing it to keep him from seeing.

"The girl, she is not coming out!" Guillaume said. He elevated his axe and had to take a step back to keep from falling.

"Have it your way, Frenchie," Ellis said, brushing past Mackenzie.

Guillaume planted his feet. He raised the axe another notch. In doing so, he grew a foot taller and fifty pounds heavier. He seemed fully capable of chopping Ellis in two.

Ellis hesitated. "Good way to get hurt, old man."

"*Le Bon Dieu* is my witness," Voisine started to say, but he didn't get to finish.

With a startling fast move that Guillaume never saw, the axe was snatched from his crippled hands. His legs were kicked out from under him, and he fell hard against the steps with a brittle snap. Guillaume screamed and kicked out, catching Ellis in the knee. Ellis sent three vicious boots into Guillaume's ribs and head. The old man was done; he grunted and lay still.

A rock crashed through the front window. The force of it pulled down the lace curtain inside and shattered an unseen object.

"Come out, teacher," the rock thrower said. "Come on out and meet your pupils." Mohl made no attempt to disguise his voice. He staggered toward the porch, sounding even drunker than Ellis. "Come out now, Sweetie, or we'll burn you out. Then we'll fuck you and the old lady." When he didn't get a response, Mohl hurled his torch, end-over-end, through the broken window. A woman screamed. "Oooh, let's hear some more of that!"

Mohl picked up another rock. "Come out, come out, wherever…" he began to chant, but the words were interrupted by an explosion and a blinding flash that filled the window frame. Behind the Klansmen, the flaming cross disintegrated, sending burning fragments skittering across yard."

Mohl tripped over old Voisine and fell backward. He scuttled away from the house like a startled crab.

A reedy voice filled the silence. Dad strained to hear it. "I'm apt to shoot again," the voice said. The front door opened, and the phantoms floated a step backward.

Wattie stepped out onto the porch. He was no bigger than Guillaume, but he was holding a shotgun and aiming it at Mackenzie's head. "You spooks had better leave," he said. "It won't take nothin' for me to pull this trigger again. To tell the truth, there are few things I'd like more."

"You can't take us all," Mackenzie said.

Wattie looked hard at Mackenzie as if straining to see him. "What you say may be true," he said, not bothering to argue. His eyes were watering, most likely from the smoke. He blinked twice and had to take a hand away from the gun to rub his eyes.

Dad shifted his gaze to the men spread out in front of the thin black man. Most of them wanted no part of the shotgun and were backing away from the house. Pete Ellis was the exception. He was sidling toward the porch, carrying Guillaume's double-bladed axe behind his back. Ellis was big, easily strong enough to cleave Wattie in two, and foolish enough to think this was still some kind of a pissing match.

"I know about niggers from long experience," Ellis said. He was only feet from Wattie. "This here tar baby is no different than the rest. He'll turn and run right after he shits his pants, just like he did at the Bucket of Blood." Ellis took two calculated steps forward. "Ain't that right?"

"Won't nobody, ever again, find me in a pile of shit," Wattie said.

"I never thought much of school," Ellis said, watching and inching forward, "but I am here to teach you a lesson, boy."

His eyes red and sore, with tears streaming down each cheek, Wattie blinked again. He reached a hand up to rub the tears away, and then thought better of it.

Ellis picked that instant to rush the small man, once again surprising everyone with his quickness. He swung the axe above his head in a powerful arc and trained its blade on the round black bull's eye in front of him.

It was as if Wattie had expected the attack, or maybe had hoped for it—at least that was how Dad described it. Wattie didn't flinch. He stared Ellis in the eye and responded to the powerful charge with an imperceptible twitch of his forefinger.

What the dead man hadn't known, would never know, was that Wattie had waited for that moment most of his life. When the shotgun jumped in Wattie's hands, Ellis probably saw the barrel spit at him, but he wouldn't have had time to register the significance of the subsequent roar. More than likely, Ellis was still concentrating on directing the axe blade into the center of Wattie's head when the twelve-gauge load blew him backward and removed his Texas-sized skull from the ears up. In addition to half his head, the blast tore away Ellis' hood and most of his robe. It left him spread-eagled on the smoldering remnants of the cross with the exposed pistol still tucked inside his belt.

Nobody moved, for sure not Wattie. He faced the flapping ghosts like an unbreakable statue. He cycled the trench sweeper's action and pumped a fresh shell into the chamber.

"I got more of the same here," he said quietly. "Everybody best go home now."

44

When Mackenzie said the strikers had run away and wouldn't be back, he was as wrong about them as no-good Marvin's dad had been about Wattie. Some hours after Wattie had used Boone's trench slayer on Ellis, they drove up the canyon highway without headlights and parked a half-mile downstream. From there, they ran the rest of the way.

Three gray figures slid through the moonlight onto the bridge. I didn't actually see them douse the planking, but I did see the torch ignite. It wasn't hard to follow the flames when they chased after the kerosene.

Babe Ashman later said that a low moisture count was the reason the bridge burned so hot, with sparks rising into the sky, but I think it was the kerosene. So much happened that night, to get it all straight, I have to go back to when Mohl broke Boone's skull with the crowbar, when the Klansmen drove off to teach Miss Cherry a lesson.

I found Boone lying face down in his blood: it everywhere, sticky and black. Two bones were sticking out of his arm, and his hand was on backward. All the fingers were darkly wrong.

"Boone?" I whispered, almost afraid to wake him up. He didn't move. I looked toward the winking taillights, hoping Dad might come back and help. I wiggled the discolored fingers, and then I shook the broken arm. "Boone, you have to wake up!" I was crying.

"You best leave them be, Teddy."

It was Wattie. He hadn't left, after all. He kneeled in the gravel and studied Boone's crooked arm.

"Mercy," he muttered. With his thin hands shaking, he pulled on the fingers. He put a foot in Boone's armpit and pulled harder. With Wattie straining, and me feeling sick, Boone's hand swung around to where it was supposed to be, and the pieces of bone that had been sticking out sucked back inside with a slurp.

Boone groaned.

"Pour this on it." Ray also had come out of nowhere. He pulled the cork out of a bottle of gin and poured the contents over Boone's arm. Working together, Wattie and Ray wrapped Boone's arm in a towel and tied it between two sticks.

"Can't have them bones flopping," Wattie said. "He surely needs a doctor."

"Doctor won't do more than what you've already done," Ray said.

"That don't seem right."

As big as Boone was, it was all we could do to roll him on his back. As soon as we did, he started choking.

"He's drowning in his blood," Ray said.

We flipped Boone face down again and left him that way while Ray ran for Boone's car. Wattie and Ray wrestled Boone onto the backseat. Ray got behind the wheel.

"Teddy, get in back with Boone," Wattie ordered. "Hold his big head up and don't let it flop. We got to keep him from choking." Wattie pushed a dirty towel into my hand. "Soak up the blood with this."

I pressed hard with the cloth, trying to stop the flow of blood. It was streaming through my fingers and down his neck. I pushed with both hands.

"Not too hard, now," Wattie said. "You got to let him breathe." He walked to the front of the car and spoke to Ray. "You and Teddy go on," he said. "I got to stay here."

"I can't drive him to town by myself," Ray said.

"Get Teddy's mother," Wattie said. "She'll know what to do. I got to go now." He disappeared inside the Bucket.

Boone was starting to wake up by the time we got to the house. He was thrashing all over the backseat, pushing the rag off his face, telling me to leave him alone.

Mother heard our honking and ran out. She took one look and shouldered me out of the way. She tried, but Boone wouldn't hold still for her either. None of us could hold him down.

"What happened to him?" she asked.

Neither of Ray nor I knew what to say, and she didn't ask again.

She pressed a hand against Boone's forehead. "Stop it, Boone!" she said sternly, "Look at me."

Boone threw her hand off, but she put it right back on, talking to him and somehow getting him to settle down. He refused to go to town. Nothing we said would change his mind. With him leaning on Mother and Ray, we moved him into our house.

Mother put Boone in her bed and gave him laudanum for the pain. "Take a sip of this," she said, supporting his head. She washed the blood off his face after he fell asleep, and then she changed the bandage on his arm.

"We'll have to wake Boone every half hour," she said. "If we don't, he might not wake up ever again."

I stayed up most of the night, dividing my time between his bedroom and the front window, rousing and shaking him every half hour until he pushed me away. That's what I was doing when the union men ran onto the bridge. Mother was with me. She saw them, too. From our window, next to the weeping willow, we watched the fire on the bridge start small and grow. We didn't bother to tell anyone.

"They'll find out soon enough," she said.

A dozen men from both sides of the river were soon clustered around the bridge. A few of them tried to fight the fire, but most saw it as a lost cause and let it burn, no different than Mother and me.

"I want to get closer," I told her.

"Stay out of the men's way," she said. She seemed so tired.

I walked over to the gramophone. "Would you like music?"

She glanced toward Boone's doorway and shook her head. "Not tonight."

"I won't be gone long."

When I returned, I could see that Mother hadn't moved. She was sitting right where I had left her, staring at the two fires.

"How is he?"

"Boone's fine."

By then, Dad's mill was on fire, too.

I stepped behind her and rested my chin on her shoulder. She felt warm and soft. "What are you doing?" I asked.

"I'm watching my ship come in," she said quietly.

"Me, too," I whispered, standing close to her, enjoying the warmth, breathing in her scent, watching reflected flames pirouette across the pond.

She reached up and touched my face with soft fingers—it had been so long since she'd done that.

I kissed them and then pressed my lips against her cheek. She stiffened and pulled away.

"Go and get some sleep," she said. "I'll sit with Boone until morning."

For once, I did just what she said, and as I slept, the heavy scent of wood smoke filled my room and my dreams.

When I awoke, I jumped from bed and ran to the window. The sun was overhead, and columns of smoke filled the sky. The bridge was gone, and so was Dad's sawmill. The few parts that remained were deformed to the point of being useless: blackened boilers, twisted smoke stacks, warped saws, and charred timbers. The pond water was as black as the timbers.

Mill hands were standing at the edge of the ruin in groups of twos and threes. Babe was with Alec and Ray. Mr. Sharpe was off to the side by himself. I didn't see Dad.

Mother stood beside me. "Boone is much better this morning. You can go in and see him." She walked back to the kitchen and started my breakfast.

Boone was sleeping when I looked in.

Mother sat with me while I ate. "Where's Dad?" I asked.

"I haven't seen him since yesterday."

"Do you think he'll be sad?"

Mother picked up my dishes and took them to the sink. "I have no idea what your dad feels."

I found my coat and went out. I circled behind the pond and followed the firebreak up the hillside, not wanting to talk to anyone because I had no idea what to say. High above it all, I could see that half of the bridge was still standing—the Dolomite half. Our end had fallen into the river. The steel rails that had run along the top of the bridge were hanging in mid-air like tightropes. Off to one side, right where the kerosene cans had been, something else was hanging.

I raced to the locomotive. My footprints from the previous night were everywhere along the path and the riverbank. I waded downstream in my shoes, purposely keeping my gaze down. I didn't look up until I had reached the bridge moorings because I already knew what a dead man looked like. At the end of his rope, Uncle Normal had been a purple jack-o'-lantern. This time, a white ghost floated above the rushing water. I was glad to see a ghost because ghosts don't have bulging eyes, purple tongues, and heads swollen to the size of harvest pumpkins.

I didn't touch him, but after a moment, I stepped back and stared at the robed Ku Klux Klan man. Unlike Wattie's brother, this ghost would never fly: his hands had been tied behind his back. I took one look at his shoes and knew who he was. If I had lifted his hood and stared at his swollen head, I couldn't have been surer.

Just as I had done the night before, I ran upstream, slipping and falling. I fought through the blackberry thorns and sprinted across the highway. I had to get to Boone, I thought. No, that wasn't right...I had to find Mother. Instead, I spilled everything to Babe and Alec, the first men I came to.

"There's a dead man hanging from the bridge!" I could hardly get the words out. "He's a ghost."

Babe didn't believe me until I started crying.

"Who is it?" Babe asked.

I couldn't say the name out loud.

The sheriff had driven up from Cottage Grove earlier in the morning. He was at Voisine's, questioning Guillaume and Françoise. It didn't take him long to get to the bridge.

"I've just been investigating the Ellis' shooting," he said, shaking his head at what he had just seen. "That was one tough lick Pete Ellis took—the man's face is completely gone. Without witnesses, there'd be no way to connect a name to the corpse."

But was it a tough enough lick to finally shut no-good Marvin up? I doubted it.

The detectives from Eugene cut the body down late in the afternoon. Since they didn't know about the secret path, it took two hours to float the body upriver and drag it through the blackberry thorns onto the bank. When they reached the highway, they laid Mr. Mackenzie out like one of Wattie's catfish. Scratches covered the detectives and mud covered Mr. Mackenzie. Had they asked me, I could have shown them a better way out of the stream, but nobody cared to ask.

According to the state doctor, who later examined the body, Mr. Mackenzie's killers brained him with a bat before they hanged him. They managed to break his neck, too, but that probably happened when he dropped off the bridge with the rope around his neck. Based on how stiff Mr. Mackenzie was, and because his clothes were scorched in places, the doctor believed that Mr. Mackenzie died before the bridge was set on fire.

The sheriff blamed Mr. Mackenzie's murder on the strikers. "Those boys had motive and opportunity." The sheriff guessed that Mackenzie must have tried to stop the arsonists, but he was wrong. I saw the whole thing, or most of it anyway. After the union men ran onto bridge, they took no more than five minutes to start the fire—nowhere near enough time for them to tie Mr. Mackenzie up, hit him over the head, and push him off the bridge. I'd have told them so if they had so much as asked me.

Mr. Mackenzie's Klansmen had a completely different idea about what happened. They remained convinced that Wattie was the murderer. They swore that Wattie had it in for Mr. Mackenzie because Wattie was colored and Mackenzie was a Ku Klux Man. "I heard that old boy threaten to kill Sid," Mr. Pingree said. "Right after that, he shot down poor Pete Ellis without so much as blinking."

The sheriff spoke some more with Guillaume, Françoise, and Miss Cherry, and after hearing their side, he said he was inclined to believe that Wattie had acted in self-defense. "I can put that much together," he said. Even so, he arrested Wattie for suspicion of murdering Mr. Mackenzie because Wattie had made threats and had a motive. For Wattie's safety, the sheriff jailed him in Eugene rather than Cottage Grove.

Guillaume, Françoise, Miss Cherry, and Mother went to court and testified about what had happened. Over a chorus of loud objections, the judge let Wattie go. "This isn't Alabama," the judge said, banging his gavel.

The Klansmen picketed the courthouse for a week, and the newspaper wasn't happy, either. Both parties threatened to have the judge run out of town. They also guaranteed he'd never be reelected. The newspaper reported that one Klansman even offered to organize an "old-fashioned lynching," but nothing like that happened.

A few weeks after Wattie got out of jail, Boone, Wattie, and I were sitting together at the Bucket of Blood. Wattie wasn't playing his music; and he hadn't played a note since getting out of jail. Boone still had trouble remembering things.

"I don't recall one thing about that night," he kept saying. "If I didn't have to look at myself in the mirror, I'd swear none of it happened. Remind me again, why the Klansmen left Guillaume's place without putting up more of a fight? There were more of them than Wattie could handle."

Wattie actually smiled. "Them spooks left because they still had a smidge of sense the good Lord gave them. Seeing me with your trench slaying shotgun, and me blinking like I was blind, probably helped grow some more of it, too."

"After that, what happened?" Boone was working hard at trying to put things together.

"Once them spooks took off," Wattie said, "I ran inside, expecting to find the house afire. I opened the door and looked in, but there was not one lick of flame to be seen."

As Wattie explained it, when Mohl's torch landed under the table, Françoise picked it up and rushed it to the kitchen sink where she doused it. But there was nothing to be done about the fire that had already started. Miss Cherry tried beating the flames with a small rug, which only made them mad. The window drapes caught fire next. Françoise ordered Miss Cherry out the back door, told her to save herself, but Miss Cherry wasn't ready to give up. She ran to the kitchen for more water, but instead grabbed the two bottles of medicine she'd had sitting on the windowsill. She splashed the contents of one bottle across the tablecloth and the other bottle against the burning drapes.

"Just like that," Wattie said, snapping his fingers, "them fires stopped cold! Like the hand of God snuffed them out. When I ran into the house, Françoise was staring at the medicine bottles like she'd seen a miracle. There wasn't one live spark left, only smoke and smolder. She sank to her knees, crossed herself, and praised her virgin. Miss Cherry got on her knees and praised the same lady."

No miracles were to be had at Dad's mill that night. The Fraser Lumber Company was gone by morning.

"Flames ten feet high exploded in the heart of the mill," Babe Ashman later said. "It was the worst fire I ever saw, except for the time lightning struck the Darby mill."

"If sparks from the bridge fire actually caused it," Ray said, thinking things through like always, "why didn't the fire start on a roof or in a pile of shavings?"

Nobody had an answer for that.

"We never had a chance," Babe said. "The mill was lost from the start. We'd a fought it like banshees, but we didn't have water. We dragged the hoses over and had them in place, but there wasn't any water pressure. The line must have been cut during the night."

Actually, the line hadn't been cut; one of the couplings had been dismantled.

45

1942

Nine years after the mill burned, with everyone assuring me it was the right thing to do, I signed up for the army air corps. I joined within two weeks of the attack on Pearl Harbor, not out of patriotism, but because it seemed to be the path of least resistance. In the time it took to lick a stamp and get a haircut, I had my orders for basic training and was bound for Amarillo. At nineteen, I was no more ready for war than were any of the other slobs on the train. We were lambs to the slaughter.

Dad and Mother saw me off at the station in Eugene. That was the first time the three of us had been together since Culp Creek. Dad slipped me ten dollars for "walking around money" and assured me I was doing my duty. While he talked and thumbed through his wallet, with Mother at his side, I felt like a mark being played.

"You know," Dad said, dropping the fat billfold into his pocket, "blood is thicker than water."

I nodded, expecting him to tell me, that in spite of things not being perfect between us, we were still family. I got that wrong. What he was saying, what he wanted me to understand, was that since we *weren't* blood, I had better use my time in the service to figure how to make my way in the world once the fighting was over. That was when Mother and Father, standing side-by-side, told me they weren't my real parents and that I'd been adopted. Why they picked that time to tell me the truth, I will never know, unless they just didn't want it on their conscience, me not knowing, if I died in the war. In retrospect, with somewhat different words, I realized that Mother had told me the same thing that night in her bedroom, but I had pushed the memory down so deep, I had actually forgotten it. This came as headline news.

Before I boarded the train, Dad took me aside and handed me an envelope. "These are your records from the Waverly Home," he said. "You'll want to read them." I took the envelope, but didn't open it. "I've given the situation serious thought," he continued. "There won't be room in the family business for you when you get out of the service." I guess that made sense because Dad was starting a new family. He had taken up with a little ballerina from Portland who must have been quite a dancer because she got the painted house Mother had always wanted, along with a green lawn, tall white fence, and a grove of trees that Dad had no intention of cutting down. In addition to the house and yard, the ballerina got a perfect baby girl.

From Eugene, the troop train traveled south. Inside, we lurched as one through three days and three nights, bathed in cigarette smoke and swaddled in each other's odor. I expected to find oranges and sunshine at the California border, but all we got was more rain. When it was time to eat, we filed back through the train to the cattle car, a semi open affair with coal-burning stoves in each corner. For breakfast, we had eggs, pota-toes, and lard; the rest I don't remember.

The ballerina's fancy new home had a red brick fireplace in the living room with a pass-through so Dad could get wood inside without making a mess. He invited me to come by and see the house before I shipped out. While I was there, he built a fire in the fireplace and made a production of it. "The best way to lay a fire," he said, leaning over the hearth, "is to twist newspapers into sticks and stack them crossways so they get air. By twisting the paper instead of crumpling it, you can do away with kindling." He must have forgotten that he'd already taught me that. "Why split kindling when you don't have to?" he said, twisting and stacking the bulk of the morning paper. "You have to be smart about these things."

By then, Dad had given up on the idea of owning his own sawmill and had gone to work for Wulf Gehring as his broker. Dad did Wulf's dirty work, and Gehring paid him enough to join the country club and buy a Cadillac. Although Dad no longer manufactured lumber—he just bought and sold it—he still considered himself a lumberman, and as it turned out, he and Wulf were plenty busy and plenty rich after Pearl Harbor. The Dolomite mill was soon cutting sixty thousand feet a day and still couldn't keep up with demand. "Nothing like a war to get the juices flowing," Wulf told me before I shipped out. "We need a good one every ten years."

Gust Backer took over the Dolomite sawmill even before Sid Mackenzie was settled in the ground. Within the week and without ceremony, he moved Mackenzie's things out of the owner's cottage to make room for his wife and children. "I have a family to think of," he said. Twinkle offered to keep house for Gust like she had done for Sid, but Gust wasn't interested. Rumor had it that Rex Pingree wanted Gust to partner up with him in the bootlegging business, but Gust had no interest in that either. It really hadn't mattered since Prohibition ended two months later.

Gust brought in a D-9 Cat. He knocked down our pond, and cleared away what was left of the mill. Wulf Gehring said that Gust was "a fine young man because he did exactly what he was told." But Gust wasn't perfect. He hired Mohl as a millwright in spite of his drinking and his other shortcomings. Not long after, Mohl was found dead, drowned one morning in the log pond with a badly broken jaw. "Hard to feel much about it one way or the other," Boone said. "He must have tripped over a log."

Boone's arm healed without getting infected, but an important nerve to his hand had been torn. He couldn't grip a wrench or a hammer with any strength, and the meat between his knuckles withered away. "Good thing it's my left hand," he said. Even so, he stayed on as bouncer and manager at the Bucket of Blood, but not Wattie. Wattie never played at the roadhouse again. "It just ain't a good idea," he confided to Boone. Within a year, Wattie moved back to Chicago to live with a sister. "I got people there, now, and I got things to do. I ain't ready for Freddy, not just yet, I ain't!" Boone and I put Wattie on the train, so I guess he got there. We never heard that he didn't.

There remained a number of theories about who killed Sid Mackenzie. Nobody but me knows for sure what happened. The jury convicted Mike Dugan, the union agitator, but the judge wasn't sure enough about it to give him the death penalty. Dugan is still screaming about the verdict, insisting he was framed, but the jury had to go with the facts: it was Dugan's fire, Dugan's rope, and Dugan's riot.

Dad had a motive, too. He hated Mackenzie for stealing the meadow and prime timber across the river. Dad's name came up a couple of times during the investigation, but murdering someone with his bare hands would have been much too direct for my father. Dad always left the dirty work to someone else.

Rex Pingree would have bet anything that Wattie was the guilty party. According to Rex, "Old Wattie showed his stripes when he blew away Pete's face the way he did." Rex couldn't prove it and Wattie had an alibi. Boone and Mother swore to the judge that Wattie never left their sight all night, which was a bald faced lie, but just because it was lie doesn't mean Wattie did it. Wattie was too crippled up with his arthritis to beat the life out of any man. If you stop to think about it, the answer is obvious. Who was there that night, and who had the most to gain? What man beside Boone had the strength to snap a scrappy man's neck, and who, above all, knew how to play ball when it counted? Who but big, dumb, and ugly Gust Backer?

Miss Cherry didn't return to school after the fire. She took a leave of absence and moved to Eugene to live with her parents— that was all our substitute teacher would tell us. She had a boy, but I never saw it, or her, again. Françoise and Miss Cherry wrote to each other every week, and, according to Françoise, she married a good man who promised to help raise her baby. She named the baby Guillaume, but called him Guy, as a good joke on the old man since he never allowed anyone to call him that while he was alive. Miss Cherry planned to teach at a Catholic school in Eugene once the baby got older.

Guillaume never got over his broken ribs. He coughed all winter long and gave up on his carving. Françoise cut their firewood because he no longer had any strength. All he wanted to do was lay in bed, but Françoise wouldn't stand for it. She threw the covers off every morning and sat him by the fire.

"You act like an old man with one foot in the grave," she said.

"Maybe I am."

Guillaume didn't make it to Christmas, even though Françoise lit candles and prayed to the *Bon Dieu*. Not long after he died, Françoise decided to leave, too. She tried to sell their little house, but couldn't find a buyer. "There is no purpose for me here," she said. "And I've got nobody left alive in Maine." Without telling a soul, she took down her lace curtains one day, boarded a train the next, and moved into a Catholic rest home in Portland. She never wrote anybody either, although I don't know who she'd have written to, with Miss Cherry gone. When Miss Cherry found out about her move, she and her husband drove to Portland and searched until they found her. I guess it didn't take much to convince Françoise to come live with them and help raise the new baby.

Dad didn't want me after the divorce, and Mother couldn't take me. "I just can't," she said. Her grief had become a circus by then. The fire, the divorce, and Uncle Normal's death were too much for her. She ran off to San Francisco and took up with a French woman named Annabelle. When that fell apart, she moved to Reno and bought a boarding house with her share of the fire insurance money. She began catering to those women who were traveling to Nevada to get their "quickie divorces."

Most of Mother's guests drove up from California, but she also nurtured young women from nearly every other state in the country. It turned out to be a good business for her because she finally got a family. She also started attending church. Reno's churches are non-denominational for the most part, but she had her favorites: The Great Provider, The Flamingo, and Harold's. Every week, she tithed like the Baptists and the Mormons, and actually got a return on her money, especially at the blackjack tables.

I stayed on at Culp Creek through the eighth grade and later went to high school in Cottage Grove, boarding with a different farm family each year. Dad covered my living expenses, and Mother sent me letters. During the summer, I worked on the Dolomite green chain and lived in their bunkhouse.

Dad bought me a car when I started high school in Cottage Grove. I spent weeks looking for Miss Cherry, driving up and down Eugene's streets, stopping at parks and circling schools, but I never found her—she had a different name by then. I wanted to know where she lived and whether she was happy or not. Most of all, I wanted to touch her. I wanted things to be the same with us. I had no feelings either way about the boy or the husband. As far as I was concerned, she had no feelings about them either. I don't know if I was searching for a mother, a wife or a whore to bed down—maybe all three. It's not a distinction I've dwelled on over the years.

Three days before I was scheduled to leave for Amarillo, I drove to Culp Creek to see the place, to satisfy some morbid curiosity, I suppose. The pond, the three massive boilers that had driven the saws, even the mill foundation were gone. It was as if our time there had been erased. I knew what I'd find before I got there, but still it hurt. That shouldn't have come as a surprise, since my only real attachment with the place was to the machines.

As I walked through the abandoned mill site, I searched the ground but found little evidence of our life there. Bolts and nails, most of them still blackened from the fire, lay encased in the soil like fossils from another era. At the edge of the clearing, where Gust's dozer had buried the mill's skeleton, ash coated the black of my boots with gray. I stirred the ash with the toe of my boot and recalled the heat from the fire that day, but even that memory brought no warmth.

46

I came across Rita's obituary in the paper this morning. She died at age sixty-two from brain cancer. I suppose I'll miss her, now that she's gone, but if you want the truth, Rita was pretty well gone before her heart stopped, at least the best parts. What the cancer didn't take, the chemotherapy killed. When her hair fell out, she wore a wig—except when she was with me—but I didn't complain. I remember her being a thirty-eight double D, but those beautiful boobs withered away, and by the end, they were nothing at all to look at. Even a training bra would have been wasted on her. So you can see, there wasn't much left for me to visit.

When Rita was still good, she bought me a George Foreman Lean Mean Grilling Machine, and she did the cooking. The last time I saw her, I asked if she wanted the grill back, but she had no use for it, which worked out well for me because I anticipate plenty of use. I remain a king bed lizard! My latest sex therapist is forty-two and stacked—no old, dried up morsels for me. She's coming over later tonight, and I promised to grill her some chicken for dinner. My first wife did the cooking when we were married, and Rita took charge of it when she was around, but I know how to do it, and I want this therapy session to go well. First thing this morning, I dragged George Foreman's grill off the patio and pulled it into the kitchen out of the rain. I rinsed the chicken breasts and peppered them, but left off the salt—no since tempting fate with a stroke.

Rita was the last woman to call me a bastard, but she wasn't anywhere near the first. Both wives, my one daughter, even my mother have used the term on me, so it doesn't carry much of a punch. If I'm a bastard, I'm a bastard through no fault of my own. I arrived without parents, and, after years with Merle and Marie, I left with none. Had Mother cared enough to touch me, she might have felt my fever. Had she thought to try, she might have dressed my wounds. In place of caring and trying, my mother looked away, and I grew to be a bastard in every sense of the word. I choose to believe that she allowed an injured child to grow into a ruined man because it had to be someone's fault. Mother found what she was looking for, but I never did.

Like so many things, most of that no longer matters. I'm content with my life, and I do what I want. I shuffle around the apartment in slippers: I've stopped wearing socks because my feet swell and my toes turn purple. Since I rarely put on shoes, I no longer need to cut my toenails. I don't care if they curl down like ram's horns and click against the linoleum like Pecky's used to do. I haven't heard anyone complain about it.

I know what they're thinking when they look at me. They'd like to zip me inside a plastic bag with the rest of the old men, and they might be right about the others, but they're dead wrong about me. Except for the foot and toenail problems, I'm not bad. Just this morning, after my shower, I stood in front of the bathroom mirror and took a long, hard look from the front and the side, and then I flexed. I've got great biceps for eighty-nine, no paunch to speak of, and I can almost always get it *up. I'll put on a clean shirt for dinner. This new babe won't be able to resist me.*

Sometime after lunch, I started up the grill and threw the chicken on. I left the sliding door open so the smoke alarm wouldn't go off, but later shut it when it got too cold inside. I remember shuffling to the bedroom for a sweater. That was when I forgot about the chicken and decided to take a nap.

Things get fuzzy after that. I woke up, coughing, with my eyes stinging. I stumbled into the kitchen and found the chicken on fire. I reached a fork into the flames and tried to pull the meat off, but it was stuck tight. Then my sleeve caught fire. The flames started at the frayed cuff and traveled up my arm. I batted at them like Boone must have done, but they had a mind of their own. Underneath the wool, my skin began to blister, and my hair caught fire. I felt my eyelids crinkle like crepe paper.

"Must be spontaneous combustion," I thought.

I know all about spontaneous combustion because Dad used to talk about it so much. That was what I was thinking about— Dad and spontaneous combustion—when I fell. The flames followed me down, painting my trousers and scorching my feet. I kicked at the pain with orange legs, but it did no good. As I lay on the linoleum and burned, it felt like God exhorting one more sinner, but no bright light joined the exhortation. In its place, I heard buzzing. I thought the main saw was starting up.

My apartment door exploded inward. Men with hoses, but no buckets, rushed in. I thought they had come to save the mill, but they had come for me. Cold water splashed over me. It brought some relief, and I began to float. I was floating even before they put me on the stretcher. When they picked me up and carried me outside, I couldn't see the sun or the clouds. What I saw was a boy on an errand.

It is night, but not dark, when the boy slips from his house. Across the highway, flames rise from the bridge and fill the night. The wind that had earlier rattled his window now carries bright embers toward his father's sawmill. The boy glances up with mild interest, but only for a moment. He begins running toward the river, and as he does, he sees movement on the bridge, but no detail. When he reaches the water's edge, the fire's heat finds him.

The boy wades into the river without rubber boots. He blindly slides his leather shoes across the rocky bottom until he locates the stolen kerosene can. Slipping and crawling backward, stopping twice to catch his breath, he drags the heavy can through the blackberry thicket and up the slope. At the highway, he sets the can down, but he doesn't rest. He uses his feet once again to search, this time shuffling them through the dry autumn grass, feeling for the four-inch waterline that supplies his father's mill. When he stumbles against the line, he drops to his knees and slides his hands along its length, feeling for a coupling. He takes a half-inch wrench from his pocket and begins to loosen the bolts. When the ends of the pipe fall apart, he steps back and listens to the sound of escaping water as it spills down the bank into the river.

With that task completed, the boy picks up the heavy can. Cradling it in both arms, he hurries as best he can across the empty highway and over the railroad tracks. His arms are shaking when he reaches the loading dock. With the bridge glowing red behind him, he moves into the shadows beneath the planking. At the sawdust pile below the main saw, he holds his breath and listens for voices above him. Hearing none, he strains to twist the metal cap. He struggles against the resistance until he feels one gritty surface slide free of the other. And then he begins to pour. Kerosene splashes over his hands and onto his shoes, but he doesn't notice. He soaks the sawdust pile. He splashes the timbers that support the mill. He stains everything.

Before the can is completely empty, he sets it down, and like he was taught, he twists strips of newspaper into kindling. He dips the final twisted strip into the remaining kerosene to make a torch out of it, and then reaches into his pocket for the small book of matches he's saved for years. Just as he is about to strike the match, he hesitates. He drops his hand and reconsiders.

The boy recalls another lesson: planer shavings burn far hotter than sawdust. He sets the match aside and scoots to the pile of shavings. He gathers up an armload and scatters the shavings over the kerosene. He makes a second trip and a third, adding more and more tinder to the mix. When he is satisfied, he wipes his hands on his pants and carefully strikes the match. He holds the paper shaft steady until it is burning well. Only then does he reach out and place the tiny flame against the kerosene-soaked newspaper. He watches. Within seconds, he knows there will be no need for the other match.

The fire immediately rises up and grows. When it snaps at him, he backs away. When the planking blackens and catches, he turns and runs back to the river, to his sanctuary on top of the locomotive, where he sits and watches both fires: the one on the bridge burning lower, dying; the other beneath his father's mill erupting like a tower. Teddy laughs. He claps his hands and giggles.

ACKNOWLEDGMENTS

This novel is a work of fiction. The characters are imagined, as are the Fraser and Dolomite mills. Several historical figures, including HJ Cox, Latin Professor Frederick Dunn and Reverend RH Sawyer, are real. A resurgence of the Ku Klux Klan throughout the U.S. did, in fact, take place during the 1920's. The Klan grew particularly strong in cities that today might surprise us: Denver, El Paso, Salt Lake City, Eugene, La Grande and Anaheim. In 1922, as a demonstration of its influence, the Klan burned a cross atop Skinner's Butte in Eugene and claimed to have 35,000 members throughout the state of Oregon. Although the Klan's apex preceded events depicted in the novel by five years, the events and timing of the Great Depression are accurate. Shawn Lay's *The Invisible Empire in the West* is an excellent account of KKK activity during the 1920's.

I am indebted to my father, Ted Scott, and his father, A.M. Scott, for adding color and texture to the Oregon lumber business. HJ Cox' *Random Lengths,* Coman & Gibbs' *Time Tide and Timber,* and Michael Thoele's *Bohemia* were particularly valuable resources. The Cottage Grove and Scott's Mills Historical Societies could not have been more gracious in assisting my research.

I would like to thank my writing group for encouragement and criticism during the past seven years: Mary, Kate, Jeana, Rachel, Suzanne, Ken, Randy, Scott, and KK (wherever you may be) thank you. Kristin Ingram, Jeff Metcalf, The Sawtooth Writers Conference, Brett Lott, David Kranes and Connie Voisine were my teachers. *Old Guillaume* was conceived while reading Ms. Voisine's poetry collection, *Cathedral of the North.* Aviva Layton's editorial insight provided a clear direction and shaped the story's final path. Most of all, my appreciation goes to the world's most wonderful wife and editor, my Teresa.

16893706R00174

Made in the USA
Charleston, SC
16 January 2013